THE LAST TO VANISH

ALSO BY MEGAN MIRANDA

Such a Quiet Place

The Girl from Widow Hills

The Last House Guest

The Perfect Stranger

All the Missing Girls

THE LAST TO VANISH

MEGAN MIRANDA

First published in the United States of America in 2022 by
Marysue Rucci Books, Scribner, an imprint of Simon & Schuster.

First published in Great Britain in 2022 by Corvus, an imprint of
Atlantic Books Ltd.

1 2 3 4 5 6 7 8 9 10

A CIP catalogue record for this book is available from the British Library.

Hardback ISBN: 978 1 83895 751 3
Trade Paperback ISBN: 978 1 83895 596 0
E-Book ISBN: 978 1 83895 597 7

Printed and bound by CPI Group (UK) Ltd, Croydon, CR0 4YY

Corvus
An imprint of Atlantic Books Ltd
Ormond House
26–27 Boswell Street
London
WC1N 3JZ

www.corvus-books.co.uk

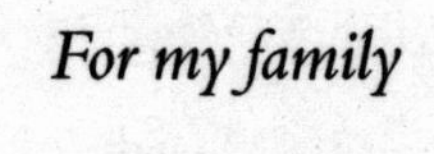

For my family

A NOTORIOUS HISTORY

These are the relevant statistics of Cutter's Pass, North Carolina: The town covers roughly four square miles of a valley, tucked against the base of a mountain ridge. Its main economy is tourism, due to the proximity of an access point to the Appalachian Trail. The most recent census puts the population at just over 1,000 permanent residents. Six visitors have gone missing in the last twenty-five years. As a result, some have called it the most dangerous town in the state.

Here's what the people of Cutter's Pass want you to know: It's a picturesque valley, named almost a century earlier for a path through the nearby mountains, which had proven historically difficult in the winter. Yes, they've had a string of bad luck with the missing visitors, but there's nothing particularly dangerous about the area now. The disappearances are just coincidence. Statistics, even. Twenty-five years, *just a few incidents*.

It's easy to believe, if you want. It's just as easy to disbelieve. But whichever person you are, believer or disbeliever, Cutter's Pass welcomes you equally.

The truth is—

PART 1

Landon West

Date missing: April 2, 2022

Last seen: Cutter's Pass, North Carolina

The Passage Inn

AUGUST 3, 2022

CHAPTER 1

HE ARRIVED AT NIGHT, in the middle of a downpour, the type of conditions more suitable for a disappearance.

I was alone in the lobby—removing the hand-carved walking sticks from the barrel beside the registration desk, replacing them with our stash of sleek navy umbrellas—when someone pushed through one of the double doors at the entrance. The sound of rain cascading over the gutters; the rustle of hiking pants; the screech of wet boots on polished floors.

A man stood just inside as the door fell shut behind him, with nothing but a black raincoat and some sob story about his camping plans.

Nothing to be afraid of: the weather, a hiker.

I was only half listening at first, his request buried under a string of apologies. *I'm so sorry, I'm usually more prepared than this* and *I know this is a huge inconvenience but—*

"We can get you taken care of," I said, making my way behind the desk, where I had the room availability list already pulled up on the single computer screen. This was the type of rain that drove hikers off the mountain—sudden and fierce enough to shake their resolve, when they'd give a second thought to their gear, their stamina, their will. Unlike him, I had been ready for this.

The back of our property ended where the local access trail began: It was marked by a small wooden sign leading day hikers on a path to the falls, but the trail then continued on in a steep ascent, pressing upward until it ultimately collided with the great Appalachian beyond. Our guests loved the convenience, the accessibility, that touch of the wild—the mountain looming, so close, from the other side of their floor-to-ceiling windows.

From the ridge of that mountain, at the T intersection of the two trails, I knew, you could see us, too: the dome of the inn, and the town just beyond, with the steeple of the church pushing up through the treetops; the promise of civilization. Sometimes, on nights like this, they spilled down the mountain like ants scurrying out of a poisoned mound, searching for a place of last resort. Our lights drawing them closer, the first sign of respite off the trail.

Sometimes if there was only one room, strangers would join forces and bunk up, in the spirit of things.

Right now, it was high season and we were booked solid in the main building, but three of the four outside cabins were vacant. The accommodations out there were more rustic, mainly used for either long-term stays or purposes such as this.

The man was still standing on the far side of the lobby, hands cupped in front of his mouth, as if the storm carried a chill. I saw his gaze flick to the freestanding fireplace in the center of the room. "You're going to have to come a little closer to check in," I said.

He laughed once and lowered the hood of his raincoat as he crossed the lobby, shaking out his hair, and then his arms, in an uncannily familiar gesture. I felt my smile falter and tried to cover for it with a glance toward the computer screen, running through the possibilities. A return visitor. Someone I'd seen in town earlier this week. Nothing. Coincidence.

"Here we go," I said, turning my attention his way again, hoping the sight of him so close would trigger a memory, place him in context: brown hair halfway between unkempt and in style; deep-set blue eyes; somewhere in his thirties; no wedding ring; the sharp line of a white scar on the underside of his jaw, which I could only see because he was a solid head taller. I imagined him falling during a hike, hands braced for impact, chin grazing rock; I imagined a hockey stick to the face, helmet dislodged, blood on ice.

I did this sometimes, imagined people's stories. It was a habit I was actively trying to break.

I was sure I knew him from somewhere, but I couldn't place it, and I was usually good at this. I remembered the repeat visitors, could pull a name from three years earlier, recognizing those who'd gotten married or divorced, even, changing names and swapping partners. I paid attention, kept notes, filed away details. The stories I imagined for them sometimes helped.

He looked behind him at the empty lobby before leaning one arm on the distressed wooden countertop between us. "I'm so sorry," he repeated, though I wasn't sure whether he was referring to his lack of reservation or the puddles of water he had trailed across the wide plank floor. "It's just, I left my wallet somewhere. Out *there*." His raincoat rustled as he gestured toward the door. He was pointing in the opposite direction of the mountain, but I let that go because of the dark and the rain, and because I knew how disorienting it could get *out there*, on a bad night. "I had some cash in my car, though," he said, hand stuffed deep into the pocket of his coat before he pulled out a damp roll of twenties. "For emergencies."

He extended the money my way, an offering held between the tips of his fingers.

Hikers sometimes arrived like this, it wasn't unheard of, but I started reassessing him. The clean fingernails. The collar of his blue T-shirt, just visible, still dry. The familiar squeak of too-new rubber-soled boots, before they'd gotten any good miles on them.

Celeste wouldn't approve of this—a man with no ID and no credit cards, showing up just before closing. She'd say I needed to look after myself first of all, and then the guests, and then the inn. Would warn me that we were alone up here, that the only way to project control was to make sure others didn't think they held the reins. Celeste would rather the lost customer than the lost upper hand. She'd say, *So sorry, we're all full*, and she'd mention the campgrounds down by the river, the rentals over the storefronts, the motel in the next town. But I'd been known to make some exceptions. I didn't like the idea of leaving anyone alone *out there*, especially on nights like this. Besides, I was sure he'd been here before at some point.

"No problem," I said, "Mr.—"

His gaze was drifting around the lobby again, taking everything in, like he'd never seen this place before: the fireplace encased in stone and glass, visible from all angles, logs piled up into perfect pyramids on either side; the two-story arch of the dome with the exposed wood beams, the large picture windows that made up the entirety of the far wall, for the best views; the keys hanging from the pegboard in a locked display behind me.

"Sir?" I repeated.

He finally made eye contact. "Clarke," he said, clearing his throat. "With an *e*." He smiled apologetically, a little lopsided, a dimple in his left cheek—another twinge of familiarity.

The name didn't ring a bell.

"Sure thing, Mr. Clarke. Let's see what I can do for you."

Cutter's Pass was a seasonal, small-town haven: river guides and zip lines; a well-maintained campground a half mile outside downtown; horseback tours and an abundance of hiking trails forking off into the surrounding mountains. There were three types of visitors we typically got at the inn. The high-end vacationers who wanted a taste of rustic without actually roughing it; the hikers who thought they were ready to rough it, and discovered they were not, asking for a cabin, or any availability *please*; and the tourists who came for our eerie history, our notoriety—usually groups of friends who asked a lot of questions and drank a lot of beer at the tavern down the road and stumbled in late, laughing and clinging to one another, like they had escaped something. They always seemed surprised by the reality of Cutter's Pass—that it was more REI and craft beer, overpriced farmers' markets and upscale accommodations, less whatever stereotype of Appalachia had taken root in their heads.

From the way this man was looking around the place, and his questionable story, I would've put my money on category three. Except. That familiar gesture. That dimple when he smiled.

I slid a sheet of paper in front of him. "All right," I said, "jot down your license plate so we don't tow you."

He blinked twice, mouth slightly open, a single drop of rain trailing along the edge of his jaw, toward the scar. "Tow me?"

"Lots of people try to park here to get to the mountain," I explained. "The spots are for guests."

"Oh, um, I don't know it by heart . . ."

God, he was bad at this.

"Make and color, then," I said. "And state, if you remember that." I smiled at him, and he laughed.

"I do," he said. I watched as he scrawled down *Audi, black. Maryland.* I felt myself holding my breath. It clicked, where I'd seen him, why he looked so familiar. The family picture with the joint statement. The reward offered in a long-shot plea for help.

I tried to keep my smile in place: cordial, careful. "Maryland, huh? Long way from home," I said.

"Yes, well, next time I'll stick to a beach vacation. Lesson learned."

He was charming, which almost made up for the lack of plan, but wouldn't get him very far here.

I felt for him, really. I'd been an outsider for years; to those who'd grown up here, I probably still was.

"Any preference on room?" I asked.

"Oh," he said, narrowing his eyes, looking toward the balcony of the second floor, just beyond the dome of the lobby. "I . . . I wouldn't know."

My heart was too soft, I knew this. I unlocked the display case on the wall behind me and took the key off the hook for Cabin Four. I knew what he wanted; what he was here for. "You look just like him," I said.

His entire body deflated, almost like he was making himself prostrate, his forehead down to the counter between us before he stood again, as if he were unveiling someone new.

"I'm sorry," he said, face contorted into a grimace. It was the first time I believed him.

"No," I said. "I get it. Really. I understand. I would do the same."

He pulled a wallet out of his back pocket, took a deep breath in and out, started again. "Trey West," he said, leaving a pause for me to fill. A question, an offering.

"Abby," I said.

"Abby," he repeated, turning over his license, a credit card. "I'm not good at pretending. It's a relief."

It was his brother, Landon, who was good at that. We didn't know he was a journalist when he came to stay. We'd thought he was trying his hand at writing a book, that he was on a personal retreat, that he needed the peace and quiet, the lack of distractions, the ambiance—that's what he'd told us. We'd thought he was here to get away from something. Not that he was here for something instead. But those things were hard to differentiate on the surface. It wasn't until he disappeared that we knew the truth.

I didn't know what Trey was looking for all these months later. Whether he thought there was still something worth finding, that the police and the searchers had all missed; whether he was here to pay his respects, hoping for some sort of closure.

Closure was a hard thing to come by here.

"It's not what I expected," Trey said as I charged the night to his card.

I wasn't sure whether he meant the inn or the entire town. The road into town climbed up for a stretch of miles before swerving down again, narrowing as it dipped from the mountains into the valley, vegetation pushing closer and creeping over the guardrails. It was a drive you didn't want to do at night, riding the brakes as the curves grew tighter, branches arcing over the pavement. But then the trees opened up, and Cutter's Pass presented itself, a lost city. A found oasis.

"It never is," I said. There was always a slight disorientation when you arrived, nothing quite as expected from the drive in. The inn appeared older than it was from the outside, with the weatherworn cabins set back from the main three-story structure, and the forest steadily encroaching over the cleared acreage, but that was just how fast nature worked. Inside, the fireplace was gas; the logs, just for show; the antique locks on all the guest room doors could be overridden with an electronic badge.

It was already clear that Trey was different from his brother, who was closed off and blended in, whom I didn't even notice for the first four days of his stay, because Georgia checked him in and could only remember, when pressed, that he had asked for the Wi-Fi password, and she had told him the service didn't reach the cabins, that it was slow and barely consistent in the main building as well, which was why we had to keep the credit card slide under the register, old-fashioned carbon copies that people thought quaint, so it worked in our favor.

Other things that worked in our favor but were neither authentic nor necessary: the wooden key rings with the room names etched in by hand; the poker beside the fireplace, angled just so.

Things here were designed to appear more fragile than they were, but reinforced, because they had to be. We lived in the mountains, on the edge of the woods, subject to the whims of weather and the forces of nature.

The large guest room windows were practically soundproof. Frosted skylights in the upper-floor halls echoed the fall of rain or sleet, but were fully resistant to a branch lost to a storm. There were tempered glass panels in the thick wooden doors at the entrance, which could hypothetically stop a bullet, but thankfully had never been tested.

I pulled one of the umbrellas from the barrel, each a uniform navy blue with a tastefully small logo: a single, bare tree, white branches unfurling against the evening sky.

"Come on," I said, "I'll show you the way."

This was not part of my job, but I couldn't help myself. I never could.

OUTSIDE, THE RAIN WAS unrelenting, puddles forming in the gravel lot, water seeping into my shoes. Trey West had to duck to fit under the shared umbrella, his arm brushing up against mine as we walked.

"The cabins are this way," I explained, gesturing to the trail of marked lighting along the brick path on the other side of the parking lot.

We passed his car, that black Audi with the Maryland plates, on the far end of the lot, and he looked at me sheepishly.

"Is it always this dark?" he asked.

"Yes," I answered, because it wasn't really that dark out front, all things considered, but he must've had an entirely different frame of reference. The lit pathway did a fair enough job, along with the lights of the main building, both kept on from dusk to dawn. From the edge of this lot, even, you could see the road slope down into the town center: a geometric grid of antique shops and breweries and cafés, stores that specialized in expert hiking apparel or kitschy tourist gear, all named for the thing that could've been our downfall, but seemed to put us on the map instead.

Down there, you could find the Last Stop Tavern; Trace of the Mountain Souvenirs; the Edge, which sold camping gear and rented out lockers but also featured a menu of coffee and hot chocolate and beer, depending on the time of day; and CJ's Hideaway, a top restaurant of the western Carolinas, with its entrance tucked in a back alley, a commitment to the con, even though it boasted a growing waiting list on most nights during peak season. Each storefront a subtle nod to what the rumors implied: that there was something hidden under the surface here. Some secret only we knew, that we weren't letting on.

The town was best known, and we weren't known for much, for the unsolved disappearance of four hikers more than two decades earlier. The Fraternity Four, they were called, even though they hadn't been members of any frat together. But they were in their twenties, youthful and carefree, and they had last been spotted here in town, had set off toward the Appalachian and were never seen again.

Here one moment in Cutter's Pass, gone the next. No clues, no leads. Just vanished. Over the years, their story had morphed into something of an urban legend, layers added with each retelling, rumors spreading in absentia.

Maybe the mystery would've faded with time, attributed to circumstance, buried with history, if not for the string of disappearances that continued to follow, with haunting regularity.

Most recently: Landon West, onetime resident of Cabin Four. He'd vanished four months before, in early April, when the inn was still ramping up to high season.

We didn't notice, at first.

His disappearance had kicked it all up again: the stories, the press, the headlines calling us *the most dangerous town in North Carolina*.

It didn't matter that the first thing a visitor saw when they passed the sign for Cutter's Pass and took the wide bridge over the river was a welcome center and, across the street, the sheriff's office. Didn't matter that there were bright painted signs for rafting and horseback riding and adventure tours around the town green, where people milled around each morning as the vendors set up for the day. Or that thousands of visitors came through our small town to experience all we had to offer. The simple truth was that Landon West had vanished on our watch, just like all the rest.

"This is you," I said as the path snaked off to the string of cabins, set back in the trees. There were technically only two cabin buildings, but we had subdivided them with a poorly insulated wall, the separate doors side by side in the middle of each log-home-style building. The only light coming from any of them was the soft glow of the floor lamp in Cabin One, visible in the curtain gaps of the front window. If Trey wanted real dark, he could walk the twenty yards into the trees around the back of his cabin and face the mountain.

I handed Trey the umbrella, slid the key into the lock of Cabin Four, felt the gust of cold as I opened the door, my hand stretching for the switch on the inside wall. Here, the wood paneling gave way to smaller windows that slid open on the front and back walls, to let in the fresh mountain air. There was a heating unit under the back window, for off-season stays.

The cabin furniture was simple and spare: a wood dresser, a nightstand, a four-poster bed with a quilted blanket, a desk and hard-back chair. Everything was shades of brown, except for the hotel guidebook, a white three-ring binder of information, perfectly centered on the surface of the desk.

Trey remained on the other side of the entrance, still holding the umbrella over his head. Now he was looking at the place Landon had once slept, the chair he'd once sat in, the place at the foot of the bed where Georgia had found his suitcase, mostly packed but still opened, only his hiking boots noticeably missing.

"Okay, well, I'll leave you to get settled," I said. I took the umbrella from his hand, which prompted him to finally step inside, switching places with me. He looked shell-shocked, unprepared. "If you need anything, the phone at the front desk will reach me."

"Thank you, Abby," he said, one hand on the door.

My hand lingered over his for a moment as I placed the key in his open palm, cold and wet and unsure. It took some time to get your bearings here. "Welcome to the Passage."

CHAPTER 2

GEORGIA WAS STANDING AT the registration desk, the inn's landline phone halfway to her ear, when I returned.

"The lines are down," she said as I shook the rain from the umbrella and leaned it in a groove beside the entrance. She held that same pose, that same haunted expression, as a door opened somewhere on the second floor—the cry of a hinge I'd have to get fixed.

"Probably the rain," I said as I crossed the lobby. It was more the wind than the rain that managed to cut us off most times, though we weren't the only ones. The entire grid of the town center had been known to lose power from a downed tree limb—or, once, a car that collided with a telephone pole. It was that sort of night.

"I heard it ringing," she said, quieter this time. "It just kept going, and I came out to answer it, but . . ." I took the phone she extended my way—*nothing.*

Well, not quite nothing. There was a low clicking sound coming from the receiver, something between dead air and static. It had happened before.

"It'll come back," I said, replacing the phone in its cradle. Georgia's gaze flicked to the dark windows, like she expected something to be out there, watching back. A year working here, and she still wasn't accustomed to the whims of the weather. The coincidences she took as signs. The sound of the local wildlife outside our windows at night. The dangers she feared could exist behind a dropped phone call, a missed connection.

When she'd first arrived, I couldn't help but notice our similarities: We'd both come to the area soon after losing a parent, and we'd both chosen to remain—a waypoint that had turned permanent. It took longer to notice our differences: Georgia seemed to process everything by sharing, expecting me to do the same. She said whatever she was thinking, airing her insecurities, and her fears.

But Georgia always seemed on high alert, just by nature of the shape of her face—narrow and fine boned, with large brown eyes and her blonde hair in a pixie cut. You could almost imagine her as some mystical creature, something you might catch a glimpse of hiding between the trees, if not for the fact that she was nearly six feet tall, sharp angles and long limbs and very hard to miss.

"Was that a hiker you just checked in?" she asked.

I shook my head, straightening the paperwork into the binder behind the desk, just to have something to do with my hands. "Actually, it was Landon West's brother," I said without making eye contact. I could imagine her expression well enough.

She stood perfectly still, waiting for me to look up. When I finally did, I lifted one shoulder, as in, *I know*.

"Are you going to tell Celeste?" she asked.

"Wasn't planning on it." After nearly a decade of working with her, Celeste now paid me to keep the details from reaching her, content to spend her time in a semiretirement. And I wasn't sure whether this was a problem just yet.

I started closing up for the evening, shutting down the computer, gathering anything of value to store in the office behind us, which would remain locked until the morning.

"How much longer until this rain breaks?" Georgia asked, pulling out her cell and taking it into the back office, which was the best place to get any signal here—the closest to the town center you could get, the better. "I can't get any bars," she added, her voice going tight. She'd been on edge to some degree since Landon West's disappearance in April, and it didn't take much to push her over now.

"Soon, I think," I said, for no other reason than wanting to ease her nervous energy, which had only succeeded in making me anxious as well. *The weather; the phone lines; Trey West's arrival*—like there was something beginning. Something gathering force. I shook it off as I tucked the locked case of receipts and cash under my arm; this was why Georgia rarely worked the late shift.

"Abby," Georgia called from the back office, her voice even higher, tighter.

I stepped around the corner, where she faced the dark windows over the table we used both as a desk and for meals. I'd often stood in that very spot to send a text, or upload a photo to the inn's social media accounts. The rain sounded like it was indeed letting up, though the weather app visible on her cell phone screen was still blank and searching. She pressed a single pointer finger against the glass, turning to face me. "Cory's on his way up with a group."

Rain or Shine, that was his motto. Pretty much the only rule of his tours, that I could tell. "I thought he only went to the woods on day trips," I said. It was too dark, too pointless, to take visitors out there in the night. Never mind the current state of things.

But I felt Georgia's eyes on me as I slid the money drawer into a secondary safe in the closet. "He added Landon West to the circuit a couple weeks back."

"You can't be serious," I said, joining her at the window, face pressed close to the cold glass. The case was barely four months old—dormant, but definitely not closed. I could just barely see the dancing beams of the flashlights heading up the steep incline in the dark.

"Someone should tell him," Georgia said.

I stared at the side of her face, the plea already forming. I'd warned her about Cory, but some people have to figure things out for themselves.

At the tail end of last summer, when I was still showing Georgia around Cutter's Pass, I brought her along on a night out, introduced her to the seasonal workers who were then in their last weeks, half of whom, despite their promises and drunken assurances, we would never see again. I felt Georgia picking up on it, sliding into it, the wild energy that pulled at everyone then, the impermanence of our choices. These people who wouldn't remember us, just as we wouldn't remember them. In a year, two, they'd be nothing more than *the redhead who broke her wrist working the zip line*; *the kid from Texas who wore a cowboy hat on the river.*

The only reliable fixture of that world was Sloane, who'd managed the river center from spring through fall for five years running. She'd become my closest friend, another in-betweener—not a temporary employee, but not someone with deep roots here, either.

That night, as we'd closed out the evening at the Last Stop—a tradition, a calling—we ran into Cory, who'd said, *Aren't you going to introduce me to your friend, Abby?* I'd given Georgia a not-so-subtle shake of the head, which she pointedly ignored. Georgia answered for herself, with one long, fine-boned arm extended his way.

Georgia barely knew me then, no better than the seasonal workers who would soon disappear. Had no reason to trust what I was saying, which was: *If you're planning to stay, Cory was unavoidable, infallible. This was not a choice that could be forgotten.*

At least it gave us something else to bond over now. Though it took everything within me to bite my tongue when she'd say, *I don't want to deal with him.*

"Abby?" she pleaded, as the shadowed mass of the tour group drew nearer.

"Shit," I said, racing for the exit, grabbing the umbrella, and pushing out into the storm once more.

FROM MY SPOT IN the parking lot, I watched as the group in dark hoods crested the top of the steep drive, huddled close together, faces low, like some sort of cult. Even in the distance, I could pick out Cory Shiles, the glow of the bottom half of his face, square jaw, a familiar regret. That tattoo of ivy creeping up the side of his neck as the light swung back and forth from his hand. He had a lantern, for God's sake.

Cory ran something between a ghost tour and an excursion for rubberneckers. Thirty bucks for an all-weather guided experience of the history of Cutter's Pass that started and ended at the Last Stop Tavern in town. So people could liquor up both before and after. He brought paying customers to the sights of the disappearances, showed them where each person had been spotted in town earlier. Told them what we knew of the missing, what the police had uncovered, and where the investigations had stalled.

Cory shared theories that none of us really believed: a hidden network of caves with an underground cult; a man in the mountains who had supposedly lived off grid for decades, protecting the land he deemed his own. And he told some we believed a little more, about animals and weather and how easy it was to disappear in a place like this; about people who might not want to be found. All mixed in with rumors about lines of latitude and magnetic fields, like this was the Bermuda Triangle and not four square miles of solid ground with a well-defined perimeter.

Cory hadn't noticed me yet, his arms wide as he was telling some story that was lost to the rain, and the crowd.

"What about the people here?" I heard one woman shout from the back of the group. "Especially since all the missing were visitors? Were there ever any suspects in town?"

"The police have been through this place with a fine-tooth comb. More times than I can remember," he answered, his voice sliding smooth as honey over the crowd. "Have you ever known a place to keep a secret for over two decades? Have you met me?"

Some laughs, a few smiles visible in the dancing lights. This was how he got the tips. That gosh-darn attitude, *I'll tell you my secrets for a beer, friend*. It wasn't true. Cory Shiles would take his secrets to the grave.

"Cory," I called, sharp and deliberate.

He turned my way, lantern illuminating the white of his teeth. "Well, hey there, Abby!" he called back, too friendly, not reading my tone—or, more likely, choosing to ignore it. "We're in luck tonight, this here is Abby Lovett, manager of—"

I gave him a single shake of the head, and he handed the lantern to the woman beside him, wide-eyed and eager. "Excuse me for one second, folks."

I waited until he was out of earshot of the group, who were watching this interaction closely. I kept my voice low, my teeth clenched. "Tell me you did not add us to your ghost tour, for the love of God," I said.

He grinned, rain hitting the hood of his coat, the top of his boots. "It's not a ghost tour, Abby. We're a historical walking tour—"

"He went missing *four months ago*, Cory. People are *still looking*."

Cory took one step back, his shoulders rising and falling. "Just giving the customers what they want."

I took a step forward, to keep this discussion private. "His brother just checked in," I said.

The smile fell from his face; he craned his neck, taking in the second-floor windows of the inn over my shoulder. "Where'd you put him?"

"Same room," I said. "Cabin Four." Out of sight, for the moment. As long as Cory's group didn't make a scene.

"Well," he said, dark eyes searching mine, "you really should've led with that." He used his left hand to wipe away a raindrop that may or may not have existed on the side of my face, his thumb rough and familiar. "You take care now, Abby."

Thank you, I mouthed, though I wasn't sure he could see.

"Folks," he said as he walked back, "there've been some flash flood warnings coming through. I think we'd better finish this up over a drink or two."

He looked back once, used his fingers to tip the hood of his raincoat my way, like he was someone from another time.

I'd met Cory at the Last Stop myself almost ten years ago now. Before I knew he was the tavern owners' son. A permanent, reliable fixture of town, whether you wanted him there or not. Ten years, and he still had that charisma, a fearlessness, the promise of secrets.

There were certain things about Cory that were still appealing, just as there were things about the inn that were not. It's all in what you chose to focus your energy on, what you wanted to see. The flattering slant of the angle. The play of shadows. What you could get people to notice. What you could convince the majority of them to believe.

GEORGIA WAS GONE BY the time I returned, the office locked up, the registration area secured. She preferred morning shifts—handling breakfast instead of happy hour; checking guests out, instead of in. But she'd finished most of the evening routine for me. Like a fair trade for me dealing with Cory.

Celeste wouldn't have hired Georgia on her own. *Are we sure about her?* she'd asked more than once. Celeste didn't want people who seemed like they couldn't do the hard things, and Georgia sure didn't look it when she arrived. She'd come to the mountains to hike a stretch of the Appalachian in the second summer of the pandemic, but five days in, she left the group she'd been with, hiked herself down that access trail, and threw her pack on the floor of the lobby, coated in dirt and fatigue, like she'd wanted any excuse to get out and misjudged herself; like she'd reassessed her life and was out to make a change, before realizing that wasn't the change she was looking for. "This isn't me. I'm out," she'd said before slapping a thick credit card on top of the registration desk.

I had imagined hard ground and poor packing; a man she was trying to impress, who was not impressed with her; I had imagined her waking up that morning, staring at the top of her tent, or the burned-out remnants of a campfire, or the heavy pack and the trail disappearing into the distance—and bailing.

It had seemed, from the way she had arrived, that she could not, in fact, do the hard things. But Celeste had been looking for more help so she could take a step back. And I thought I saw something in Georgia, something I recognized. So when Georgia extended her stay, asking around about jobs, I jumped.

A year later, for all our differences, I was glad to have her. The guests connected with her, and she was easy to work with, easy to live with. She might not have needed the money (a warning from Celeste, after she saw the car she'd returned with), but she did need something—and whatever it was, it kept her here, kept her loyal.

I lifted the phone from the cradle, pressed the power button, and listened to the soft familiar hum of the dial tone. *See? Everything's okay.* Some line must have come down in town, and now it was back; and Trey West would spend a night in the place his brother was last seen, and come to terms with something, then head out in the morning; the storm would pass and tomorrow the mountain sun would creep across the sky, drying the earth in steady patches.

By tomorrow evening, all evidence of this would have disappeared, as so often happened here.

I left the phone on top of the desk, angled toward the lobby, and placed the sign beside it, designating my apartment number as the line to call for assistance. I checked the office locks one last time and peered around the common area, making sure everything was as it should be. Last, I hit the light switch hidden behind the registration area that turned off the upper lights, leaving only the soft glow of the gas lanterns in my wake.

Then I walked down the main hall, passing the series of framed black-and-white photographs showing the construction of the inn. First, Celeste and her late husband, Vincent, both with windswept hair: Vincent, with a strong jaw and chiseled face, smile turned toward her, sleeves of a button-down rolled up, like he'd just come from the office; Celeste with her head tipped back, wide smile, like she'd been starting to laugh. She must've been close to my age then. Both of them were standing beside the lumber that would one day become the dome of the lobby. The next pictures captured the various stages of the build, the main structure in skeleton form, all wood beams and open air, so that now, standing in this hall, I could almost smell the raw lumber under the drywall and paint.

Near the end of the hall, I pressed my thumb to a nail hole that still needed repair, visible under a patch of paint that hadn't been spackled first. No one here visiting would notice, probably. But it was our job to find the imperfections and correct them, even in the rustic allure. The only flaws here were deliberate and curated. But there was never any time for a complete job until the off-season. Anytime I got started with a paint touch-up, I only noticed the borders where the color didn't blend right, older sections that had faded or dulled from sunlight and time. The full repaint would have to wait for the string of winter days in January when we shut the inn for all the work we'd been putting off throughout the year.

I used my badge to unlock the nondescript door just before the back exit. Inside, the steps led down to the lower level, for employees, where we stopped pretending. Here, the doors had regular keys, regular locks—nothing that could be overridden with an electronic card. Along the hallway, scuff marks marred the walls, from furniture and supply deliveries, year after year.

Down the hall, I could hear music coming from Georgia's apartment. She kept the radio on whenever she was in, even when she was sleeping, as if to confirm that she was there. As if she had listened to Cory's talk one too many times, had started to believe the rumors herself—that an unknown danger could approach from the woods at any time.

My apartment was just past Georgia's. I let myself in and locked up behind me. The noise from her room fell to silence. The walls on the lower level were built thick, for structure and support, and noise didn't carry like it did out in the halls. Georgia and I each had a one-bedroom unit with a kitchenette and bathroom off a small all-purpose living space—the mirror image of each other's.

Without turning on the light, I dropped my keys on the laminate counter, stepped out of my damp shoes, peeled off my socks. I removed the pins from my bun as I crossed the room, worked my fingers through the deep brown layers, feeling them slowly unspool.

The inn was built into a slope, so that our rooms on the lower level actually looked out onto the mountain, too, tucked into the side of the incline. Personally, I believed these were the best views, because you could see near and far equally—the blades of grass just on the other side of the glass, an animal tracking by, leaves falling over the sill; and the mountains in the distance, seeming even more massive, given the lower perspective.

My living room curtains remained closed, since guests sometimes explored the grounds directly outside. But my bedroom had a view that remained unobstructed and uncovered at all times. Upper windows that slanted outward, halfway to being skylights, giving way to a rocky overlook below, difficult to reach from the outside.

When I'd first arrived, I used to jolt alert in the night, listening for whatever had startled me, before realizing it must've been the silence itself. And I'd wake each morning disoriented by the perspective, taking a moment to recenter myself, remember where I was.

People seemed to think this place would settle into me immediately, that it was in my bones, somehow, as Celeste's niece, even if we weren't related by blood. But it had happened gradually, in a way that caught me by surprise. Ten years later, and it held the familiar comfort of home: It was private and perfect and mine.

I felt my way in the dark, pulling my pajamas from the drawer underneath my bed, brushing my teeth by the glow of the bathroom night-light, slipping into the familiar sheets.

Then it was just me, and the rain. I felt my pulse, two fingers at the base of my neck. Counted my breaths, in and out, in and out. Stared up, out the bedroom windows, at the water streaking across the glass, and the night sky beyond. The view familiar, if ever-changing.

There was a subtle shift in the pattern of the raindrops on my windows. Something in the chaos that told me the storm was over, though it still sounded like it was raining—the kind of thing you only came to recognize with time. The drops continued to fall from the trees around us, and would continue to do so, hours later, in a delayed echo, like the light of a dying star.

Looking up at night here, the universe felt so alive—not that you were really looking into the past, at things that may not exist anymore. At times, everything about this place felt like we were circling things that had already happened. The photos in the hall; the people who had gone missing; the stories Cory told, down at the tavern. Like you were always running behind—whether by hours or light-years. By the time you realized what you were seeing here, it was too late. It was already gone.

CHAPTER 3

THERE WAS NO NEED for an alarm clock in the summer months—the sun rose before any work needed to be done, and I wasn't due in an official capacity until the afternoon.

The windows above my bed were slightly fogged, and I could feel the morning chill as my feet planted onto the floor beside my bed. Outside the window, a scattering of pebbles cascaded down the rocky outcropping—a squirrel or two, making their way down from the roof, I was guessing. They were nearly impossible to deter, leaping from tree to roof, gnawing their way into the eaves with a relentless, single-minded focus. No matter how frequently we patched over the problem, no matter how much we tried to stop them, we'd hear the telltale scratching within weeks again.

My apartment phone hadn't rung through the night, so I assumed everyone had gotten through the storm okay. No power outages, or leaks, or requests for the number of a late-night delivery service so guests wouldn't have to venture out into the weather.

A good night. A quiet night.

I caught sight of myself in the bedroom mirror, dark hair down past my shoulders and a tattoo on my collarbone that I very much regretted from when I was a teenager, three tiny birds taking flight.

I'd imagined it as my future, then—my mom used to joke that I always had one foot out the door, ready to take off.

Even though I wasn't on shift yet, I got myself ready for the day, gathered my hair into a low bun and dressed in my uniform—black pants and navy polo, bare-branched tree logo on the upper left corner. As the manager of the inn, there was a constantly growing list of things to keep on top of, from coordinating repairs to checking the grounds, and it was less concerning for guests to see someone in uniform slipping in and out of previously unnoticed doorways. The only difference in my work attire right now was my choice of footwear—sneakers, for walking the grounds or pacing the halls while keeping a low profile.

Georgia's room was quiet. She was either on her morning run or already up in the lobby, opening for the day, preparing the continental breakfast that guests would take from the lobby to the seats by the windows scattered throughout the inn, or, more likely, to the bistro tables on the deck out back, where you could have your coffee while watching the sky turn colors over the mountain ridge.

I took the private exit at the end of the employee hall, barely visible from the back of the building, painted to blend in. It was only accessible with an employee badge, just like from the upstairs hallway, so that maintenance and Celeste could access the storage closets, where we kept an assortment of supplies, outdoor furniture, old records, and fresh linens. But it was also the entrance most often used by me and Georgia—a private door to our home.

Now, as I emerged on the back corner of our property, under the deck that extended off the main level, I could already hear chairs shifting above. Beyond the stairs to the deck was a line of trees that concealed a garage with a carriage home over top, where Celeste lived.

In the distance, the fog was lifting off the mountain, like smoke. Wisps of heavy gray still clung to the trees in sections, muting everything. It was my favorite kind of morning, haunting and beautiful.

I took a picture to send to Sloane later in the week, when I knew she'd be back in cell phone range. When Sloane took a promotion to start up her company's new rafting center in Virginia, she pulled me in tight and whispered, "Don't disappear on me." The day after she'd left, I'd sent her a photo from the town green at three p.m.—what Sloane called ice cream hour, for the prevalence of tourists who took their cones to the lawn at the same time, as if coordinated. I'd bought a cone from the corner shop just for the shot, captioned the photo: *Proof of Life*. I'd received a photo in response that evening: Sloane, looking tired, long wavy hair, unimpressed expression as she stood in front of a room full of moving boxes, bottle of beer raised.

We continued sending proof-of-life photos back and forth, at least once a week—it had become a way to stay connected during busy days and opposite schedules. In the last few weeks, I'd received: an oar stuck in mud; a heap of life jackets in an open truck bed; legs crossed on a wooden deck railing, dirty sneakers half blocking the sunset.

I slid my phone into my back pocket and began my morning routine, tracing a path across our property. A decade here, and I could walk the grounds with my eyes closed, day or night. First, the expanse of back greenway with the periodic bench swing, where guests often had picnics and occasionally forgot a blanket, or an empty bottle, or food (but that would be gone by morning, if so). Then, the gated section along the side wall, with the hot tub, where there was currently one inn-issued towel forgotten on the brick patio, which I shook out and tossed in the bin against the wall.

Along the perimeter of the building, I checked the flower beds for any damage from animals, and the path lights for tangled cords or stakes that had become dislodged. I glanced toward the cabins, but nothing was stirring. Nothing but green grass and rocky outcrops from here to the trees.

A rustle in the tree line, and I froze. It wouldn't be the first time a bear emerged onto the clearing, drawn by curiosity, or food left behind by a guest. But it was just a deer there now, staring back at me on its own high alert. I took a single step forward, and it darted back into the woods. A quick flutter of movement through the brush, and then it was gone.

As I turned back, I noticed movement through the trees by the employee lot: Someone crouched low near the carriage house.

My heart stilled, and I walked quietly in that direction, careful not to give myself away. The person stood, and I caught a clearer glimpse—a familiar, slightly hunched figure: Celeste.

She raised a hand as I approached, waiting for me to close the distance. The Celeste I knew looked much different from the Celeste in the photos that hung from the inn. As if, when she'd molded this place to her liking, it had molded her in return. The windswept brown hair now heavily laced through with gray, like the fog rolling through. Calloused hands and nails kept short, everything about her efficient. She projected a steadiness, a seriousness.

"Good morning, Celeste," I said as I approached the back garden gate. Celeste was even shorter than I was, with hair falling to her midback. Up close, she had wide-set features, striking green eyes, and a downturned mouth that gave her an air of gravity. She was also generous and protective, with a wild and unrestrained laugh if you could surprise her into it, and the three great loves of her life were: this inn, her husband Vincent, and the mountain, in that order. Her husband had died a decade earlier, in the year before I arrived, so the mountain was bumped up a spot. She was up and on that trail more mornings than not, at dawn, like there was something new to discover each day.

But she wasn't wearing her hiking boots this morning. Just khakis and a brown T-shirt and dark sneakers, which were currently toeing the mud in front of her.

"Someone left a cigarette out here, can you believe it?" she said with her trademark raspy voice. "Look around at this place." She held her arms out wide. "How fast do they think it would take for everything to burn?"

Judging by the mud, and by the water I felt under the soles of my shoes as I approached, I didn't think there was much of a fire hazard right now, but that was beside the point. She was probably more upset about the lack of courtesy, the fact that someone had encroached so far onto the territory she considered her own. Though there was nothing to designate it as such.

"We can put up a sign," I said, not for the first time.

Celeste frowned, lines deepening between her eyes, around the corners of her mouth. "We don't need signs, just common sense." Then her focus shifted to somewhere over my shoulder. "Tell me about our mystery guest," she said.

I smiled tightly. Celeste was probably out here waiting for me, for this very purpose. I ran through the possibilities of how she had heard so quickly: Georgia, even though I thought she would've left that up to me; Cory, who could've called her directly; or someone down at the tavern, who had heard about it from him. A place like this, a place with our type of history, information had a way of moving fast through the channel of people who had lived here forever.

"He's in Cabin Four," I answered.

"I see." I heard it in her voice: A disappointment. A warning. "And tell me," she said, turning back toward her house. "Is he leaving today?"

I fell into stride beside her. "I think, but I'm not sure." I had charged a single night to his credit card, but had not confirmed. Maybe I didn't want to know the answer.

"Well, let's go ahead and be sure, dear." Celeste attempted to soften her critiques by including herself in them. *We should be more careful with the glass*; and *We don't want to upset the guests*; and *Let's try to keep up*. The *dear* was new. It didn't sound particularly gentle, but I took what I could get. Celeste didn't give a compliment that hadn't been earned, and often not even then. But I felt them in the things she entrusted to my care.

"Of course," I said.

She stopped just outside the small gated garden at the back of the carriage house. "We could even find out what he wanted, while we were at it."

"We will," I said, my hand resting on a white picket fence.

That got a begrudging rise of the corner of her mouth, before she reached a hand over mine. "We need to be careful, Abigail," she said, which she only called me when she was serious, commanding my attention, pronouncing each syllable carefully.

No one else ever called me that, not even my own mother when she'd been angry. But Celeste had taken up the practice in the way a parent might. It was less tied to her mood or any transgression I had committed, and more a warning she was trying to impart. She'd used it over the years, when I'd head out late after a shift to meet up with Sloane, or a short-term fling with a seasonal worker: *Good night, Abigail.* When a group was getting too rowdy at happy hour, an energy buzzing, a tension in the air: *Let's start closing up, Abigail.* And now, *We need to be careful, Abigail,* as if I had failed to notice something important.

Family members, she had once told me, put everyone on edge, more than most. They shook and rattled, driven more by desperation than logic. Compelled by something deeper. You could never be sure what they wanted, exactly—if they even knew themselves. It made them reckless, unpredictable.

Though four months had passed since Landon's disappearance, the chaos of the investigation was still fresh. The publicity. The blame. I'd had to let all calls go to voice mail for weeks. I'd had to lock the comments on our social media accounts for far longer. But we had survived it. Still, I understood: This was supposed to be behind us.

"Celeste," I said. "He's probably just here to see it for himself. Everything's okay." I pictured him waking up and looking out the back window of the cabin this morning, straight to the mountain, breathing the crisp morning air, understanding the pull Landon must've felt. Watching as the ghost of his brother stepped into the trees, wishing he could go back and stop him—but accepting he could not. I couldn't imagine him staying for long. I pictured him packing his bag, tossing it into his trunk, driving away, back to the life that was waiting for him.

"I hope so," she said with a pointed look toward the cabin path on the other side of the grounds. She squeezed my hand once before releasing me.

I turned back as she opened her garden gate, the white pickets scratching against the brick path inside. "And let's keep Georgia out of it," she called after me.

I raised a hand in understanding. Georgia had been the one to find Landon West's things, had been the one first interviewed by the sheriff, and more. It took a solid month for her to stop jumping whenever someone called her name. For her not to pale at the sight of an empty room. For her not to check and recheck the guest list, walking by the rooms at night, listening for movement within.

For a time, I was worried she might leave over it. She didn't. Still, she shouldn't have to face it all over again.

I knew in Celeste's mind, this was my mistake. I had misjudged the threat here. And it was therefore my job to fix it.

THE CABINS WERE SILENT. I trekked carefully to the grounds around back, where the lawn gave way to forest, but none of the occupants were out here, either. Cabin One had been rented as a home base by two women who were serious hikers while they took a few camping routes, so they weren't planning to be here every day. And Trey either was still sleeping or had already vacated Cabin Four, having experienced whatever it was he was hoping for.

Celeste was less inclined than I was to take people at their word, trusting actions above all else. She'd watched over my work closely during my first months here. It took a while to see it not as a slight against me, but an indicator of how much she cared. The time she put into me was because she thought I was worth it, and I'd spent the years since trying to prove her right.

I felt borderline hopeful as I followed the path, now unlit, back toward the parking lot. Until I saw his black Audi in the same spot. I circled it slowly, getting a better look this time: mud-streaked tires from his drive in last night; a dent in the passenger door and a series of scratches on the back bumper; tinted windows, so I couldn't see much of anything that might be worth seeing inside.

The birds were calling, and so were the insects, and it wouldn't be long until he was up, if he was like a normal person, accustomed to the dark shades and insulation of home. Instead of circling around back to our private entrance, I entered the inn through the lobby, where I was greeted by the sound of utensils on plates, the low shuffling of footsteps and clothing and voices, and Georgia behind the front desk, highlighter in hand, tracing a route on a map for an older couple in hiking gear—the Shermans, in Mountain View Two, here for three nights and making the most of every hour. They each had one of our walking sticks in hand, and I waited for them to head off before joining Georgia behind the desk.

"He hasn't checked out," she said, practically reading my mind.

"I noticed. I think he's still sleeping." I drummed my fingers on the counter. "I'm heading into town. Do me a favor and call me if he leaves. Or if he comes in for anything."

She pushed her short hair off her forehead, a nervous habit. "What if he asks about his brother?"

"There's nothing more to say, Georgia," I repeated, which was what I told her every time she brought it up. She had given a statement to the police; we had let them search the inn, had turned over everything they had asked for. Sheriff Stamer told us to send any calls his way. It wasn't our job to spread rumors. But it didn't stop others from trying. Our phone rang off the hook for months after—with tips, with questions, with people pretending to be visitors who were instead fishing for information.

It wasn't hard to say nothing. But Georgia asked every time, as if someone could trick her into revealing something new. As if she had done anything wrong, and was just waiting to be found out.

I assured her she hadn't. But when someone goes missing, I had learned, every action is reevaluated, our motivations probed and judged. So that, at night, alone, when it's just you and the dark, it's hard not to do the same. To revisit not just the things we had done, but the things we had missed.

In truth, all of us at the inn had done exactly what had been expected. Georgia had only entered Cabin Four when Landon West missed his checkout. It was then that she found the luggage, the laptop, all still in his room. His car was still in the lot. We all searched the grounds, and I called the Last Stop Tavern before Celeste called the sheriff. He could've walked into town just as readily as he could've walked into the woods.

But the woods were what everyone was worried about.

Still, the inn was not at fault.

There was a guidebook in each room, with brochures for bicycle rentals, river rafting trips, horseback excursions. We included a map of all the surrounding trails, with details on the difficulty of each. And we took extra precautions in warning about the dangers one might encounter on the mountain. Bears, snakes, poisonous plants, and dangerous terrain. We offered walking sticks at the front desk, made sure everyone knew that there was no cell phone signal; we told people to travel together, to pack food and water, to stay on the trail. We even offered guided hikes, free of charge.

All these things, to keep them safe.

We reminded them that the number one cause of death out there was exposure, which could only happen if you made a mistake or got lost.

We did not mention the second cause, or the third.

IT WASN'T YET NINE a.m. when I pulled my car out of the small employee lot, coasted down the drive, and headed toward the center of town. I didn't bother calling first; I knew exactly where everyone would be at this time on a Thursday morning. The guests who rented apartments over the storefronts would be checking to see what was open for breakfast; the tourists from the campground would soon begin walking across the bridge into downtown, just as the huts on the border of the town green opened up to sell tickets and check people in for excursions; and Sheriff Stamer would be making his morning rounds:

A coffee to go from the Edge, where tourists stocked up on both caffeine and supplies; a paper from the stand outside Trace of the Mountain Souvenirs; and then a seat at the bar at the Last Stop Tavern, where he'd catch up with the owners before their official opening.

By the time he finished his circuit, he'd know anything worth knowing about the day prior, and anything to look out for in the day to come. I kept an eye out for his uniform as I looked for a parking spot along his route.

Up ahead, Jack Olivier was loading the back of his van with a few tents, probably making a personal delivery from the Edge.

Jack was a twentysomething lifer of Cutter's Pass who split his time between leading Outward Bound youth programs and working at the outfitting store, his hours flexible enough that you could often rely on him to lend a hand when needed. He was tall and thin, all gangly limbs, so it wasn't hard to imagine him scaling the face of a rock or lunging across a crevasse.

He climbed into the driver's seat of his van, leaned his head out the window, and called something across the street. Rochelle, another lifer, was out there now, heading toward the sheriff's office, where she'd worked for as long as I'd been here.

Rochelle pushed her long dark hair over her shoulder and shook her head with a small grin, never breaking stride.

I pulled into the spot Jack had just vacated, and circled back to the tavern, deciding to wait for the sheriff at the end of his route. Marina and Ray never minded if you sat at one of their outdoor tables off-hours.

But when I passed the front of the tavern, Sheriff Stamer was already visible through the front window. He was seated at the bar, a newspaper rolled up on the counter beside him, hands circling a to-go coffee cup, while Marina and Ray worked on the other side of the counter. Marina had a laptop propped up on the surface, and Ray moved quickly and efficiently behind her, unloading crates from a delivery.

I knocked on the glass beside the door, and Marina startled before raising one hand. I couldn't hear what she said to the others, but they both watched as she crossed the room, unlocked the door, and propped it open on her hip.

"Speak of the devil," she said with a wide, gap-toothed grin. Her brown curly hair was held back in a haphazard ponytail, pieces falling forward. "The line at the inn has been busy all morning."

I pictured Georgia, her worried face, the phone lines out again. I pictured a string of callers, all asking for information about Landon West, and her leaving the phone off the hook, to escape.

"Sorry about that. I think the storm messed up the phones," I said.

She nodded. "Power surge took out the entire left side of the street last night. Sheriff's got Harris rebooting systems down at the office, if you need him to take a look."

"I'll check it out first," I said. Besides, if Harris's van was in sight, he'd probably end up working his way up and down the street all morning, people stopping him to *just take a quick look at something*, while he was around.

"I was hoping to catch the sheriff here, actually," I said, tipping my chin to the bar, where Ray kept glancing in our direction.

"Sure thing, just, while I have you, any changes to the order this week?" The Last Stop supplied the drinks and appetizers for our nightly happy hours. Georgia typically confirmed the orders each morning, adding more if the wine supply was running low. I would have to check when I was back.

"Let's keep it the same," I said.

She opened the door wider, gesturing me inside. "You've got a visitor, boss," she called with a lopsided smile.

This was also why I remained in uniform. I knew I looked younger than twenty-eight, that without makeup, without the right attire, people were quick to overlook me otherwise. The memory of Cutter's Pass was predominantly long-term, and I lacked the roots that tied so many of them together. Sheriff Stamer only paid me more attention than he would have otherwise because I was Celeste's niece.

"What can I do for you, Abby?" the sheriff asked, swiveling on the stool. He looked as if he'd just gotten back from vacation, his pale skin pink across the bridge of his nose and his forehead, where his reddish-brown hair had begun to recede.

"I was wondering if there've been any recent updates to the West case," I said, shifting on my feet. Something, I didn't yet add, that might've drawn his brother here.

His mouth was a flat line, and Marina cast a quick glance to her husband. Ray looked down, dropping a crate on the countertop too hard, dishes rattling inside. Behind him, on the wall beside the liquor shelves, was the small photo of the Fraternity Four, the last picture of record, where visitors could raise a glass to the lost from the other side of the bar. The wooden frame had been securely nailed into the wall, after several unsuccessful attempts by visitors to nab it.

"You're not the only one asking about that," he said. "There's definitely been some renewed interest the last couple weeks, but nothing to report."

I imagined Trey at the sheriff's office, attempting to nudge the gossip out of Rochelle at the front desk. I imagined him here at the tavern, acting like a tourist and nothing more.

"I told Cory not to talk about that case yet," Ray mumbled. Cory was more like his mother in personality, who greeted everyone by name, always ready to lend an encouraging ear. But he looked more like his father—squared-off jawline, deep-set eyes, light brown skin, but with hair that fell like Marina's, whenever he was in need of a haircut.

"It's not his fault," Sheriff Stamer said, brushing his arm across the countertop, as if cutting off a well-worn argument at the roots.

Long before he was the sheriff, Patrick Stamer and Ray Shiles grew up here together, friends since they were neighbors in childhood—and always a study in opposites, to hear anyone tell it. Patrick, redheaded and pale, skinny and tall. Whereas Ray was broad shouldered and stocky, with black hair, brown skin, dark eyes. As kids, the sheriff was loud and hot tempered, where Ray was the steady one.

Still, no one was surprised when Patrick became a deputy, as his father had been the sheriff then; or that Ray took over the tavern his parents had run for years prior. There was a sense of order here, of established expectations and stability. But since Patrick hadn't married or had children, Ray and Marina were as close to family as he had, and any benefits of nepotism from the sheriff fell to Cory Shiles.

"It's true," Marina said. "The visitors this summer have all been asking about it."

Marina loved town gossip, but Ray was opposed on principle, for the same reason as the sheriff.

They had been here when Landon West went missing this spring. And when Farrah Jordan disappeared, three winters earlier. And Alice Kelly, before that. And, of course, they had been here for the Fraternity Four, the start of it all. Back then, neither was much older than the missing young men. The Last Stop was just the Tavern, owned by Ray's parents. The sheriff was just a new deputy. And Cutter's Pass was just a small mountain town, known for its hiking and river activities, and its proximity to a steep and narrow pass that led to the Appalachian Trail.

Now Sheriff Stamer stood, smoothed out the sides of his beige pants, readjusted his thin brown tie. "It's nothing, Abby. Just some of the tourists thinking they'll be the ones to find something. This is how they get each time." He almost smiled, the lines at the corners of his eyes radiating outward. He'd aged a lot in the decade I'd known him, with the receding hairline, the weathered skin. But it fit him. Gave him that authority, that trustworthiness. "They're not coming up your way asking questions, are they?" he asked.

"His brother checked in to the inn last night," I said. "I wondered if something specific brought him here. Or if he's just staying there for . . . sentimental reasons."

The entire room fell silent. The only sign of movement was a twitch at the corner of the sheriff's eye.

The details surrounding Landon West's case were not easy for the town. The fact that he was a journalist, that he'd been working on a story about the string of disappearances here—it was hard to reconcile as coincidence. *Bad optics*, the sheriff had said. *Difficult*, for all involved.

It was clear that none of them had heard about Trey West's arrival yet.

Sheriff Stamer breathed in deeply, splintering the moment. "He hasn't come my way, if that's what you're asking." He hitched his pants by the belt loops, tucked the paper under his arm. "Listen, Abby, the brother wasn't around in the spring when it all went down. My guess, he's here to pay his respects. Deal with his guilt. His grief. Best to let him do that."

"Okay. Thanks," I said, nodding.

"Someone better tell Cory to stop with his tours up there," Ray said, eyes to his wife.

"I already did," I said, more sharply than I intended, already regretting coming here. Imagining all the gears I'd kicked into motion, with a simple question, a careless statement.

I should have known better than to think this place would have answers. This was supposed to be behind us. And now all I'd done was spread the gossip. By the time I made it back to the inn, the rest of the town would probably know. The sheriff to Rochelle, and then up and down the storefronts. From Jack at the Edge to the booths on the town green, tendrils spreading outward.

This was why I knew there couldn't be some deep secret at the heart of the town that had been kept, incident after incident, for decades. Because word travels fast here, and we're opinionated and stubborn, each in our own way. Because the PTA presidents can't hold their posts for more than one term before being voted out, and even the town slogan on the welcome sign was up for debate every year.

Because, for as many people who wanted things to stay exactly the same as they had always been here, just as many others wanted a change. A new perspective, a new vision. To shake our notoriety, and there were only so many ways to do it.

Because I'd listened closely, and I paid attention, and I'd been here long enough by now to believe I could see the town for what it was. It was just a place.

Being called the most dangerous town in North Carolina was a joke. I could count the number of actual crimes that had been committed here on one hand—I knew them all.

As for the disappearances, we had rehashed, with one another, all the nondangerous options: Maybe there was some mistake—that they went missing from somewhere else, another town, farther along the trail. Maybe the Fraternity Four had always planned to live off grid, had set up a community, of sorts, for themselves. Maybe those who had vanished simply didn't want to be found.

But danger was a concept fueled by uncertainty, that grew stronger the longer we went with no answers. Time kept expanding here.

With every new, unanswered question, something stirred.

CHAPTER 4

TREY WEST'S CAR WAS still in the lot when I returned from town. And it was still there when it was time for the shift change at one p.m.

Georgia filled me in on the guest updates just as a man from the laundry service left with the linens. "The Shermans are out on a hike," she said, sliding the binder across the surface of the registration desk. The binder served as both a daily record and an ongoing conversation between the two of us. It was more reliable than any computer program, and we could adjust it at will. She'd made two tally marks beside the Shermans' name on the open page—a running inventory of the walking sticks.

"Got it. Anything else?" I asked.

"Mountain View One lost their key," she said with an eye roll.

"Did you give them the spare?"

"Yes, and cataloged the loss." She pushed her hair to the side, eyes to the double doors. "He hasn't checked out yet, you know," she said.

"I can see that." I grinned. "I'll handle it. Hey, did the line go down again?" I asked, remembering what Marina had told me earlier in the day.

She frowned, a single worry line appearing in her forehead. "I don't think so—"

I put a hand on her wrist as she reached for the phone. "Don't worry about it. I was just checking."

Georgia shrugged, then slipped into the back office, where I heard her dragging a chair across the floor—I could picture her, feet propped up, cell in hand, scrolling the news while she ate beside the windows, in the one location with the prime service. Since April, she always brought her lunch up here at the start of the day and stored it in the mini-fridge beside the cabinet with the safe, instead of sneaking back to her apartment for a bite or heading into town.

I picked up the phone, listened to the steady dial tone, then called the line for Cabin Four. By the fifth ring, I was about to hang up, when the line finally connected. A rustling, a pause, and then: "Hello?"

His voice sounded tentative and far away, like the receiver was nowhere near his face.

"Mr. West?" I said, leaning over the counter, to keep the conversation from drifting toward Georgia in the office. "This is Abby, at reception."

"Oh." I heard the phone juggling, coming closer to his face. "Hi."

"I only ran your card for the single night, I'm sorry. How long were you planning to stay, so I can update your reservation?"

There was a delayed pause. "To be honest, I hadn't thought about it," he said. "I took off from work for the week, came down on impulse . . ." He trailed off, cleared his throat. "Sorry, is the room available for the rest of the week?"

"Through the weekend, yes." I had a group of hikers on the calendar for two cabins next week, but they weren't set to arrive until Monday. The cabins were never all booked far in advance.

"Okay, if you give me a minute, I'll bring over the credit card."

But Georgia was still in the office, and I was trying to keep her *out of it*, like Celeste requested.

"Actually, we have a happy hour each night, at five. Some drinks and appetizers in the lobby. I didn't give you the full overview of our services last night, but if you swing by this evening, I'll run your card then. And we can go over anything else."

"Five," he repeated. "Yes. Hey, is there food on-site normally? Like, for lunch?"

"No," I said. "There's a tavern at the edge of town." I couldn't bring myself to say the name, which now seemed offensive, in bad taste. "It's the first place you'll hit if you walk down. There are plenty of cafés scattered through the downtown, and ice cream shops. Sometimes there'll be other vendors set up on the green. It's all walkable. You can't miss it."

"Thanks, Abby."

When I hung up, Georgia traipsed out of the back room. "Doing a walk-through before calling it a day," she said. "Anything else you need after?"

Most afternoons, she handled the room turnover; said she found the cleaning and prepping a soothing routine. A simple monotony. Which was how she discovered Landon West's empty cabin at one in the afternoon on his checkout date, two hours after it should've been vacated.

The problem, the police quickly realized, was that we weren't sure *exactly* which day he went missing. He'd kept largely to himself, for his stay. And there wasn't a daily cleaning service in the outside cabins.

By the time he was discovered missing, any trail that might've existed was untraceable. It had rained early that morning, a quick rush of water over the trails, the roads, the grass in front of the cabin.

It still haunted her, I knew. It haunted all of us.

"Go," I said. "Enjoy your afternoon." Even though I knew Georgia would spend the rest of the day keeping to the grounds, as she'd been doing ever since Landon West's disappearance. She'd change first, thinking she could blend in with the guests—so different from my own approach. I felt the opposite: Always in danger of fading into the background. Always feeling the need to remind people I was here.

THIRTY MINUTES LATER, A pizza delivery arrived in the lobby. A teen I had come to recognize as a regular throughout the summer popped his head inside but remained in the entrance. "Cabin Four?" he asked.

I waved him on, sure he already knew the layout of the property.

It occurred to me that Trey West hadn't left that room since he arrived last night.

I started watching the clock as it crept closer to the time I would see him again. Imagining a do-over of the night before, where this time I was capable, no longer caught on my heels: *What are you interested in doing while you're here? Anything I can help set up? What do you* want*?*

The Shermans returned just before three. They appeared to be somewhere in their fifties, and both seemed relatively fit, but they looked a little worse for the wear after their hike.

"Which trail did you do today?" I asked, smiling.

"Shallow Falls," the wife answered, peering out the window for a moment.

"How was it?" I asked.

"Took twice as long coming back than going," the husband said, running his palm across his forehead, leaving a streak of dirt behind. "But worth it," he added, smiling at his wife.

The Shallow Falls Trail was tricky like that. You had to be

careful not to misjudge when you left. The path to the falls was rocky and meandering, weaving around roots—and the addition of a recent rain made the footing unstable on the way down.

"The falls were beautiful. Stunning, really," she added. She had a metal water bottle in her free hand, and she passed it to her husband.

"Please thank Georgia for us," the husband said, still a little out of breath. "She was right, about the map, and about needing these." He dropped the walking sticks in the bin, the bases most likely coated in mud—I'd take care of that when they were out of sight.

When they were halfway down the hall, heading toward the stairs that would take them to one of the three Mountain View rooms on the second floor, I checked them off Georgia's list for today, then closed the binder, slipped it under the countertop. Everyone safe and accounted for.

The Shallow Falls Trail—that was the one behind our property. The one made famous for the disappearances. We were more careful now. We kept a closer watch.

BY THE TIME HAPPY hour was approaching, I hadn't received the food delivery yet, and I was getting anxious. Or maybe it was the thought of Trey West, due any moment.

I kept peering out the office window, in between people stopping by the lobby. And when the older couple staying in Eagle's Nest on the top floor came down fifteen minutes early, completely in character—early for check-in, early for happy hour, early for breakfast—I went ahead and gathered a crate of the wine from inventory.

Through the tempered glass panel, I could see a blue vehicle parked in front of the doors, and I breathed a sigh of relief. The

Last Stop Tavern owned a blue, nondescript van, driven by a variety of their employees.

I opened a few of the bottles, setting out the glassware and the small plates, when Marina opened the front door, propping it ajar.

"Sorry, running a little behind today," she said while I pasted on a grin.

I was too surprised by her presence to react. Usually, one of their teenage employees brought up the trays of food, wearing jeans and a T-shirt with the Last Stop logo.

But Marina was out of uniform, and looked like she had plans for the evening. Her hair was uncharacteristically down, curls defined with gel, and she'd lined her eyes, wore her wedding rings—which I never saw while she was working, typically.

She set up the appetizers on the warming trays, then stood off to the side as the early couple started piling their small plates with an assortment of bruschetta and mini mozzarella sticks, heat visibly escaping at first bite.

It occurred to me, then, that Marina intended to stay. Which was the point of these happy hours, really. Celeste wanted the inn to be open to the community, a place where visitors could mingle with one another, but also a place to help local businesses, to meet someone who might share details about a river trip, a horseback tour, or the best place to hike. And for the locals to share a taste of the authentic Cutter's Pass. We wanted the inn to look alive, and this was a way to achieve it, while supporting the community at the same time.

The wine was procured from the Last Stop, but the label matched the logo that had adorned the inn since its inception—that tree with the bare branches spreading across the sky, in inverse colors from the umbrella: navy blue on a white label, *The Passage Inn* written in small cursive letters underneath.

"How are things going?" Marina asked as she fidgeted with a

stack of napkins, turning them side to side on the counter, accomplishing nothing.

I knew why she was here. She was waiting to see what would happen. She was waiting to see him.

Footsteps approached from down the hall, and her eyes betrayed her, shifting over my shoulder. But it was just the trio of couples from the Forest View rooms on the second floor, traveling together.

I smiled, poked a cherry tomato with a toothpick. "He's not staying upstairs," I said before popping it into my mouth.

"Has he seen the room?" she asked.

"He's staying in it."

She raised her eyebrows, surprised. "You're kidding." She laughed. "Well, I guess that's one way to get him out of here."

I shook my head, slightly startled. I'd thought it would be what he wanted, to be as close as he could, to feel the echo of his brother left behind. But now I wasn't so sure.

Marina stepped closer, just as more guests filed into the lobby. "What do you know about him, Abby?"

In truth, I knew almost nothing of Trey West: He shared a few mannerisms with his brother, something I couldn't quite place when he'd first walked into the inn. He'd been overseas when his brother went missing, and as far as I knew, he didn't come home when he heard. He was a nonentity, then. Someone who contributed to a joint statement, but remained far removed from reality. It had not concerned me to find out why. Maybe others knew more. Maybe I was missing something.

"Not much," I said. "Why?"

"I just think it's weird, him coming here now, after all this time. What's the point?"

"Closure?" I asked. Like the sheriff said, maybe he was here to pay his respects. Maybe he felt a pull, had to see it for himself.

She gave me *a look*, like I should know better. "Wishful thinking doesn't help anyone."

Neither Marina nor I grew up here, didn't have the history of her husband or the sheriff, or Cory, even, who only saw this place for how he wanted to see it. Ray had vouched for her, just as Celeste for me. Marina had grown up only two towns east, but she said it had still taken her years to be accepted as a true resident of Cutter's Pass.

"People want action. Even if it's just for show." She paused. "Maybe especially then."

The front doors opened behind her then, and she must've seen it in my face, because she turned slowly to see who had just arrived.

My stomach sank. He didn't look good.

I wasn't sure what I expected, but Trey West seemed transformed by his stay in Cabin Four. Hollow-eyed and unsure, hair unruly, like he hadn't slept.

I imagined him up all night, picturing his brother's last movements. Falling asleep in the morning, in a fitful exhaustion, until my call after noon had roused him. The disorientation that comes from sleeping the wrong hours. Like stepping out of a dark room after too long.

It was a common refrain from anyone who's lived here for a time that Cutter's Pass changes you. There was an atmosphere that drew people here, or kept people returning. While this town was most known for those who had disappeared, many others seemed to find what they were looking for instead: people from the outside who would find a way to remain, uprooting their entire lives. Like there was something you might discover here, about yourself.

I thought of Georgia, stumbling out of the woods, with blisters and ill-fitting shoes, like some ethereal being made solid. Becoming, in time, more grounded, and real. Cleaning the corners of the halls with a set determination. Celeste's husband, Vincent, transforming from a man in a suit working with numbers in a back office to one whose imagination could turn a plot of land and a heap of wood into *this*. *Like magic*, Celeste had said. Even me, learning to move in harmony with the town, and the inn.

It wasn't magic so much as the crisp mountain air. The necessity of everything in town, and the familiar routine of all the pieces working together. It was the contribution you brought to the order here, and the confidence in the choice you've made to be here. Just like the choice I'd made ten years earlier, and the choice I continued to make, in staying.

So maybe I shouldn't have been surprised to see Trey West differently one day in, uncertain about his choice to come, his purpose for staying, after spending the night alone in the spot his brother was last seen.

But the town had done the opposite to him; Cutter's Pass had complicated his understanding, taken something instead. Marina was right—there was one sure way to get him out of here, and I was well on my way to achieving it, by putting him in that room. Not in an act of kindness, as I'd thought, but cruelty.

Marina stepped aside as Trey approached the registration desk, and I tried to look unfazed by the pronounced shift in his demeanor. "Glad you could make it," I said.

He nodded, distracted, as he pulled out his credit card, a faint tremble to his hand this time. There was a scratch on the back of his wrist that I didn't remember seeing yesterday.

As I ran his card, his gaze drifted to the barrel of walking sticks. "Weren't there umbrellas in this yesterday?"

"There were," I said. "Today seemed like more of a walking stick day." I smiled, trying to get his face to mirror my own. Standing so close, I could see the twitch of a muscle at the corner of his eye.

"That's it, right?" he began, turning to the back window for a moment. The mountain, invisible last night, now the million-dollar view. "The Vanishing Trail?" His voice dropped, and my throat tightened.

That's what they called it, the visitors who were more interested in the myth than the people. Who were more captivated by the mystery than the reality.

"Yes, that's the trail to Shallow Falls," I corrected. "But you can't do it now." Not with the rapidly setting sun, the narrowing of the path, the lack of clarity and direction. "You'll never make it back in time."

His gaze was hooked on that mountain still, and I needed to pull him back.

"You know, we offer guided tours. For safety. I can take you tomorrow." The words were out before I could consider them, weigh them. I cleared my throat. "But it would have to be early. I need to be back by lunch."

He slowly turned my way, eyes slightly unfocused. "That would be great," he said.

Sheriff Stamer walked in just then. He was in uniform, and he surveyed the room, shaking hands and greeting guests. He smiled at Marina, and I wondered if they had coordinated their visits. Whether they'd returned to whispering across the bar top after I left the tavern this morning, formulating a plan. Or if each was just drawn here by their own curiosity, no better than the trauma tourists. But then, the sheriff was here enough on his own—he'd been known to bring groceries and deliveries for Celeste, and often picked her up for the Sunday-morning service at the chapel in town.

"Hi, Abby," the sheriff called just as Trey retreated toward the display of drinks. "Is Celeste making an appearance tonight?"

"No, she—"

But then there she was, as if manifested by his words, coming around the corner of the hall, in a flowing green tunic that brought out her eyes, transformed her to something at one with this place, with the surroundings. When you couldn't help but remember that these were the walls she had built, the floor she had laid, on her knees beside Vincent, in prayer to something else. That there was a history inside these rooms, and every marred surface, every chosen detail. It was no surprise that her beaded bracelet matched the bowl on the end table by the window, both made from the same artist and sold at the farmers' market on the town green on Saturday mornings.

"Glad you could make it, Patrick," she said, joining the group, and now I was wondering if it was she who had orchestrated this. She extended her hand, and the sheriff took it between the two of his, giving her a soft squeeze, a gentle smile, before moving on.

The lobby had filled up with guests, with visitors, with *us*. Only Georgia was missing.

I sank back against the wall, taking in the entirety of the room, the way everything clicked and moved and connected.

There were the Shermans, cleaned up from their hike, talking with Celeste, who nodded along to their animated story.

There were the trio of room reservations who had coordinated their trip together, now gathered in a boisterous circle in front of the windows, laughing too loudly and going through their drinks at a pace that even I found impressive.

There was the small child, a rarity, hands reaching up to sort through a plate of warm chocolate chip cookies. I quickly followed behind, removing the food he'd touched.

When I looked up again, Marina and Sheriff Stamer were standing in a small circle with Trey West.

Marina handed Trey a fresh glass of red wine, which he took, depositing his empty one on the counter beside him. The sheriff was patting his shoulder. I couldn't hear what they were saying, but Trey still had that glazed look on his face, and didn't seem to be contributing much to the conversation.

The sheriff quickly moved on, only for Celeste to slide into his place. I heard her welcoming him, hands clasped together, *I hope you're having a lovely stay*, like she had no idea who he was.

"Abby?" A man with ruddy cheeks and an empty wineglass stepped into my vision.

It took me a moment to pull his name. "Mr. Lorenzo, how can I help you?"

It turned out, *how I could help* was by making a reservation for their group of six during peak season at peak hours at CJ's Hideaway, which required a text to the hostess's cell from the back office, and the luck of a cancellation.

When I returned to the lobby, eyes skimming the crowd, Trey was gone.

Sheriff Stamer ambled my way, wide stance, straight posture, like he knew he was being watched. He rested an arm on the counter, turned so he was partly facing the room while speaking with me. "I feel bad for the kid," he said. "But he seems like he's processing." Even though Trey was nowhere near a kid, probably older than I was, even.

"What did he say?" I asked.

"Not much at all. I told him I'd be happy to walk him through the case, if he comes by the office. Gave him my card, told him to make an appointment with Rochelle." He smiled tightly. "I doubt he will."

He tapped the counter twice with an open palm. "Have a good one, Abby." And then he stopped to speak with Celeste for a moment before heading out.

I waited as the rest of the guests finished up, or at least took the hint as I started cleaning. There were always stragglers—those who waited until you officially closed up, before moving on.

Marina lent me a hand stacking the trays, and I helped her carry her supplies out to the van. "I should come more often," she said, sliding the back door closed. "Better than handling our happy hour crowd, for sure."

"You're always welcome," I said as she lingered in the parking lot, squinting against the lowering sun.

"You're a good one, Abby. Celeste is lucky to have you," she said, and I smiled, out of politeness.

Children hadn't been a part of Celeste's plans, and though at eighteen I had considered myself an adult, looking back, I could see how she had shifted her life to accommodate my own. Pretending Sunday dinners were part of the work arrangement, telling me things I could imagine a parent saying instead, under the guise of my job. Raising an eyebrow at me and Cory and saying, in her frank way: *That's going to get you nowhere.* And she was right. Things became clearer the older I got. I was lucky to have her, and everyone knew it.

I watched as Marina climbed into the driver's seat of the van, the wheels kicking up gravel in the lot, as she took the exit too quickly.

Back inside, I found myself alone once more, nothing but the scent of food and perfume and a tinny ringing in my ears, like the absence of something.

I hurried to wipe up the wine stains before they set in, then removed the empty wine bottles, counting as I went, for inventory. There were three full bottles still unopened, but we seemed to be missing two. Which also happened—guests taking a bottle back to their room.

I didn't think more of it until later, when I was back at the registration desk, pulling the walking sticks from the barrel—noticing I was a count short.

Thinking of the Shermans leaving their two behind. No other tallies on the page from Georgia. No one else talking about hiking this evening.

Just Trey, eyes to the barrel, asking about the start of *the vanishing trail*.

I thought of the dark. Of the stories. His questions about the trail.

Of Trey with a bottle of wine and a walking stick and some purpose most of us were just guessing at—and I felt a chill, a precursor, the same feeling I'd gotten when I stood in his brother's empty room for the first time.

The thing about a disappearance here was that our history made it somehow more unlikely, harder to comprehend. Like you've been playing a role in a production for too long. Something tongue-in-cheek, not quite a joke, but not quite the absence of one, either. So at the first sign of a disappearance, you had to shake the smile, fight back the nervous laughter threatening to bubble up. It's a slowly creeping horror. Something you have to check and double-check, a hypothetical monster under the bed. Where the only thing you can think is: *No. Please, no.*

I picked up the phone at the front desk to call Trey. But the line just clicked steadily with dead air.

Something was wrong. *Of course* something was wrong. Something was very wrong here. I understood that. We all must've understood that, on some level, whether we wanted to face it.

There were a lot of rumors about us here, as a collective—about the things we knew, the secrets we kept. But they ignored the obvious.

Georgia with her always-on music, and me with my proof-of-life photos to Sloane. Cory, outgoing and charming, making it impossible to miss him for long, and Marina, always bringing in the latest news. Celeste, who hosts nightly happy hours, and the sheriff who makes his regular visits, keeps to his schedule. Even the notes Georgia and I leave for each other at the front desk, a reminder that we were just there.

Everyone here is afraid of disappearing. And that no one else would notice before it was too late.

The missing hiking stick. The bottles of wine. His questions about the trail. His frame of mind.

I could not leave him out there alone.

CHAPTER 5

I QUICKLY SECURED THE OFFICE behind the registration desk before racing out into the evening, where the sun had begun to set, and hoped I wasn't too late to catch him.

The path lights to the cabins switched on as I jogged past, triggered by the settling dark. I raced up the cabin stairs, my steps echoing on the wood, when I heard something moving inside the cabin. Something heavy.

I breathed a sigh of relief, realizing I wasn't too late, and pounded on the door with the side of my closed fist. The moving stopped, but no one approached. No steps across the floor, or a muffled call of *Just a minute.*

Silence.

I knocked again. "Mr. West? It's Abby. Can I speak with you please?"

Footsteps this time, and the door swung partly open. Trey had a faint gleam of sweat covering his face, hair disheveled, with the room in total disarray behind him. I could smell the booze coming off him—wasn't sure it was just the wine after all.

Instinctively, I took a step back. "What's going on?" I asked, trying to keep my voice steady, calm, and controlled.

This time, he flung the door wide open, like some grand gesture. "I don't know, why don't you tell me."

I shook my head, still standing in the entrance, as I surveyed the room. The dresser drawers had each been removed, laying empty on the floor. The bed had been pushed out from the wall. The wooden desk chair had been relocated below a vent, the grating removed.

And the metal grate was now on the surface of the desk, tossed on top of the open guest book binder. There was a screwdriver beside it, along with one of the missing bottles of wine—now empty. The walking stick was resting on the floor beside the chair, like he'd been using it to prod the space behind the missing grate.

I swallowed, stood my ground. "If you don't tell me what's going on, I'm going to have to ask you to leave."

"Come on," he said, taking a few unbalanced steps backward, steadying himself on a bedpost, "from the second I've been here, I'm being watched."

"That's ridiculous. No, you're not." On the contrary, the three of us here had done our best to keep our distance.

He let out one loud, sharp laugh. "Oh, the sheriff just happens to be there tonight? Pulls me aside to ask if he can help me with anything while I'm in town?" He smirked, like he thought he'd uncovered my game. "And the noises last night, my god. If I didn't know any better, I'd think someone was trying to drive me out of here. So tell me, Abby, am I close?"

"No, that's not . . . the sheriff showing up, it was a coincidence . . . What noises?" I asked.

He swung his arm out to the side, gesturing to the wood-paneled wall that divided his room from Cabin Three. "From next door. The scratching. The moving. All. Fucking. Night."

"There's no one there," I said. "It's the squirrels. They get in the eaves, and—"

He started laughing again. Head tipped back, unhinged. I thought about calling someone. Backing down the steps, locking myself in the lobby, safe behind tempered glass and solid wood and locks made of steel.

"Squirrels. Coincidence. Answer me this, then. Where is my brother's phone? He always recorded his interviews with it."

My eyes went wide. "If you have questions about the investigation, you should talk to the sheriff. *All of us* looked for him. Here, and out *there*." He flinched, but I continued. "My guess? His phone was on him." I looked around the chaos again, an understanding slowly setting in. "Is that what you're looking for? You think there's a missing phone in here?"

He rounded the room, to the far side of the bed. "No," he said as he pushed the bed farther away from the wall, leveraging his weight behind the headboard. And then he shook his head. "I don't *know*."

I saw him differently then. Not at all how the sheriff implied—as some kid worthy of our sympathy—but something more: illogical, panicked, something on the cusp of dangerous. I squeezed my eyes shut, desperate for control of the situation. "Stop," I said. "Just, stop." I gripped the closest bedpost, like that could stop him. "Please just calm down."

The desk light caught on the scar below his jaw, and this time, I imagined a fight. A hotheaded punch, a returning jab, a knockout blow, and his chin colliding with the surface of a bar.

I ran through the possibilities of who to call. The sheriff; Celeste; Ray at the tavern, who might get someone here faster than the police; Cory, even, who was probably somewhere out there, right now.

But suddenly, Trey stilled. His hands were still gripping the headboard, but he was looking at me closely now, like he was reclassifying me, just as I was doing to him. "Was it you, Abby, who noticed he was missing?"

I shook my head. "I didn't notice," I said. "None of us did. Not until he missed checkout. I'm sorry."

"I didn't, either," he said. He deflated, looking around the room, like he could see himself finally as I did.

Okay, everything was okay. He was coming down from the episode. His reaction tonight was just the setting, his guilt, the lack of information. All of us, bombarding him at once.

"We weren't close," he said, in a confessional tone that belied our relationship. "I was away on business." An excuse that sounded like an alibi he'd had to give to the police. "It was the start of a new consulting assignment, and when my mom called, I didn't see what difference it would make if I were here or there. He was a grown man, we both were, he had his own life, his own way of doing things. We weren't cut from the same cloth, him and me. Do you have siblings?"

I shook my head. Had imagined it sometimes, how different my life would've been if the makeup of my family had been just a little different, a little larger. The small shifts that changed the entire trajectory of a life.

"Well," he said, like I couldn't possibly understand the dynamics of such things—of people forced to occupy the same space, with little in common. Of growing apart. "I thought maybe he was trying to emulate the experience at first, you know? The disappearances. He wasn't . . . He got his stories in . . . nontraditional ways."

I guessed that *nontraditional* was a generous way of saying that Landon West did not find himself beholden to the same ethics as others. The papers had reported that he had a reputation of keeping his stories and his progress under tight wraps until they were ready. Whatever he'd been working on, it was never printed. No details had emerged. His editors at the magazine he often freelanced for didn't know much about it, other than he had said he had a fresh lead into the mysteries of Cutter's Pass. His friends knew less, just that he was planning to be off grid for a time.

Whatever that lead was, it didn't exist in any email correspondences with colleagues. It hadn't been shared with anybody who came forward, looking for him, or looking for the reward offered by his family. It hadn't been stored on his laptop, either, which was left behind in his room on the surface of that desk

"My parents went through all his things, I know. But *I* didn't."

"You think they missed something? That you're going to find it now?"

"I think if there's something worth finding, it'll be me, yeah."

Everyone who arrived here came with that same feeling—that they would be the one to crack it, somehow. It was almost a compulsion, but it never played out.

Trey sighed. "It's not just the phone. He also kept a notebook on him, one of those small leather ones. Always had it. I thought it was so fucking pretentious." He laughed to himself before dropping onto the edge of the bed.

"You think you're going to find a notebook?"

I looked at the surface of the desk again. Trey had packed a screwdriver, had come here with the intention of taking this place apart. But there weren't many hiding places.

He raised his arms in some exaggerated, exhausted shrug. "When we were teenagers, he hid things from our parents in a vent like that . . ." His eyes drifted to the open grate, and he shook his head. "It was stupid to think. But there has to be *something*. There's nothing on his computer? He was here for almost a week. What the hell was he doing here, then?"

"I'm sorry, I wish I had answers for you. But there's nothing in this room. Everyone has already been through it." I swallowed. "We all searched for him. Went out every morning. For weeks, Trey."

He looked over at me, mouth slightly parted, before his eyes drifted shut. "Yeah," he said, still sitting on the edge of the bed, running his hand through his hair. "I'm sorry about . . ." He waved his hand around the cabin. "He's not an experienced hiker. Do you think . . ."

I didn't like to think about it, didn't want to talk about all the ways something could go wrong out there. The rumors of people who tried to take shelter in some hidden place in bad weather, becoming trapped. The stories of hikers stepping off trail, getting disoriented and unable to find their way back.

"Here," I said, "just, let's move this back. Help me with the bed."

He returned to the headboard, and I braced my hands on the nearest post, but when I put my weight behind it, the oval top of the wooden post popped off in my hand, the sound reverberating.

I had maybe two seconds to decide what to do, and by then, it was too late. Trey's eyes locked on mine.

I waited for him to look first, in case he didn't think of it.

He quickly circled the bed, reached his fingers inside the wood cavity, his fingers coming out coated in dust and black glue. It was empty. But now we knew: these posts weren't firmly secured. A new possibility suddenly revealed itself.

Trey went around to the second post and pulled off the oval top with little effort—empty—and then the third, while I stood there, frozen and useless.

His hand stilled inside the third cavity. He stood on his toes, his breathing coming too fast as he peered inside before revealing something small and black inside the palm of his fist.

There was a moment I thought: bug, cockroach, something gross but safer, in the long run. He held his arm in my direction, slowly unfurling his fist: a small, black, rectangular square. It was a flash drive.

We stared at each other, and I knew we both believed that this had once belonged to Landon West.

IT TOOK FIVE MINUTES for Trey to realize he had nothing to read it with. His laptop, which he'd dug out of his bag, didn't have a port to read this flash drive directly, and he didn't have the right attachment. He leaned over the desk, cursing at the screen, while I hovered behind him, picking the side of my nail, wondering what to do, what to say.

"It might not be his," I said.

But all he did was shoot an incredulous look over his shoulder. I imagined him leaving. Going back home. Taking whatever that rectangular drive contained with him—any answers, out of reach.

"I think the computer at reception might have a port," I said, breaking the silence.

Trey straightened, staring back at me, like he was deciding something. Then he nodded quickly, the idea gathering momentum. "Okay, yes, let's go."

Outside the cabin, he led the way down the lit path, and I could suddenly see a thousand possibilities branching out in front of me. A thousand directions this could go.

Inside, the lobby was empty, the steady flame in the gas fireplace the only movement. I brought the computer to life, then waited while it prompted me for a password.

Trey took the hint and stepped back, so I signed in and held out my hand for the flash drive.

My hand shook as I slid it in, and I was half-surprised when a drive popped up on the screen in front of me. For the briefest second, I considered wiping it clean. Maybe the answers we searched for were not the ones we wanted.

But then Trey leaned in close, and I clicked it open. A password box appeared, and Trey sighed just next to my ear. "Try 9-8-7-6. It was his password for everything growing up, and I swear he never changed it. He's always been a creature of habit."

I entered the code, and the box disappeared, displaying the contents of the drive. "Holy shit," he said. Any question whether this belonged to Landon West was gone.

Inside, there was a single Word document, unnamed. And a folder, labeled with one word, in all caps.

FARRAH.

I sucked in a breath. Farrah Jordan. The woman with the dark hair and haunted expression, whose icy gaze had stared back at me from every frost-coated storefront window in town, three years earlier.

I closed my eyes, the room spinning, time splintering.

Most people who went digging through the history of Cutter's Pass started at the beginning, with the flashiest story. The Fraternity Four. As if that case could solve all the rest, in simple succession.

But new cases brought new information, and Landon West must've understood the trick. You had to start at the most recent, the freshest trail—and work back.

"Oh my god," Trey said, his face so close to mine.

I watched as something settled onto his features: A sobering. A sharpening.

I knew that look—it was foolish and reckless and too far gone. I'd seen that look reflected in each person who came here with a new theory, a new spark. There was no going back now. I saw it in his eyes.

He believed he could find him.

He believed he could find them all.

PART 2

Farrah Jordan

Date missing: January 16, 2019

Last seen: Cutter's Pass, North Carolina

Shallow Falls Trailhead

CHAPTER 6

"**OPEN THAT FOLDER," TREY** said. Too much time had passed as I stared at the contents of the flash drive, my inaction veering too close to being interpreted as a choice.

I could feel his breath at my shoulder and the proximity of his body hovering over mine, could see both our faces reflected in the glow of the computer screen, as I clicked the folder marked FARRAH.

A grid of thumbnails loaded across the page, and a wave of nausea rolled through me, as Trey cursed under his breath. These were photos. Photos in a folder marked with her name.

Farrah Jordan had disappeared three winters earlier. She had arrived in town one morning in January and was last seen at the wooden sign that marked the Shallow Falls Trailhead, with a camera hanging around her neck.

Everyone said it had been bad luck. Bad luck, that she had stopped in Cutter's Pass on a frozen Wednesday, drawn by the beauty of the landscape, lured in to take a closer look. Bad luck, that her car had been found abandoned between the Edge and Trace of the Mountain Souvenirs, covered in a heavy snowfall, three days after she'd presumably gone missing.

I clicked the first photo, preparing myself for her image, her stare, something that dragged her across the past, brought her abruptly into focus. Something sharper than the image we'd all been shown later that week, driver's license quality, reducing her to the haunting eyes, the set of her mouth.

But this was a photograph of nothing. A white blur, a camera in motion. I clicked the next picture, and it was more of the same, but slightly more in focus. In this image, I could make out the vague definition of the tread of a snow boot on white earth. Like she'd snapped these pictures inadvertently, camera pointing at the ground, while she was doing something else.

Maybe outside the Edge, where she'd stopped for a coffee and asked for the way to the Shallow Falls Trailhead. *Beautiful morning*, Jack had said. He'd stepped out front and pointed down the snow-lined road, past the Last Stop Tavern, a straight shot from Main Street to the rise of Mountain Pass, leading the way.

Can I walk it from here? The last words on record of Farrah Jordan.

Sure, most people do. His reply still haunted him, three years later.

Now I could feel the tension building in Trey's breathing beside me. These images were useless, nothing worth hiding on a flash drive in a hollow bedpost.

One more click, and suddenly the room chilled, the world expanded. We were staring at a crisp photograph of bare branches against a pale gray sky.

Trey released a sharp exhale. "Is that here?" he asked.

"I can't tell," I said. I couldn't even tell if the photo was in color—all the warmth had been leached out of the winter landscape. I moved on to the next: more bare trees, narrow trunks and crooked branches overlapping, fading into the distance, giving the illusion of something disappearing. Next: a circle of bare branches against the winter sky, as if someone had taken this while lying on the cold earth. As if the thing disappearing in the previous photo all along was you.

I shivered as Trey leaned across me, impatient, and I moved to the side as he began scrolling faster—searching for her, for *Farrah*, or maybe something else—and gripped the edge of the reception desk.

But the only images, passing one by one across my screen, were of trees, of sky, of snowy ground and a cold, barren landscape. They felt *wrong* somehow, disconnected from the name on the folder.

I knew before he'd reached the end: We wouldn't find her in these pictures. There would be no haunting gaze staring back at us, or glimpse of her in town. There wasn't even a strand of dark hair that had fallen across the frame, or her unsettling reflection against the frozen landscape.

"She was a nature photographer," I told Trey as he hit the arrow key again. "Lived in South Carolina, but taught courses all across the Southeast. She'd been on her way to Asheville, to teach a course for the spring semester. Stayed in Springwood the night before she disappeared, about thirty minutes from here." We had learned, during the search, that she'd told her family she would be taking her time on the way up, would be in and out of cell phone range. They didn't worry at first—she was independent, thirty-six, and often off the grid for work.

For the investigators, Jack's statement indicated that this was probably an unfortunate accident; that she may not have even realized she was in a town notorious for the disappeared when she set out. And the state of her car: back seat piled high with a duffel bag of luggage, a camera bag with several attachments and a battery charger, sneakers tossed on the floor—like she'd just been passing through and got caught up in the beauty of the moment, went angling for a closer shot.

Looking at these images now—trees, snow, sky—I couldn't even say that these had been taken here, on our trail. In the woods, in the winter, everything had a tendency to look the same. Just bare crooked branches, and barren ground, as far as you could see.

"These could be from anywhere," I said. It was even possible that this arrived in Landon West's possession from some other time, some other work trip. That these were not the last images that Farrah Jordan had ever taken.

Trey paused scrolling only for a second before shaking his head and continuing. "Then why the hell did my brother have them?"

My back teeth clenched together, because that was the question. That was the big question. Because, in all the searching, in the list of things that were never seen, that camera—and any presumed contents—had disappeared along with her.

"We don't even know these were hers," I said. They didn't look like art, didn't look like shots taken by a professional photographer, documenting the beauty of a place.

He turned his head toward me, disbelief radiating off him, in a way that made me lean back. He moved the cursor up to the file properties, and a list of details filled the screen to the right. "What day did she disappear?" he asked.

He had highlighted the date in the photo properties, and my stomach sank. "January sixteenth," I said; I knew the date by heart. The same date currently on display in the properties.

"It's hers," he said, and I nodded once. I imagined her surrounded by trees, tipping the camera upward—

Trey clicked forward again, and this time, my mouth started to form a word—*Wait, what*—as the landscape slowly gained context. A snowy trail, seemingly untouched, and I heard the crunch of ice and snow beneath my boots. The next photo: a curve of a rock wall, icicles hanging from the grooves, and I felt the cold texture of the stone ledge under my fingers. Next: a set of ice-slicked rock steps stretching down, and suddenly I knew exactly where we were.

"I know that place," I said. My heart was racing. It was an identifiable location. Would be memorable to anyone who had done the hike. "It's on the way to the falls." It was the last stretch before the end of the trail, when the sound of the cascading water carried around the curve but still remained out of sight. The air cooled by the mist of water and the shade of the rock as the trail veered suddenly downward—a place of expectation.

Trey clicked forward again, but we had reached the end of the photos, the icy steps frozen on the screen.

I closed my eyes, just as a noise escaped my throat. After all this time, I had given up on answers. I'd given up on the idea that anything had been left behind at all.

Until now, there had been no evidence that Farrah Jordan had made it any farther than the trailhead by our property, but seeing these, I knew she'd gone on to the falls, at least. Maybe farther. And she'd documented it all before she'd disappeared.

I should've felt relief: It was the mountain, the weather, *exposure*, as we made sure to warn the visitors. It was not something intrinsically, disturbingly dangerous at the heart of the town itself.

Except. Someone had recovered this camera, and kept it hidden.

Somehow these photos had ended up on a flash drive in Landon West's possession. A tip, sent to a journalist. *A new angle into Cutter's Pass.*

Farrah Jordan's stay in Cutter's Pass had been short and succinct, her movements cataloged up to her last sighting at the trailhead. It was Celeste who was the last to officially see her, later that morning. We'd closed the inn that week for the renovations we put off throughout the past year, and she'd been checking the outside for signs of weather damage.

"What time," I said. "What time were these taken."

Trey clicked over to the file properties again, leaning closer to read the fine print. "January sixteenth," he repeated. "At 3:06 p.m."

I swallowed nothing. Dry air. Fear.

Celeste remembered her because Farrah Jordan didn't seem dressed for a hike in the snow-covered woods. She wore a brown hat, or maybe it was gray. A red scarf. There was no backpack, just a small case, to protect her equipment; just that red scarf slung around her neck, dangling over her shoulder, and a camera in front of her face, angled toward the mountain.

Celeste figured she didn't plan to go very far. Anyone would know better. *We* certainly knew better.

But of course, that was after. We didn't know for several days that she was missing, that this was the last moment anyone would see her. By the time the sheriff called for her abandoned car to be towed, any footprints that marked her route had long since been buried under the fresh layer of snow that blanketed the ground the evening of her arrival and had continued to fall for days after.

I imagined her now, taking a step forward onto the trail, watching the view through the lens of the camera. Another step, crunching the snow, a track she had left for others to follow. A blanket of white sweeping in behind her, erasing it; any trace of her, vanishing.

Trey closed the folder, and my tentative grasp on Farrah went with it. He clicked on the unmarked Word document.

The first thing I noticed was the heading: *A Notorious History*

The document was just a few paragraphs long, and it seemed to be the introduction to whatever piece Landon West was planning to write. I leaned close to Trey, my eyes burning, as I skimmed the words. He listed the statistics of our town, from our geography to our population, capping it off with the *six visitors* who had gone missing. I did not miss the thinly veiled accusations within: the fact that the people in Cutter's Pass wanted you to believe it was just coincidence.

But whichever person you are, believer or disbeliever, Cutter's Pass welcomes you equally.

The truth is—

And then, midline, the document just stopped.

"What the hell?" Trey said, moving the cursor down, as if more of his brother's thoughts would magically appear. A thought frustratingly unfinished, forever lost to us. "What was he starting to write? The truth is *what*?"

I read it again, searching for more. Trey must've been doing the same, because just as I finished, he muttered, "Goddammit, Landon. Of course he would just leave it unfinished." As if this were all Landon's fault, some selfishness that managed to carry over even now, never thinking of the people who might be searching for him.

I imagined Landon sitting at the small wooden desk in Cabin Four, a noise outside the window distracting him. I imagined a sudden knock on his door and Landon calling back, *One moment*, as he frantically removed the drive, hiding it away in the one place he thought no one would go looking. I imagined the precursors to danger, something that had gone horribly wrong.

Trey stepped back from the computer, took out his cell, and held it in front of him. "I can't get any signal," he said, crossing the lobby, holding his phone closer to the windows facing the mountain—which was the very wrong direction to try.

I quickly copied the contents of the flash drive onto the lobby computer, before Trey took it all back, out of reach. Things had a way of disappearing here, after all.

"Who are you calling?" I asked, my mind running through the sequence of events about to be unleashed once more: a thorough search of the cabin and maybe more, a series of interviews asking us to confirm and reconfirm each other's statements—our memories harder to be sure of now, suspicion taking root in the gaps.

"I don't . . ." He turned slowly to face me, corners of his mouth tipped down, like he hadn't quite considered that point. "He *hid* this, Abby. He knew he was in danger."

"Just—" I held my hands out, trying to get him to calm down, think things through. There were other possibilities; it didn't have to be true.

I imagined, instead, Landon West cleaning up before he went hiking for the day. Protective of his work. Worried, more, about someone snooping through his things, uncovering what he was working on.

"You said he was secretive about his work," I said. "Right?"

Trey tilted his head. "There's a difference between not telling your colleagues what you're working on and hiding a flash drive inside a piece of furniture in a shitty cabin in the middle of nowhere." A pause. "No offense." His words were starting to slur, and I remembered the empty bottles of wine, the state of his room, the threat of danger lingering just under the surface of him.

"Look, everyone knew he was working on a new angle into Cutter's Pass. And here it is." I gestured at the computer screen with the unfinished document currently front and center. "There's nothing here, really. Nothing he would need to be worried about. This isn't new information." Other than the folder marked with Farrah's name—a tip. A way in.

"Or," he said, "someone could've gone through his room, taken his journal and phone, and this was the only thing they missed."

There were only so many of us who had access to that cabin. He seemed to be forgetting that he was accusing me, just as much as anyone else. If this was what he believed, if this was what he told someone, I knew exactly how the investigation would go: Celeste, Georgia, me. Those were the options. There would be no escaping it.

He started pacing again, staring at the screen of his cell. "It's like we're in a fucking dead zone," he mumbled.

"You can use the lobby phone," I said, picking up the receiver from its spot at the reception desk. But, once more, it wasn't connecting. I replaced it in the cradle, knew I'd have to call Harris in the morning to check the lines for damage. I took out my cell instead. "I can usually get service in the office. The sheriff's office is closed, but I can probably reach him, if that's who you want." I'd have to go through Rochelle, or Cory, but I could do it. A reminder—to him, to myself—that I was a part of this place. That there was a web binding us all together.

But Trey just frowned. "I don't know . . ." The purpose seemed to be draining from him, like he had only just realized the hour. Maybe he was thinking of calling his parents, a girlfriend, a friend— "The FBI has jurisdiction on the Appalachian Trail, right?"

I cleared my throat, remembering the waves of investigators who had been involved in the disappearances in the past, the way their presence had altered everything, changing your perspective, your behavior. "That," I said, gesturing toward the computer, the photos that we'd just seen, "isn't the Appalachian." Maybe Farrah had made it that far, but there was no evidence of it. No, this was still just a trail in Cutter's Pass, a town famous for disappearing people.

"Give me a minute to think," he said, shaking his head, stumbling into a bench beside the fireplace.

A noise from upstairs jolted us both. My gaze went to the second-story balcony, a shadow stretching and disappearing down the hall, which served as a reminder that this place was full of guests, and it was nearing midnight, and Trey was on the cusp of making a scene.

Trey stood, stared out the windows, into the dark. "That place, in the photo. That's where you're taking me in the morning, right?"

Were we really still doing this? How had this discovery not

altered his plans? But maybe the images only tightened his resolve. Confirming the belief that his brother had set out on that trail, and now Farrah Jordan was leading us to the same spot. A connection; a *possibility*. It was the one certain path he could continue to follow.

"Yes," I said, after a pause, knowing there wouldn't be anything there after all this time. Nothing solid for him to bring to his family, or the police, or the press, or wherever he was planning to go. Visitors never seemed to notice that the mountain range was a living thing all on its own. The landscape was constantly shifting, purging itself of what had existed before, showing you only *this* moment and what it wanted you to see. A season later might as well have been a year. A year might as well have been a decade. Time moved faster up there.

Trey circled back to the reception desk, where he removed the flash drive, storing it in the pocket of his pants. "I just feel like . . ." He trailed off. "Look, the police had their shot four months ago, and did absolutely nothing."

He wasn't here. Of course it wasn't *nothing*—they combed over this place, over all the steps that had brought Landon West to the Passage Inn, searching his apartment, his car, that cabin. But the sheriff probably hadn't made the best first impression on Trey at happy hour, showing up unannounced, catching him off guard. I could understand why Trey distrusted his intentions.

"If you want to go, it has to be early," I said. A pointed remark, that he should go back to his cabin.

"Okay," he said, growing more confident. "Tomorrow, we go to the falls. If Farrah took these pictures, and my brother had them, then he must've gone out there, too, don't you think? He must've wanted to see it for himself."

We had all searched these places, back when it counted. But it couldn't hurt to go again. The sheriff would be sleeping anyway, and this would not count as an emergency. Contacting him at this hour would, however, spread news faster than I could stop it.

"Six a.m., then," I said. "You should get some sleep."

"Okay, yeah." Even though I knew he wouldn't. Neither of us would.

"He was looking for them," he said. "Six missing visitors," he mumbled, hand in his pocket, where I imagined it clenched around the flash drive, his brother's words. Trying to chase his thoughts, follow them to the right path. Tell us what he was trying to say. To warn.

I didn't bother correcting him. That his brother made seven.

I waited until the front door fell shut behind him, and his footsteps faded into the distance, before saving the copied images in a password-protected folder with my name.

The truth is—

The truth is, I felt a pull, too. Farrah, gesturing for me to follow, from the other side of the dark window, red scarf blowing in the night wind. Who knew where she might lead? All these strangers who had come so close. All these people who could've been us.

CHAPTER 7

AFTER TWO A.M., MY senses were on high alert. Unnerved, even, by the bugs that flew into the bedroom windows at night, imagining, instead, someone gently tapping. I kept my eyes trained to the dark, the stars hidden behind the clouds tonight. And then: a light flickering in the distance, on the other side of the rocky outcrop just outside my window. I bolted upright in bed. A flashlight? More likely, I decided, a path light, slowly dying, on the other side of the rocks.

There was no way I would be getting any sleep—not before I had to be up to take Trey down to the falls. And not with the past suddenly rising up in figments, one by one—first Landon, then Farrah—out of the dark.

Instead, I was thinking of all the things Trey had seen in this place. The way people turned up at the happy hour as if coordinated: the sheriff, Marina, Celeste. The noises he'd heard the night before, coming from the next room—he'd been so sure that someone had been in the cabin beside his, listening in. Maybe even watching him. And I couldn't convince myself that he was wrong. Not anymore. Not now, with Farrah Jordan's photographs turning up in that very room.

I picked up the phone in my room, just to check—this was the number I left on a sign at the lobby, where guests could reach me during my nights on call. The dial tone connected, and I felt something unfurl inside my chest. Relieved that the issue with the phone lines did not stretch across the entire property. That we were not being targeted by some unseen force or threat.

The flicker of light outside the windows finally dimmed to nothing. I left the lights off, suddenly aware of all that might be out there instead, looking in.

When I'd first arrived, a decade earlier, it was easy to feel isolated and removed from everything and everyone, to let my imagination run wild. The drive into town alone was narrow and winding, the trees stretching over the asphalt. We were fifteen miles from the next town, but it felt like longer on the mountain roads. Alone at the inn, with the spotty cell phone service, that feeling only grew, especially in the bad weather, especially when a heavy windstorm cut us off from the rest of town.

But over time, I'd come to appreciate it—love it, even. I grew to know this place through Celeste's eyes, her perspective bleeding over into mine. She had a faith in this world she had built that was impossible to doubt. A belief in the decency and ability of the people she surrounded herself with, a group that now included me—so that it was impossible not to see those same traits in myself. This inn, she believed, would withstand anything, with its strong foundation and reinforced walls. We were a self-contained universe, and I was a necessary part of it.

Even with all of its *notorious history*—from the Fraternity Four to Landon West—most days, I still saw it that way.

But now I felt unsettled by those same elements, bound by the concrete walls, unable to hear anything that might be happening beyond the confines of my apartment. I needed to hear someone else's voice on the other end of the line. A connection. Georgia was just across the hall, but nothing comforting could come from waking her up at this time of night. Sloane would probably still be camping out of range—and if not, she'd be catching up on some much-needed sleep. I stared at the phone, considering. Remembering, years earlier, calling Cory deep in the night, just to hear the familiar rumble of his voice, feel that connection.

Instead, I slipped on my sneakers, tucked my key card into my back pocket, and ventured out of my room. The basement was lit by the always-on soft-glow safety lights in the stairwell, leading up.

The inn was entirely quiet as I stepped out from the employee entrance to the first-floor hallway, slowly easing the door shut behind me. The gas lamps that lined the lobby gave it a gentle ambiance—but were dim enough to remind our guests that this was not a place to linger after hours.

On the wall behind the registration desk hung the locked display case of room keys. This was a danger, of course, if you were looking for it: an inventory of which rooms were occupied, and which were not. It didn't matter, typically, since most every room was booked inside the main building. And we had an electronic badge that could be placed on the silver square above each room handle, disengaging the lock.

But not for the cabins. Nothing had been upgraded, technology-wise, out there. Those accommodations generally appealed to a different clientele.

We had a master set of keys to every room, which we kept in the lockbox in the back office, along with the key for the display case, each labeled in a small manila envelope. This was where Georgia would've gone to replace the lost key to Mountain View One. Eventually I'd have to call in for a replacement to be made. But for now, I riffled through the manila envelopes until I found the one marked *Cabin 3*.

To avoid the front-path lights, I exited out the back onto the deck. In the mornings, we propped this door open for the breakfast crowd, but now, as the door swung shut behind me, the light went with it. I leaned forward until my hands brushed the iron rungs of the chair at the nearest table, using the furniture to guide myself until my eyes adjusted to the dark. I inched down the steps by memory, onto the grassy expanse, tracing the edge of the inn, hand grazing stone, until the outlines of the cabins appeared in the distance, darker shadows against the night.

A small line of path lights trailed from the cabins toward the front of the inn, but there were no lights coming from any of the cabins themselves. Not even from Cabin Four, where I couldn't imagine Trey West actually sleeping. Unless he'd had even more wine than I'd thought.

I approached the cabin steps carefully, quietly, making sure the curtains on his front window were closed before easing my key into the lock for the cabin next door, all too aware of every noise. I was used to the nighttime sounds, but now, I felt overexposed and vulnerable.

A twig cracking to my right; something rustling in the leaves overhead; the gentle thud of the lock disengaging.

I eased the door closed behind me, holding my breath as the latch clicked shut, then used the light on my phone to illuminate the corners of the room. Empty, as expected. And undisturbed. Just an unexpected chill circulating through the room, but that could've been the hour, the dark, all the things I had been imagining that had brought me to this point.

The queen bed was made; the bathroom door was closed; the guidebook was left on the center of the desk. Nothing appeared out of place. All the furniture had been positioned in the mirror image of the cabin next door, so that the desk in this room was pressed up against the same spot as the desk in Trey West's room.

And then I listened: silence, mostly. Except for a faint whistling coming from the back wall. I took a step in that direction, thinking there might be a crack in the window frame. The closer I got, the more I could feel it—a hiss of cool night air filtering through a gap somewhere.

I ran my fingers along the borders of the window frame, but instead of finding a crack, there was an open expanse between the glass and the frame. The window was unlatched, pushed slightly ajar, probably from the last time someone was staying here. Something Georgia must've missed in her follow-up routine. Out of character, considering how she'd been almost compulsive in her routines since Landon West's disappearance, checking and rechecking rooms and guest lists, as if everyone was always in danger of disappearing.

My fingers stretched through the gap into the open air—the screen worked in a similar way, sliding open and closed, and it, too, was currently ajar. Most likely, the noises Trey heard last night had indeed been an animal. Maybe not a squirrel in the eaves, but something else: a nocturnal creature slipping in through the gap of the window, flying or scampering around the abandoned room.

Though I knew a person could slip through the window just as easily. One foot on an outer log, elbows on the windowsill, a body climbing through. I shuddered, brushing the image aside.

I slid the screen closed, and then the window, but when I tried to latch it shut, it wouldn't engage at first. The slide was old and weatherworn, and I had to put my weight behind it to close the final gap. I cringed as the sound broke the silence.

A noise resounded from the wall to my right, almost in echo. I spun, expecting to confront whatever animal had found its way inside, but the room remained still. Nothing moved as I scanned the beam of light from my phone slowly across the wall.

Another scratching sound began from the space behind the

wall, just as I was staring at it. Like an animal had become caught between the wood framing.

But then the noise deepened, solidified; too large to be a squirrel or mouse. No, something was scraping against the base of the wall. It had to be Trey West, on the other side of the divider. Shifting the desk. Dragging a suitcase.

I held my breath, tried not to make a sound. Had he heard me when I closed the window? Would he come to investigate and find me here, thinking I had been spying on him the night before? *I couldn't sleep, couldn't get it out of my head, the noises you said you heard, and came to check*— Would he believe me?

The sudden sound of glass on glass made me jump. I tried to imagine it: Throwing a glass at the wall? An empty wine bottle, ricocheting to the floor? The noise didn't seem violent enough. I was still trying to picture it when the distinct sound of a wooden chair scraped against the floor, like nails on a chalkboard. And suddenly I knew exactly what he was doing on the other side of the wall: He was cleaning the mess. Tossing the empty bottles of wine into the trash. Moving the rest of the furniture back to where it belonged.

I crept closer, ear to the wall, until I could imagine him clearly, the steps he was taking, the expression on his face. Coming toward me, turning away. Running his hand through his hair, bloodshot eyes searching the corners of the room for anything he had missed.

I decided to wait him out. I slid to the base of the wall, listening to his movements on the other side of the wood paneling, until I could imagine my breath syncing with his. Until I could feel his loss.

My mom used to tell me I should be careful not to let my imagination get the best of me, but then, she had always been a realist. She said she had to be, that life didn't hand you any favors. She'd had me in her early twenties, raised me on her own, quit the job she'd loved, with the irregular hours running camps and clinics at the stables, for the steady and dependable one instead.

But her practicality hadn't done her any favors in the long run. She had died from a quick and aggressive bout with cancer when I was eighteen.

I'd done the only thing I could imagine doing in those months leading up to her death—I'd changed my mind about college, put my future on hold to stay with her; and then after, I'd packed up the things she'd left behind, and had no idea where to go next. The person I had been before felt like a stranger, like the future I'd once imagined belonged to someone else.

This, *here*, was never a future I'd have pictured for myself. But now I couldn't imagine anything else.

If she were still alive, I knew she'd see nothing practical about me being here, either, but then, I had never been much like her in any way that counted.

I heard the soft shift of mattress springs, and I imagined Trey sitting on the edge of that four-poster bed, head in his hands, finally processing everything that had happened. The not knowing leading him down too many paths, dredging up too many memories. It felt too intimate, too close, and I wondered if he could sense me here, too.

Finally, the springs creaked again as he stood, and I heard his footsteps cross the room. Then: the hinge of the bathroom door, the squeak of a knob, and the shudder of pipes before the sound of running water in his shower muffled all the rest.

I took my chance, sneaking out as silently as I had entered. Locking the door behind me. Darting through the night, undetected, the same way I had arrived. Like a ghost.

I WAS PACKED AND ready to go for the hike by 5:45, riding the wave of adrenaline. I knew, even then, that I was on my way toward a crash—but I also knew from experience that it wouldn't hit yet. You just had to keep moving. If nothing else, the mountain taught you that.

It was why, when hiking, I didn't look too far ahead or too far back. In truth, I didn't consider myself an expert, either. My primary experience was with this single expanse of trail to Shallow Falls. I knew it well, but I knew very little of what lay beyond it—I'd only done the trek up to the Appalachian once, with Sloane, through the famous pass that hugged the ravine, and I had no interest in doing it again.

I hadn't even gone out on our trail since the search for Landon West. At first, it was a choice: I couldn't walk out of sight of the inn alone without getting a chill, imagining all the things that could've happened to him. The pull of the safety of the inn, and the town full of people—people who would notice, look out for you, keep track of you. Eventually, like all things, it became habit. A *thing*. We'd hired Jack to be on call for summer weekends when he wasn't leading Outward Bound programs in the deeper parts of the mountain. And, as much as I hated to admit it, I knew I could count on Cory to handle a last-minute request for a guided hike in the mornings during the week, without question. The guests loved him.

Still, I had to get back out there, and this was as good a time as any. But I was struck by an extra surge of nerves, and I wasn't sure whether it was from the prolonged time away, or Trey's presence, or the images on Farrah's camera. The feeling that there *were* secrets here.

I performed one last check of my gear, trying to get back in the habit:

Bear spray in the side compartment of my pack, which had never had to be deployed, and was probably expired by now. Snacks and metal bottles full of water and a pre-packed first aid kit. A small poncho rolled up in case of rain; a knife, folded up, in the outer pocket of my hiking pants.

Most of my gear had been acquired from the lost and found bin we kept in the storage area of the basement, full of the clothes and supplies that guests had forgotten over the years. We labeled what we knew of—if something was left in a room, we'd place it in a bag with their name, in case they called. But after enough time had passed, those items, too, joined the bin with what had been abandoned in common areas across the property.

Our guests left behind brand-name gear I could've never afforded on my own, and the consistency with which they did not seem to miss it was something I still couldn't get used to. When I started working here, Celeste had told me to help myself to anything I needed—I wasn't sure how long I'd stay, couldn't justify buying anything on my own—and this pack was the first thing I'd claimed, from the place it had been buried, for who knows how long, all the way at the bottom. The pack was a dark beige, so you couldn't tell whether it was particularly dirty, and the straps had a bright orange threading running down the center. The only imperfections were the label that had torn off the back, leaving a darker rectangle underneath, and a broken zipper clasp on the smallest pocket. I'd threaded an orange zip tie through the loop of the zipper, and then it felt like mine. It continued to serve me well a decade later.

I rarely brought my phone on hikes; it was pointless, since there was no service from the span of the inn to the intersection with the Appalachian. But this morning I slid it into the other pocket of my pants, thinking of Farrah's pictures. Wondering if I could try to stand in that same spot, see what it was she was looking for, capture that same image, and feel what must've happened next.

Then I laced up my boots, hoisted the bag onto my shoulders, and passed Georgia's room on the way out, where the blare of her alarm clock was cutting through the sound of the radio.

Upstairs, the lobby was empty, but I saw a shadow through

the glass of the front doors, shifting back and forth. I left Georgia a note beside the computer, still shut down: *Went on AM hike with guest.* I couldn't bring myself to leave his name. Then I added two hash marks to tally the walking sticks we'd be bringing and grabbed one from the barrel. The sticks wouldn't really be necessary today, but I knew Trey had one already, and I didn't want to be without my own. There was a safety in the grip, in the solid wood. An extra layer of protection against both falling and predators.

I stepped outside and found him waiting, as the sky was lightening in shades of pinkish purple behind him. He looked, somehow, like he'd slept, which I didn't think was possible. He had his own bag, which didn't look new, but also didn't look like it was best suited for a day trek—it was mostly empty, built more for camping, meant to carry a sleeping bag, a tent. And he wore those same hiking boots that had squealed against the lobby floor, a telltale sign of disuse. He would probably have blisters by the time we reached the falls.

"Ready?" I asked.

Trey stepped to the side, letting me take the lead as we veered right from the entrance of the parking lot—in the opposite direction from town. There was no paved road here, but loose gravel gradually gave way to a dirt trail marked by time and use. People sometimes tried to park here, tucked just out of sight, and there was an old dirt-streaked sedan there now, with a bumper sticker of a multicolored peace sign.

The air was crisp and the sun was rising behind us, casting the trees in an eerie glow, shadows stretching into the distance. I heard nothing but the sound of the morning birds, our steady breathing, and our steps falling in unison as we approached the wooden sign for the trailhead.

The letters were carved into the wood post, just before the tree line. I stopped once, gazed over my shoulder, and had to shield my eyes from the rays of light coming up over the inn.

"This," I told Trey, "is the last place Farrah Jordan was seen." I imagined her feet planted into this very earth. The others who had stood here before and felt the pull of what awaited just inside the tree line. Her thinking, *Just one step. Just one more. Just a little farther—*

"How far to the falls?" he asked.

"It's about two and half miles," I said. And then, imagining Farrah taking a step across some unseen threshold, I did the same.

The trail started in a steady, gradual incline before dipping down toward the falls. We had only been walking about five minutes when Trey stopped. He had turned around, staring back at the trees and rhododendron, our path narrowing. "You can't even see the exit anymore," he said, with the vegetation pushing tighter and tighter, a tunnel-like descent.

"It happens fast," I said, the foliage growing in thicker each year, and every spring, a volunteer team coming through to keep nature from encroaching too far. Making sure the ground beneath the flat rocks that worked as steps hadn't eroded too much; checking that the path was wide enough; adding a fresh flash of yellow paint to a tree trunk at each switchback, to mark the way.

"This must be impossible at night," he said. It wasn't, actually, as long as you had a headlamp, a friend, good instincts. But now I was following his line of sight, imagining the scene from Trey's perspective. His brother, trying to find his way back, unable to make it. How this place looked in the dark when you weren't familiar with it, with no landmarks to guide you home. How easy it would be to take a wrong step, head deeper into the woods. How difficult to reorient yourself toward the exit.

The danger wasn't the trail; the danger was in stepping off and not being able to find your way back. I'd heard about hikers' bodies found years later, on other sections of the Appalachian, mere yards from the trail—never knowing how close they were. Perishing, tragically, so close to safety.

"Come on," I said, and listened as his steps continued behind my own. I appreciated the silence of the early morning, but I was on edge, waiting for the questions to begin. It didn't take long.

"I read up on the disappearances," Trey said. "Before I came." A thought he'd obviously considered sharing for some time. This was also not a surprise.

I tried to keep my pace steady. "Most people do," I said. It was easier to discuss this with him behind me. I imagined Celeste's voice in my ear. *We should be careful, Abigail.*

"All of the cases, they have a tie to the trail now, right? Not just the town of Cutter's Pass. But this. *Here.*" Like this ground we were walking was hallowed, dangerous. Either. Both.

"Depends what you mean by tie," I said. "There's not a lot of hard evidence that any of them came this way. The cases aren't similar. They're not related." There wasn't even proof, in a few of the cases, that some had even set foot in these woods, though that was certainly what most of us believed.

"The Fraternity Four, on a camping trip," he began, as if he were suddenly the expert, two days in to his first visit to Cutter's Pass. "Alice Kelly, leaving her group on the Appalachian, to hike out by herself. My brother, with his boots missing. And now Farrah Jordan. The pictures put her here."

It was easy to see the woods as the tie, if you wanted. It was just as easy not to. "The Fraternity Four *said* they were heading for the trail, but no one saw them out here," I explained. They had set out in the evening, which they had been warned not to do. It was too late, the sun setting too fast; they wouldn't make it to a campsite on time. But they had flashlights and charisma and strong will and good humor, and they were up for an adventure, they said.

"And Alice Kelly made it *out*," I continued. "All the way into town, to the tavern, where she made a phone call. And *then* she disappeared." The woods were not the last place she was seen. The woods were not the last place *any* of them were seen. Farrah Jordan, at the trailhead. Landon West, at the inn.

We continued on, the uncertainty hanging between us, when I realized we were the only two people who knew about the flash drive. And then for a moment, we felt like the only two people in the world. Nothing but our heavy breathing, our steady steps, a chill at my back at the sound of his hiking stick striking dirt between each step.

And then, something else. Up ahead. The soft sound of footsteps, coming closer, but out of sight, around the next bend. I thought of that car tucked around the corner, by the trailhead.

I stopped walking so suddenly that Trey nearly collided with my back. I moved the walking stick to my left hand, as my right went instinctively to my pocket—with the knife.

But the person rounding the corner was only Celeste, with her trademark walking stick, on her trademark walk.

"Well, good morning, you two," she said as she approached. Her hair was in a braid that hung down her back, and her strides were deceptively long for a woman just over five feet tall, who had recently celebrated her fifty-eighth birthday. With her graying hair, and skin that had seen three decades of working outdoors on the mountain, she often appeared older than her age. Until you saw her on the move.

"Good morning, Celeste." I stepped to the side to let her pass but gave her a look as our eyes locked. We'd had words, before, about her coming out here alone. Especially since Landon West's disappearance. This was her home, as she'd told me more than once. But that was the illusion of safety that people here clung to: It was always visitors. Everyone who grew up here seemed to feel a sense of immunity, justified or not. And Celeste's roots ran deep:

Both of her parents had grown up here, and when they died soon after she finished college, instead of her tie to this place being severed, it only seemed to pull tighter, calling her back.

She paused as she approached Trey, raised her sharp green-eyed gaze, and then the corners of her mouth. "I'm glad you're getting the full service from this one," she said, one hand reaching out for my upper arm, giving it a firm squeeze. "She knows these woods like the back of her hand." Which was generous and not entirely true.

"She's a pretty good guide," he said, which was also generous and even less true.

"We wanted to get an early start," I said, taking the moment to drop my pack to the ground and hand a metal water bottle to Trey. "Thought we'd be the first ones on the trail. Everything okay out there?" I asked, my words heavy with meaning.

She smiled tightly. "I wasn't even the first. Passed a hiker coming out as I was on my way in. This is practically midmorning on the mountain." She pressed her walking stick into the dirt, twisted it back and forth before stepping to the next rock protruding from the trail. "Be safe, Abigail." Her words carrying their own warning.

Trey took a deep drink as Celeste continued on, alone. We both watched as she disappeared behind the next switchback, swallowed up by the rhododendron. The sound of her footsteps quickly faded to nothing under the breeze rustling through the leaves.

He handed me the bottle. "She's not worried? Being out here alone?" he asked.

"No," I said, my back teeth clenched together. Celeste was stubborn in a way that did nothing to ease my concern. "She thinks the fact that she comes out here every day means that nothing can touch her. That just because nothing has happened before, nothing ever will." I took a deep breath. Although we always warned our guests to go with a partner, Celeste rarely did. "After her husband died, she scattered his ashes on the mountain. She says she likes to start her day talking to him each morning, just like she always did. I guess she thinks it's worth the risk."

In truth, I sometimes felt Vincent's presence out here, too, in the same way I felt him at the inn. I'd asked about him a lot when I first arrived, when the loss of him was still heavy, and recent, and I wanted to get to know him however I could. Celeste revisited the same stories, the same moments, until I could feel her memories as if they were my own: the first time they met, at a work event, when she had just started at the same design company, where he was an architect; the first time he saw this place, when they were still just dating; the fact that they couldn't even remember whose idea it was to buy the land and build the inn, as if the thought had always existed, like magic. Listening to Celeste, I could picture him carrying a guest's luggage effortlessly up the steps, could hear his deep laugh echoing through the lobby. But I found that over time, I got to know Vincent from his absence best of all.

When I arrived, I could still see his shadow in everything. His loss was tangible in the things that suddenly fell to disrepair. Vincent came into focus in these gaps, and I imagined him organizing the receipts, and sweeping the entrance, and straightening the picture frames that had fallen off kilter. All these tasks I picked up in his absence. I grew into the places that Vincent had left vacant.

"Well," Trey said, "she's a little intimidating, despite her size."

I nodded, listening closer to the woods, trying in vain to track her back to the exit. "I think you'd have to be, to build this place from scratch and run it pretty much by yourself for thirty years."

His eyes were narrowed, still watching the corner, as if she might be waiting there all along. "You know her well?" he asked.

I started walking again, felt Trey falling into stride. "She's family," I said. I always felt protective of her, admired her for what she'd created and everything she'd done for this place, and the people within it. Everything good about this place was because of her, and I wanted Trey to know it. She'd given me a home when I had no place else to go; her car when mine had died; a job when I'd needed one most. I knew, from the way people talked in town, that she'd done the same for others over the years. People thought highly of the inn primarily because they thought highly of Celeste herself.

We walked for a few more moments in silence before he continued. "What was it like, growing up here, with a town with this sort of history?"

"I didn't." When Celeste introduced me to the others in town, all she'd ever had to say was, *This is Abby, Vincent's niece*, and nothing else needed to be said. "Her husband was my uncle," I explained. "But he was older than her, and I didn't know him growing up, either. They built this place together. I came to visit after he died. And then . . . I never left."

"How come?"

The reasons one leaves, the reasons one comes . . . impossible to say which was the stronger. "Well," I said, "I had just lost my mother." By then, most of my friends had left for college, and the calls and texts had grown farther and farther apart, and even then, I didn't feel there was anything to talk about, anything to connect over anymore. It was like we were living in alternate realities, and I couldn't breach the divide. In the end, it wasn't just my mother I had lost, but the momentum of my own life, the person I might've become, the others who I'd have made the journey with.

"I'm sorry." He had stopped walking, and now he called out to me. "I'm so sorry," he repeated, looking at me, like he understood.

I waved him off. "It was a long time ago." And it wasn't the same. There was no mystery to it: a diagnosis, a passage of time, a result. Not the ending I'd hoped for, but a definitive and permanent resolution. That's not what had brought him here—that's not what brought *anyone* here. It was the mysteries that drew people closer.

We were approaching a clearing, with a drop-off to the right, which would give him the first unobstructed view of the ridge in the distance. "Look at this," I said, as if the open air, the looming mountains, could answer all his questions. The people you could feel out there, those who had come before. I imagined all of us stopping at this point, seeing the same thing, a moment that bound us all together, across time.

But he furrowed his brow and leaned forward, eyes downward instead—to the open air of the drop-off beyond the trees. "Who would hike this in the winter?" Trey asked, seeing something very different in the exposure. A missed step. A stomach-dropping precipice.

"People do," I said. "When there isn't too much ice, or snow." There was something haunting about the winter. Not like in the summer, with the vegetation growing in thick and tight in sections, obscuring your vision. After the leaves fell, and the landscape turned brown, and then gray, everything felt so vast and exposed. Like the photos on Farrah's camera, stark branches overlapping as far as the eye could see. You couldn't hide in the winter. The mountain knew you were here. But there was also a safety in it: Nothing could hide from you, either.

The rest of the hike passed in silence—with Trey in his head, and me in my own. Until finally, the path narrowed before us, curving against a rock face, makeshift steps leading down and disappearing out of sight.

"We're almost there," I said, slowing my pace. "It can get slippery. Be careful."

I imagined Farrah leaning back for a better angle to her shot, losing her grip, losing the camera. I imagined Farrah slipping, head colliding with rock.

It was treacherous in the winter, and Farrah was unprepared. How easy it could've been for her to slip, get hurt on the steep steps down to the falls. To succumb to exposure. It could've been an accident, easily.

But whoever had found her camera hadn't helped. Hadn't turned it in. Had let her disappear, just like all the rest.

I let Trey go in front of me, hand on the wooden rail, while I took my phone out of my pocket, trying to imagine Farrah standing in this very spot, wondering what she might've seen down there. Wondering what she might've been looking for. And what she didn't notice coming.

The perspective of her photo seemed to match up *right here*. The rocky ledge, the path descending. I brought my phone into my line of vision and snapped a photo, then slid it into my pocket just as Trey turned back to check what I was doing.

"Watch your step," I called.

CHAPTER 8

THE FALLS WERE THE same as every other time I'd been out here—a surge of water that grows louder in the approach, cool mist hanging in the air, a slickening of the surrounding rocks.

Unlike Celeste, I didn't gain any solace from this place. I could not imagine safety anymore, not after standing in front of Landon West's empty cabin, allowing his things to be cataloged. Not after joining the search.

The trail had felt like something different then. A place where the sun set too quickly. A place where the present slipped effortlessly into the past.

We had gone out in groups of three and four, weaving down the path, stepping off to the side but staying a fingertip's length from each other, at most. The creeping spring foliage had made everyone nervous, desperate to remain in sight. The scent of the blooming rhododendron turned the air too cloying, too suffocating.

We'd all joined in the search. Celeste sometimes leading the way, and Sloane, before she took the new assignment, and Georgia keeping close behind, with a hand on my shoulder, an unbreakable chain. Sometimes I'd see Cory, or Ray and Marina; Sheriff Stamer himself, or Rochelle, when she could get away from the phone lines at the sheriff's office, out of her jewelry and sandals and transformed into something entirely different; Barbara and Stu Schultz, the owners of the Edge, and Charlie Jameson, who ran CJ's Hideaway; and Jack Olivier, who was still haunted by being the last person to talk to Farrah Jordan. Even Harris, who had a young daughter at home and normally preferred to stay on the outskirts of Cutter's Pass, even though he'd grown up here.

We all rotated through, the trail constantly monitored and explored, with someone venturing as far off the marked trail as others could see, in case Landon West had done the same. The official search and rescue crews went farther, brought in dogs, used drones to make it to the places we couldn't—or wouldn't. And still, there was no sign of him.

When Farrah had disappeared three years earlier, we weren't able to search as well. We were limited by the snow, the weather, the lack of appropriate resources, when we weren't even sure she'd been out there. Only those with experience had set out then: Sheriff Stamer, Cory, Celeste, and Jack, particularly shaken and committed to bringing her back.

Back at the inn, I set out hot chocolate for the crew, and they would reconvene in the lobby after, as I sat in the back office, my cell in hand, refreshing the news, looking for any trace of her. But all I ever found were personal statements from her friends and colleagues: *She knows the woods. She's spent days in them before, on assignment. She teaches others. She's calm, and smart. She can survive it.*

Celeste was glad we were closed for the winter renovations, and so was I. I couldn't concentrate on anything but Farrah's face, her haunting gaze. That dark hair, the red scarf. It was all I saw anytime I closed my eyes.

Cory had come to me once in the back office after a day of searching, an extra paper cup in his hand, steam and the scent of chocolate rising from the top. He'd placed the cup on the table, looked at me closely, head tilted to the side. The tips of his hair were coated in ice, and I could practically feel the cold coming off him. He'd smiled slightly, scanned me up and down. *Baby's first disappearance*, he'd said. Then he took a sip, took a step back.

I had jolted. Literally, metaphorically. Everything shuttered, and slid, and I felt adrift. The vanishing was no longer just a story Cory told down at the tavern at night. She was a real person, and she was gone, and he was making light of it, even then. How could anyone be found in a place like this?

Farrah Jordan was a turning point, when the press started calling Cutter's Pass *the most dangerous town in North Carolina*. I imagined her, cold and alone, staring up at the barren sky—a flash of red among the white. But the drones and helicopters had found no sight of her—no dark hair splayed in the white snow; no red scarf in the colorless landscape.

The snow and ice melted, and the color came back to the landscape, and still, she wasn't found. And without a resolution, I could imagine a different outcome. Over time, I found the fear dulling, the sharpness of her disappearance slipping away behind a facade again. It was a mystery, but it wasn't our fault. The visitors returned, and they went up the mountain, and they came back laughing, smiling. I updated our guidebook to warn the guests about the dangers of exposure, of getting lost. I started leading hikes, an extra way to keep them safe.

But now, I was noticing the slickness of the rock wall, the weeds that had taken root in the grooves, pushing outward from the small pockets of soil. The jagged edge of the rocks used as steps, not rounded or softened by erosion. The sound of pebbles underfoot, kicked loose with the lack of traction.

At the bottom, the trail ended in a widening of dirt and rock and soil, like it was beckoning you closer, to the pool of water. Standing at the bottom, looking up, I realized you'd be visible from all directions. Like a funneling, with you at the center.

The Shallow Falls Trail officially ended here. There was a system of logs suspended over the stream, which brought you to the smaller clearing on the far side of the pool. Beyond lay the narrow, meandering push toward the Appalachian.

Now that we were here, I wasn't sure what Trey was expecting. There would be no sign of his brother. No footprints to follow. No phone or missing journal suddenly revealing themselves from a thicket of brush.

Trey stood with his hands on his hips, staring at the falls, three levels of cold mountain water gently cascading over a sloping rock face. I dropped my pack beside us in the clearing of dirt, and took the water bottles out of the bag, handing one to Trey again.

"Thanks," he said, barely glancing my way, dropping his own bag to the dirt beside him. He drained half the container while I stared at his exposed throat. He wiped the back of his hand across his mouth, eyes narrowed at the pool of water before us.

Celeste once told me, over one of our Sunday dinners soon after I'd arrived, that most people have one thing they try to protect. One thing they value most of all—and once you find out what it is, you know how to work with them. How to work them. She had shared this in reference to building the inn, all the steps they needed to go through to turn their vision into reality. But it was something I thought about often, when confronted with someone difficult—in work, and in life.

I watched Trey closely, wondering, again, what it was he hoped to find here. What had brought him here, in the night.

Careful, Abigail.

Trey's eyes shifted to me briefly. "How deep is that?" he asked.

"Shallow," I said.

A twitch at the side of his mouth. "Guess that was to be expected, given the name."

You could wade in up to your knees in most places. There was no true peril.

But now I was picturing Farrah standing alone here in the winter. I imagined her slipping at the edge, losing her footing, caught, stuck, facedown—breathing in the icy water. I imagined her standing on the other side, startled by something in the trees, losing her grip on the camera, dropping it into the water, as she ran deeper into the woods.

Trey sat on the edge of the rocks and pulled off his boots, stuffing his new hiking socks inside of them, then rolled up his pant legs over his knees. He stepped into the water and stared down at his feet.

I crossed the log bridge so I could keep an eye on him from afar, to watch him without being watched in return.

My steps echoed over the sound of flowing water. On the other side of the falls, the rocks were smoother, better for picnics and for parents to sit on while younger kids splashed in the water.

The wind moving through the trees felt alive, like something coming.

Trey was wading deeper into the center of the pool, water up to his knees, like he was testing the truth of my words. He raised his head periodically, looking for me, and I made a show of looking down at the earth, as if there would be anything left behind.

A flash of red caught my eye at the edge of the woods, and for a second, I thought *Farrah*. Something near the ground, tucked behind a pile of rocks. A cairn—like the markers sometimes used to guide the way on other trails. Though we'd always used flashes of paint on the bark of a tree here.

Beyond, the trail narrowed in a steep ascent. I knew it had been searched—all the way from the falls to the Appalachian—but not by me. Now, I approached the start of the second trail. The cairn had been constructed from flat river rocks. Like someone had fished them out of the stream, or the bottom of the pool where Trey now stood.

I hadn't been here in months, couldn't be sure when this had been added. Or whether it had been here all along.

On the other side of the cairn was a single flower, bright red, leaning against the rocks. Like from a blooming rhododendron. Nothing too unusual, except that there weren't any in bloom on the bushes surrounding us, that I could tell. And there was something about the way it was positioned, at rest, melancholy. Like a memorial, instead of a trail marker.

I kept my back to Trey as I squatted down for a closer look. The stem was clean cut, at an angle, like someone had taken a knife to it. Deliberate.

"The trail keeps going?" Trey called, startling me. He was out of the water now, legs pale and dripping wet, standing on my side of the falls.

I stood, positioning myself between his view of the cairn and the bright red flower. "This is the end of the Shallow Falls Trail," I said. I jutted my thumb over my shoulder. "But the trail keeps going, up to the Appalachian." His gaze was focused on the spot over my shoulder. "It's not easy," I added.

There was a distinct difference between the trail we'd just taken and the trail in front of us.

He stepped carefully, barefoot, in my direction. "How long would it take?" he asked.

"A couple more hours, probably. It's beautiful if you catch the sunset up there, but you want to be prepared." More food, more water, a lot of *just in cases*. "There's a pretty deep ravine on the way, which is how this town got its name. Cutter's Pass through the mountains. You've got to hug the mountain wall." There were handholds bolted into the rock face on the side of the ravine path, just in case. A rope you could hold on to while you crossed, just in case. "I wouldn't recommend it at night. And definitely not in the winter." The hikers who made it down in the dark had headlamps, experience, a pressing need to get down from the mountain. It's not something you did on a whim.

"You've done it, though, right?"

"Only once."

He seemed surprised, but these were two very different experiences. I'd come up on a trip with Sloane and a group of summer workers a couple years back, near the end of the season, one last hurrah, and listened while they laughed at the stories they told around the campfire, like the ghosts were long gone and not barely two decades old.

The noises of the night felt closer up there, more predatory. I didn't feel the awe of the mountain then. I felt only the reality of being exposed in the night, the possibilities laid stark before me. "I hike, I don't camp. And that," I said, gesturing into the dense woods, "is for camping."

"Landon didn't have camping gear. But I could see him going for it," he said, teeth pressed together, a comment made in irritation, as opposed to pride.

"It was searched," I added. "I promise." The ravine was always one of the first places that the rescue crews checked. If someone fell in, and if they survived the fall, they wouldn't be able to climb back out.

"People live out here, don't they?"

"Here? No."

"I meant—" He extended his hand to the mountain, beyond.

I swallowed. I knew what he was asking. It was long rumored that there was a man who lived out here, whom none of us had ever seen. Warnings passed around with the seasonal workers, who saw the remnants of a burned-out campfire along the river, and shivered. Who spotted a flash of color in their peripheral vision as they navigated downstream and looked again. It was a legend that continued to grow with nothing to disprove it.

Other visitors had asked about it as well, something to tie each case together. A singular danger they could understand. That the threat was not the things we warned them about (exposure; animals; dehydration and disorientation), but human. "Well, there's not really a census," I said.

"Isn't that exactly the problem? No one knows who might be out there. But people talk, right?"

People talk? Not about anything that mattered. Not about anything *real*.

"You think someone's been out here, just waiting, for the last twenty-five years?" I asked. It was a stretch to believe that over that amount of time, one person had tracked the Fraternity Four—four strong young men, armed with knives and bear spray, traveling together; had seen Landon West, and done the same; had followed Alice Kelly out of the woods. Had done something to Farrah, right here, in the snow.

"I don't know *what* to think. My brother disappeared in sight of these woods, and no one has seen him, and he wasn't some *small guy*." He blew out a sharp breath, ran a hand down his face, shook his head. "Okay then, Abby," he said, changing his demeanor, trying again. "If it's not someone out here, what do *you* think?"

That was a dangerous question. Of course, the visitors asked from time to time, and we had each developed our rote responses. Cory, with a smirk: *You won't find any secrets here.* Sheriff Stamer, grim and serious expression: *It's statistics.* Which wasn't really an answer at all.

"I think twenty-five years is a long time for anything to be relevant from back then," I said. "I think there are plenty of places where people get injured, or worse, year after year, and it doesn't become a *thing*." There was a waterfall in this very state, not too far from here, where seven people had died in the last two decades, while hiking off the side trails. But I couldn't say that to Trey, looking for his brother.

"But," Trey said, "in those places, where people get injured, *or worse*—they find the bodies."

And that was the mystery. The thing that kept people coming, kept people wondering.

It was dangerous, to go looking for a way to connect everything. Because there was only one thing you could circle back to with certainty. There were no commonalities between the people who disappeared. There was no trend. There was no type.

There was just this place, and us.

I had considered some of the theories myself: copycat crimes and predatory animals. I knew that people, by nature, did not share *everything* they knew, or saw. None of which would help to say now.

"I think some people don't want to be found," I said.

Trey flinched, eyes wide. He stared back at me before responding, voice low. "My brother might be kind of a jerk, but he wouldn't do this to my parents."

"I didn't mean . . ." I shook my head, looked away. This was why I didn't usually answer the question. There was no good answer. And now I was alone in the woods with a man I didn't know, his demeanor vacillating between hope and anger. I'd seen the swing in him the night before, in the chaos of his room. How quickly that switch could be triggered.

In the absence of answers, a lot of things could grow.

"We should get back," I said, checking my watch. I crossed the log bridge, slightly unsteady, felt Trey's footsteps reverberating in the wood as he followed close behind.

I didn't pause, didn't wait. I hitched my bag onto my back, pulled the straps to tighten it, and started walking. Nothing good ever happened out here.

TWO AND A HALF miles in silence was a different type of grueling, and I endured it trying to figure out what he was thinking. What he would do next. The trail was much more populated at this time, with day hikers coming in from town, setting out with picnics on their backs, and I was glad for the existence of them. I thought of Farrah, the possibility that someone had followed behind as she descended the steps, without her knowing. I thought of the cairn again, with that single red flower: a memorial; a warning.

At the exit to the trailhead, Trey stopped walking.

"There's nothing out there," he said, and I shook my head.

"No," I said. "Not now."

"There's nothing in this flash drive, either." He took it from the outer pocket of his pants, had carried it with him to the falls. Like he believed in the danger in leaving it behind, just as Landon must have.

I pressed my lips together, agreeing. Nothing that would get him any closer to finding his brother, at least.

"I'm going to bring it to the sheriff," he said.

I remembered what Marina said, about Trey being here for a reason. "I can set it up for you," I said. *Just being helpful. Just an extension of my job.* I started walking toward the parking lot, where I could get the best signal.

"Abby," he called until I stopped walking, turned back. "He was afraid. You can feel it, right?"

The flash drive hidden in the bedpost. The lies he told at the inn—*I'm working on a book*—to keep this place from knowing what he was looking for.

I sensed it in myself, something steadily building.

"Yes," I told Trey honestly. "I can feel it."

CHAPTER 9

I CALLED ROCHELLE AT THE sheriff's office as soon as my phone registered a bar of signal, standing at the intersection of the gravel path and our parking lot. We weren't exactly friends, but I had her number in my phone as a necessity by nature of our jobs. So the sheriff could reach the inn; so the inn could reach them.

I listened to the phone ringing as Trey sat on a log at the perimeter of the parking lot, walking stick resting beside him, unlacing his boots, pulling them off carefully. He winced, and I looked away. Blisters that would take days to heal, I was sure.

Rochelle didn't pick up, but instead of leaving a message, I sent a text: *Landon West's brother would like an appt to see the sheriff today*

Almost immediately, I could see she was responding. Rochelle was an excellent multitasker, had worked at the sheriff's office since she was a high school intern in the summers, and now no one was sure if the place could run without her. I pictured her with the office phone tucked to her shoulder on some other call while she pulled up his calendar on the computer to respond to me.

"You can get service out here?" Trey asked, pulling out his own cell to check.

"This is the best spot," I said.

My phone dinged with a text from Rochelle: *Can he be here in an hour?*

Yes, thanks. I responded without asking. "One hour," I said. I checked my watch again, knowing I'd be pushing things with the start of my shift. "How about I take you? The parking situation will be ridiculous right now." It was high season, and it was a beautiful day, and the streets would be packed with people we didn't know, pouring in on foot and by car, walking from shop to shop or mingling on the town green, taking photos in the middle of the road, in the spot with the best view of the mountain in the distance, framed in the background as the road curved up toward the inn.

"Yeah, okay, thanks," he said. "Just give me a chance to clean up first?" He handed me his walking stick as he stood barefoot in the gravel lot. Now I was the one to wince.

"I'll meet you out here in forty-five," I said as he turned away, walking tentatively across the lot, heavy on his heels.

WHEN I ENTERED THE lobby, there was a woman standing next to the fireplace, checking her watch. Midthirties, blond hair in two thick French braids, a line of piercings up her left ear. Mountain View Two. The Millers.

Georgia was nowhere to be seen.

I dropped the two walking sticks into the bin. "Hi, can I help you with something, Mrs. Miller?" I asked, hoping she recognized me from check-in, even though I was in hiking gear and sweating and carrying a pack.

She looked up, face relaxing. "Yes, thanks. We were trying to get some extra towels upstairs, but the line was busy. Thought it would be quicker to come down here myself." From the expression on her face, it was clear that it had not been quicker.

"Let me get that for you," I said, sliding my backpack against the wall, unzipping the pouch where I stored my master set of keys. But they were unnecessary—the door to the back office was unlocked, and Georgia was situated at the table, pen in hand, a pile of receipts to the side and a list of names in front of her.

"Oh my god, you scared me," she said, hand to heart. She looked at the clock hanging on the wall and started stacking the receipts together.

"Mountain View Two is out there, looking for towels."

She craned her long neck toward the door. "Shit, I'm sorry. I lost track of time."

I grabbed two towels from the supply we kept here in the storage cabinets, just in case of situations like this. "I need you to cover another hour. Sorry," I added, since we were throwing apologies around.

"Oh, I—" Her eyes skimmed the room, like she was searching for an excuse.

"Please," I added, which was something I rarely had to ask her.

She nodded once, mouth a set line, then seemed to finally notice my attire. "How did it go?" She must've seen the note I'd left her this morning about taking a guest on a hike.

"It was fine," I said. "I just need to shower before running into town for a bit."

I wasn't sure why I was keeping the details from Georgia. Whether I was trying to protect her or him. Whether I felt there was something worth hiding.

"I've got this." Georgia stood and took the towels from me, heading for the lobby. "So sorry, Mrs. Miller, I didn't notice you out here."

While she was handling the towel situation, I pulled out my phone and placed a call to Harris. He dealt with a variety of the inn's maintenance issues, as needed, but he specialized in cables and electricity. Like most people at the inn other than Celeste and Georgia and me, Harris was someone we contracted with, rather than employed. He didn't live in Cutter's Pass, but just outside the town perimeter, on a plot of land between jurisdictions that had been in his family for several generations. He hadn't lived here when I'd first arrived. He moved back about five years ago when he was starting his business, and now he was often the first place I called.

When he didn't pick up, I left a message. "Harris, it's Abby at the inn. We're having some issues with the phone line. Do you have some time to swing by to check it out?"

Georgia was still in conversation with Mrs. Miller when I left the office. I swooped my pack onto one shoulder, lifted my hand as I passed, mouthed a quick *Thank you*, caught a slight smile in response.

I wasn't paying attention as I descended the steps toward the basement, but as I stood in the fluorescent-lit hall, I immediately felt the presence of someone else: The sound of heavy breathing. Something shuffling nearby.

Georgia was upstairs and Celeste moved with a distinct lightness and no one else was on the schedule to be here. Housekeeping came in the afternoon. The linens had been delivered yesterday.

My heart was pounding as I let the bag slide from my shoulder. I propped it against the wall as quietly as I could.

Keeping my eyes forward, I reached for the bear spray in the side compartment, instead of my knife. It felt more realistic, more useful.

And then a familiar voice came from the nearest storage room. "Someone out there?" His voice was muffled through the closed door.

"Jesus, Cory," I said, leaving the bear spray where it was.

The door of the storage room swung open, and he stepped

out, a sheen of sweat coating his forehead. Then he smirked as he looked at the bag and the way I was hovered over it. "What were you doing? Planning your attack?" He leaned forward, nudged the bag with his foot. "What were you going for?"

I crossed my arms. "Bear spray," I said, and he laughed once, loudly, head thrown back. "What are you doing down here, Cory?"

He shrugged, stepped back inside the storage unit. "Celeste asked for some help."

Inside, he had a metal dolly, stacked with boxes that had been pulled down from the shelves that lined the cinder-block walls, each marked with Vincent's name. Behind him, the back wall was lined with boxes—financial documents from years past, in case we were ever audited, old photos and personal items that had been here for thirty years but didn't fit in any closets in the carriage house, and labeled bags of things left behind by guests. The other shelves held packs of toiletries and new pillows, fresh linens and towels that we had delivered each week. There was one large gray garbage-can-style bin just inside the door—the lost and found bin.

The other storage closet, closer to the exit, held the outdoor furniture, the cleaning supplies, tools, and maintenance gear. But the personal stuff was all in here. The material that kept things moving, kept our history. I watched as Cory moved a few boxes off the top shelf of the far wall, finding another labeled *Vincent*. "You're taking Vincent's things?"

He dropped a box onto the dolly with a huff. "She wants to organize the paperwork. Apparently everything is in his name. I don't ask questions."

No, no one here did. And that was the problem.

Celeste commanded an unparalleled respect here in Cutter's Pass, especially from those in the younger generation. It wasn't just me who had come to see her as a parent-adjacent figure. At some point, many of them had worked here—either officially or unofficially. When I'd first met Rochelle and Jack, it had been at an inn happy hour, just after the winter renovation when I'd arrived. They had been running some supplies up to Celeste as a favor, and she'd invited them to stay. They'd peppered me with questions—*Where are you from* and *How long are you staying* and *What brought you to Cutter's Pass of all places*—and Celeste had stepped into our circle, a hand on my shoulder, and said, *This is Abby, Vincent's niece. She's going to be helping me here.* And that was all that ever needed to be said. People in town knew who I was before I'd even had a chance to meet them. They called me by name when I passed in the street, and I felt a close familiarity to these people I had yet to know deeply.

Cory had his sleeves rolled up, hands on his hips, tattoo on his forearm visible—a swooping vine, sliding back under the edge of his sleeve. Everything about him was ivy and vine, and he could tell the stories marked across his body the same as he could tell the history of this place.

He saw me looking and dropped his arms to his sides. "What have you been doing?" he asked, finally taking me in.

"I took Trey West down to Shallow Falls."

He stared at me. "And?"

"And now I'm taking him to talk to the sheriff."

He turned back to the shelves, dropped another box onto the concrete with purpose. "You don't have to do this, Abby."

"Yeah well." I shrugged with one shoulder, even though he wasn't looking.

"Abby, seriously." He stopped what he was doing, turned to face me. "We don't owe him anything."

"Don't we?" His brother disappeared on my watch. "He was going to do that hike on his own if I didn't offer to take him. Would've probably kept going through the pass, totally unprepared. Last thing the inn needs is another guest getting lost out there."

"Then he's reckless, Abby. Keep out of it. Keep away from him."

How could I expect Cory to understand—the feeling that the answers could be found through Trey, somehow, danger or not. I raised a hand, cutting off the line of discussion. There was no point in arguing with Cory. Neither of us would give an inch. "When's the last time you were down at the falls?"

He rubbed the side of his face. "Last week sometime. Why?"

"I didn't remember cairns on the trail on the other side."

He shook his head. "We use paint on the trail. Probably just kids. People on a picnic, building a pile of stones. You know how it gets in the summer. It's a well-traveled trail, Abby."

I nodded, noncommittally, and it was like he could see right through me. Every thought. Every worry.

He took a step closer, lowered his voice. "There's nothing out there. I promise. I've lived here my whole life." A smirk that brought me back ten years, to the both of us in almost this very same spot.

I smiled tightly. "I've gotta run. Georgia's only giving me an extra hour."

And with the mention of her name, any thread of nostalgia between us was severed.

I WAS USED TO seeing Cory everywhere. I wasn't even surprised to see him here now, in a place that should've felt private and mine.

When I'd officially met Cory for the first time, I didn't know anything about who he was. Just that he stood behind the bar at the tavern and poured me a drink without asking for ID, and when I slid some cash across the bar top, he said, *Oh, I'm not working here tonight.* He had the pronounced lightness of being a decade younger then, at least one fewer tattoo, a future that was still more promise than expectation. He slid onto the bar stool beside me, told me his name, and said if I was going to be staying awhile, he was a good person to know. That he knew everything about this place.

I asked him the species of trees that lined the streets, and he didn't know. I asked him the annual rainfall, and he laughed.

Two visits later, and I told him, in the hesitant way that I presented all information then, that I was going to be working at the inn, and he said he knew that, with a small smile. And when I left that night, I told him I'd be staying there, too. He said he knew that, too, and this time I laughed.

And later that night, when I went downstairs to the otherwise unoccupied basement, he was standing near the back entrance, the private one hidden at the back of the inn, and I said, *How did you get in here?*

I told you, he'd said, *I know everything about this place*. And then his smile faltered, and he looked behind him, toward the door, and he said, *I wasn't sure if—*

I knew what he meant before he finished. He wasn't sure if it was an invitation. But it was.

The thing about Cory then was he was both cocky and unsure at the same time, a little overexposed, never paying much attention to the times his heart was on his sleeve or his foot in his mouth. And for a time, I'd fallen for both.

It was lonely down there, in a different way than I'd been lonely before, after my mother's death, finding myself on my own, with no direction—like time had stopped. At the inn, time kept moving, but sometimes I wasn't sure if this place was real. Whether *I* was. I felt so far from the person I'd once been, not sure what I was really doing here. Like someone new being forged in the bones of this place. I imagined myself rising out of the concrete floor, made of intricate locks and steel and unbreakable glass. For that first year, my world shrank to a bubble, and the things that I loved in it were: this place, that mountain, and him.

But then he started pulling away, and I realized he was a walled thing all of his own. That, if I asked him something, anything real about Cutter's Pass—*What was it like, when Alice Kelly went missing? What do you think happened to the Fraternity Four?*—he would tell me nothing more than the lines I'd heard him give to paying customers. If he knew things, he wouldn't tell me, saying only, when I pressed, *You won't find any secrets here*, with a sly grin, like it was all in jest. And I realized that Cutter's Pass would only exist for you in the parts you were here for, and the rest would remain an impenetrable history. I'd learned I'd find more camaraderie and friendship in those that were like me—not from here.

It took the last two disappearances to make me feel like one of them, and only because I was here when they happened. To understand that the truth was something you couldn't just explain to someone else, but had to experience for yourself, come to terms with in your own way.

By then, I had let Cory go. Unsettled by the lightness with which he approached everything. The carefree surface, the exterior charm. He capitalized on the disappearances, accepted the mysteries as something not too serious. He made all stories seem trivial, even mine. He had a distinct lack of gravity, in a way that felt unsustainable.

But Cory was never something that could slip into the past. In a way, I felt like Cory was a part of this place, set deep in its foundation. Something that would always be a part of me, whether we were together or not.

And then last year, a week after Georgia's arrival, I saw him in the basement again, standing near that back entrance, like he was waiting for her to find him there. A rehearsed move in a play. And I'd recast our entire history, every memory. Whatever spell remained was then finally and permanently broken. I imagined the people who had come before me, the history that had once existed but remained beyond my reach. The secrets Cory knew, and kept.

AFTER I'D FINISHED MY shower and threw on my work clothes, I still heard him in that storage room. But I passed without saying goodbye as I exited. It didn't matter whether I locked up behind me. In the end, you had to choose to trust Cory, to believe his intentions.

I found out later that Cory had worked here once. When he'd wanted out of his parents' house, before he could afford his own place—he'd come here, to Celeste and Vincent. Had lived in the very same apartment that Celeste gave me later. Of course he knew how to get in.

I had thought of what Celeste had told me, about needing to discover what's most important to people to know how to navigate them. I could never figure it out, with him. And it was then I understood the problem with Cory: The one thing he was most interested in was himself.

IF CORY LACKED A sense of gravity, then Trey West was the opposite, standing in the parking lot as I backed my car up the slope of the employee drive. He was a black hole, a pull I couldn't resist and didn't want to, for fear I might miss something. I was starting to believe that the answers to this place somehow lay within him. That, despite Celeste's disapproval and Cory's warning, this was the way to find them.

I lowered the window, called his name, watched as he tried to place me in context again. I was dressed for work now, hair pulled back tightly, in the hand-me-down car from Celeste.

My own car had only lasted my first winter here. By the time the next fall was approaching—the leaves changing colors, crisp and swirling in the wind, brittle under our steps—the battery was on its way out, and the tires needed replacing, and my car, the very last thing that had once belonged to my mother, was dying. I didn't want to admit it. Of all the things I had lost, the car shouldn't have hurt as much as it did. It was just a car, and it had gotten me here, but it wouldn't change the past. It was the insult of it—just *one more thing*—and after the engine sputtered, I'd slammed a door, kicked a tire, felt my eyes burning with tears in frustration.

And then Celeste was there, outside the carriage house, watching closely. *What's the matter?* she asked.

I gestured to the car wordlessly, thinking of how I would need to call someone to tow it to the shop just out of town, tell me how much I'd owe this time.

She stepped closer as I was mentally tallying the money in my bank account, adding up my upcoming pay, when she handed me the keys to her car, her fingers shaking gently. *I don't need these.*

I didn't understand at first. Said, *I'll have it back in an hour.*

No, she said, *Abigail, I don't need it. Everything I need is here, and besides, I can roll out Vincent's old truck if I ever truly need it, see if it starts*. She tried to make a joke to cover the gravity of the moment. She was still holding that key in her hand, extended my way. A gift, an offering.

But it was a question as much as an offer. And when I raised my hand out to hers, closing my fist around the metal key, it was also an answer. A promise that I would stay.

Celeste seemed to understand my attachment to my mother's old car and offered to drag it into the garage, join the *graveyard of unused vehicles*, along with Vincent's truck. When I arrived, that truck had sat, unused and unlocked, at the top of the lot, a perpetual reminder. Which somehow seemed worse than a car that wouldn't start. I had moved it to the garage myself for her, before the high season. She didn't want to part with Vincent's truck, just as much as I didn't want to part with this.

But in the end, I did. I could only accept so much of her generosity, for fear I might find its limits.

Now Celeste's gray sedan was probably twenty years old, officially on its way out. The locks hadn't worked in two years. This past winter, I'd held my breath every time I turned the ignition, willing it to start. I didn't think it would last another. It was an inevitability that this, too, would go—and now I could only feel how I didn't want to part with this, either.

Trey opened the passenger side door and folded himself into the seat. The outside of the car may have been dirt streaked and weatherworn, but the inside was immaculate. I cared for it in a way that I imagined Celeste would approve. He would find no stray receipt or candy wrapper inside. I saw him frowning at the dirt his shoes left on the passenger side floor mat.

"It'll just take a second to get there," I said. "It'll probably take longer to find parking."

I was right. Downtown had transformed with the start of the weekend. The Friday crowd was parked along curbs that lined the storefronts and town green and in parking lots that specified *For post office customers only*. As if the rules didn't apply to them.

Beyond the welcome center, just before the bridge, I turned the car abruptly out of downtown, heading down a side street that traced the river. Then I circled back through a meandering residential road, parking where the street dead-ended at a row of evergreens. "Don't tell," I said as Trey looked over at me with his eyebrows raised. It had taken me two full summer seasons to figure out where to park on a busy tourist weekend. I assumed every local had their prime secret spot, and this was mine.

I led Trey down the narrow dirt path through the hedges, where we emerged behind the station at the corner, a few official sheriff vehicles in the lot, alongside Rochelle's red pickup. The entrance was positioned catty-corner to the main street, technically facing toward the welcome center, though the wall of front windows gave Rochelle a clear view of several storefronts along Main Street.

She was sitting behind the front desk as we entered, empty to-go coffee cup in front of her, dark red lipstick marking the paper rim. She had a diamond stud nose ring, expertly lined eyes, a way of looking at you that made you feel as if she could see everything underneath.

She was the same age as me, but remained the one person in town who could make me feel self-conscious in my uniform shirt and work bun. Like I was just playing a part, and she could tell.

She stood to meet us, silver bangles sliding down her wrist as she pushed her hair back off her shoulders. You could see her Cherokee heritage in her long dark hair, her deep brown eyes and high cheekbones. She extended her hand to Trey across the desk. "You must be Trey West," she said. "The sheriff will be back in just a moment."

Rochelle had graduated from high school the same year as I did, had just started working here full-time by the time I'd arrived. We all understood that the sheriff relied on her heavily. She'd set up her own system over the years, and others had to abide by it, by default.

She was also secure in her opinions, and had been the only one to tell me, years ago, several shots of tequila in at the tavern when I'd thought we might still be friends, what she thought had happened to the Fraternity Four. I hated tequila, scrunched my nose when she'd ordered it, but joined her anyway. Back then, I wanted her to talk to me, to like me. At first, when I'd asked, she'd been annoyed: *You're just like all the rest, of course.* A roll of her eyes. *Rubberneckers, everywhere.*

But then, just when I thought she wouldn't say any more, that she'd shut me down, she tipped a shot glass back effortlessly and continued: *They fell, of course. They went out in the dark, and they fell in the ravine.* Simple and succinct, not offering any follow-up until I pressed. Not worrying about the holes in the logic, the pieces you couldn't slip together. Speaking with a sort of confidence that bordered on vigilance.

But they were never found, I'd said. Because wasn't that the mystery, really, at the heart?

She'd thrown up her hands, irritated with either me or the details that refused to connect. *Animals. That place is littered with bones, from long ago.*

Someone would've seen them. They searched.

Jesus, seriously? She'd blinked at me, long dark lashes and deep brown eyes. *How would you even know? You weren't here.* She held my gaze until I looked away first.

The fact that she'd worked at the sheriff's office for a decade, and I assumed she had access to all the files, should've been enough. If there was anything worth knowing, any secrets stored in locked file cabinets, any rumors whispered in back offices, she would know. And, from what I knew of her personality, I didn't believe she would've kept it to herself.

"You sticking around, Abby?" she asked as I took a seat in the small waiting area beside Trey.

It was Trey who answered. "Abby's been kind enough to act as my guide around here. Even took me out to Shallow Falls this morning."

Just then, the sheriff came in off the street with a single cup of coffee, which he placed on Rochelle's desk.

"Thanks, boss," she said.

I had to hand it to her; she was the only person I knew whose boss brought *her* coffee throughout the day. She tipped her head in our direction. "Trey West, here to see you."

Trey stood and stuck out his hand.

"Mr. West," the sheriff said, the sunburn across the bridge of his nose extra pink, either from the heat or exertion. He clasped two hands around Trey's. "I'm glad you decided to come in after all." And then, to me, "Do you need to get back to the inn?"

"She's my ride," Trey explained. I got the sense he wanted me here. Wanted a witness, someone on his side to help navigate the intricacies of Cutter's Pass.

But Sheriff Stamer was already gesturing him past reception, a hand on his shoulder. "We can get you right back after," he said, a tight-lipped smile at me as he peered back. "I don't think we need you in any official capacity for this, Abby."

I nodded, taking the hint.

Once the door to the offices shut behind them, Rochelle jutted her thumb over her shoulder, pointing in their general direction, and said, "*That* is not a good idea."

"I just took him on a hike," I said. Her directness always managed to keep me off kilter, as if I needed to defend myself against something that hadn't happened yet.

She smirked. "Also not a good idea, if you want my opinion."

I didn't. "Just trying to help," I said. There was something unsettling in the way she always seemed to be assessing me. I had a feeling I would always be an outsider to Rochelle, no matter how long I lived here.

"You know—" she began, just as the phone rang. She raised

one manicured finger, bracelets jangling on her wrist as she did. "Sheriff's office," she said, holding the phone between her cheek and shoulder, hands poised over the keyboard in front of her.

I took one of the wrapped mints from the dish on her desk and headed for the exit before she could finish her thought.

"Hey," I heard her call after me, just as the door swung shut, but I kept walking. I could imagine the warnings well enough; I'd lived here long enough to know them myself: *You shouldn't get involved* and *Don't encourage this, there's nothing left to find.* But for once, they were wrong. And for once, I knew it first.

CHAPTER 10

I SAT IN MY CAR, wanting to hear whatever the sheriff was going to tell Trey. Whatever Trey was going to tell the sheriff. Thinking of how I could find a way to linger—

My cell rang in my purse, making me jump, then fumble for the device. It was Georgia, calling from her cell.

"Abby," she began, as greeting. "Are you still in town?" I could hear the wind moving across the microphone, knew she was outside, where she could get the best signal.

I closed my eyes, pressed my fingers to the bridge of my nose. "Yes, I'm heading back soon."

"No, it's fine. Just, that group in the Forest View rooms, they went out on a hike and asked if we could schedule a horseback tour for tomorrow. The computers are down, something's definitely happening with the lines here."

"I already called it in to Harris," I said.

"Great. But could you swing by, while you're down there? They're always more likely to move things around for you anyway."

I couldn't argue with her assessment. When I'd first arrived, I'd spent a lot of my downtime there, visiting with the horses, something that always calmed me, reminded me of home. "I got it," I said. I'd rather go there than back to the inn right now anyway.

"Thanks . . ." Her voice trailed off. "Hold on." The sound of feet on gravel, and I pictured her walking across the lot. "Is Cory here? Is that his car in the employee lot?"

She must've been able to see it from where she was standing.

"Yeah, Celeste had him doing some grunt work today."

"Great," she said again, this time dry and monotone. "All right, see you soon," she said before disconnecting. It sounded like both a question and a plea.

BEYOND THE BRIDGE, PAST the campgrounds, I first saw the sign for the zip lines, tucked into a canopy of trees. A right at the next intersection and a narrow road wove up a hill before the entrance for the stables. An arch over the dirt road, bronze lettering, bracketed by horseshoes on either side. There were several other cars in the lot, including Jack's van.

It was hard to miss: Jack's permanent residence was an old-school van he'd converted into a living arrangement, which apparently suited him just perfectly. When he was in town, he generally parked it on his parents' land and used their shower and laundry. Otherwise, the van served as his own home base that he brought out on trips.

A cloud of dust hung in the hot air as I exited my car, heading for the barn with a sign over the door, instructing visitors to *enter here for check-in.*

The owners' daughter was behind the front desk, drawing in a sketchbook; Sylvie had large brown eyes and hair the same shade, currently parted sharply down the middle, tied up in two buns.

"Hey, Abby," she said, closing the black book, sticking the pencil behind her ear. She looked so young; I couldn't believe I'd been her age when I'd arrived here, on my own. She was just a few months out of high school—I'd been here for her graduation party earlier in the summer—but I'd known her since she was a child weaving between her parents' legs as they ran lessons and tours from the barn.

"Hi, Sylvie." I leaned one arm on the counter. "Is that Jack I see here?"

She shook her head. "No, he's out. We were short-staffed, and he's been staying here on and off, so . . ."

"I didn't know he was staying here." Over the years, I'd seen his van in downtown, at the campground, off the road down by the river, and occasionally, at Cory's.

She leaned forward, a child with a secret. "His parents are selling. Retiring and—" She wiped her hands quickly against one another, twice: *Gone*. "Apparently it's not good for showings if there's a van on the property. You can wait for him, if you want?"

"I'm actually here to see you. Any chance you can squeeze in a group of six tomorrow?"

Sylvie pulled a laptop from under the counter, slid on a pair of blue-rimmed glasses, and leaned close to the screen. "Only in the afternoon."

It would be sweltering, but so be it. "I'll take it."

She wrote the details on a beige ticket. "Heard you've got company up at the inn," she said, head still down.

I shouldn't have been surprised, especially if Jack was staying here. Still. "What'd you hear?" I asked, trying to keep my voice level.

She stopped writing, head slightly to the side, assessing me. "Just that the family of the guy who went missing from the inn is up there now." She raised one eyebrow, like she was asking me to confirm.

"Just for a short stay," I said.

She blinked twice, like she was waiting for something else, then held the paper my way. "They can pay when they get here," she said.

"Thanks," I said, "I owe you one."

CORY'S CAR WAS STILL at the inn when I returned, tucked beside Georgia's. But I didn't want to answer any of his questions, about Trey, about the sheriff's office, about anything at all. So I left my car on the other side of Georgia's and trudged up the drive on foot.

Georgia's head darted up as I pushed through the entrance, face shifting to relief when she saw it was me.

"Got the tickets." I held out the reservation page. "And you're officially free," I said, joining her behind the counter.

She slid the binder my way. "They haven't come back from the hike yet," she said. "I'm pretty sure one of them had a flask full of liquor, too." She cleared her throat.

"I'll keep an eye out," I said. They were the type of people who were easy to be annoyed by from the outside, easy to envy on the inside. I could almost imagine the Fraternity Four like this—a few decades later, spouses in tow, maybe children, too. Telling stories of their adventures, decades earlier. Bound by a shared history.

She hitched her purse onto her shoulder, the key ring to her car dangling on her pointer finger, like she'd been waiting for her chance of escape. "Heading to the store for groceries. Need anything?"

"I'm good, thanks," I said. I was sure her trip was timed to avoid running into Cory, too.

As soon as she left, I took my cell to the back office. My phone had access to the inn's email account, and I waited for the page to slowly load. I cringed as I saw the unread messages filing down the page, with subjects ranging from *Phones down?* to *Labor Day weekend* to *Question!* But giving no indication what that question might be.

"Hello?" a deep, familiar voice rumbled from the lobby.

"In here!" I called. Harris slid into sight in the office doorway, then smiled slightly as he noticed me holding my cell against the window.

"I see I came just in time," he said. Already, I was feeling more relaxed. Harris had a way of making every issue seem small and manageable. Like all you'd ever need was a fresh bit of wire, a new bolt, all of which really meant a call to the right person.

"Thanks for coming out so quick," I said, leaving my phone on the window ledge to give time for all the emails to finish loading.

Harris had curly brown hair, a pronounced widow's peak, a full beard that matched. It made him seem older, or like he was comfortable in the role he'd settled in to. He was in his own version of a uniform: baggy jeans, plaid button-down, brown tool belt, homemade beaded bracelet tight on his wrist, usually more string than bead. The current version had a row of blue stars framing three white letter tiles, spelling the word DAD.

"Got your message just as I was finishing up at the elementary school. Figured I'd swing by and take a look on my way back." He placed his metal workbox on the long table.

I pointed to his bracelet. "I like the stars." Last time he'd been here, it had been a seashell motif.

"Elsie got a new kit for her birthday." He smiled, as he always did when talking about his daughter, though I imagined his wife had a hand in the spelling, considering Elsie was only three. "Tell me what's going on with the lines."

"The one at the main desk has been out, along with the internet. But it felt like it was going even before that, cutting in and out."

He disappeared out to the main desk while I scrolled through the emails on my phone, jotting down names and numbers to call back from my own apartment line later. I hit "delete" on the emails fishing for information—I could never tell for sure whether they were journalists or amateurs, but every email unrelated to a reservation became an autodelete. The frequency of those inquiries had slowed through the spring, but there seemed to be a recent uptick again, with the summer season, just like the sheriff and Marina said—people talking. People digging. *Bad optics.*

"Hey." Harris stood in the doorway again, taking up most of the door frame. "Any of the other lines having an issue?"

"Well, my apartment is fine, and none of the guests have mentioned anything. But the internet isn't reliable as it is."

He nodded. "Probably not the main outside line, then. Sounds like a short, or a loose wire. I'm gonna need to take a look at the junction box in the basement."

"Sure," I said, fishing my badge from my purse, hanging it around my neck.

Harris followed me down the hall, stopping at the old photos of the inn. "You change something?" he asked.

Of course he would be the one to notice. Harris had an attention to detail I generally appreciated. "Celeste is getting a frame replaced," I said. "But you know how it is. Everything gets pushed to the off-season."

I swiped my badge against the employee door, then led him down the stairwell.

Cory was just pulling the storage door shut as I exited the stairwell. "Hey," he said, taking a step closer, like he was going to tell me something. But then he stopped, his face falling flat, eyes to Harris behind me.

Cory didn't like Harris, or Harris didn't like Cory. I was never sure which came first. Only that they had gone to school together and knew versions of each other that I never would.

Not that I assumed they ever had much cause to be friends: They were almost the same age, but Harris had a steady job and a kid, while Cory took cash under the table for guided tours that capitalized on tragedy, worked periodic shifts at his parents' place, and was presumably just passing the time until the tavern fell to him, just as it had to his father before.

Harris cleared his throat.

Cory watched closely for a second, not asking any question. "See you round, Abby," he said before pushing through the entrance at the end of the hall, straight to the outside.

I pointed Harris to the closet just before the exit. That was the storage area with the patio furniture and hot tub chemicals, and we never kept it locked, since entry to the basement area itself was already limited, and a variety of workers needed access to the supplies. Celeste and I were the only ones with a master set of keys to the other rooms. Well, and maybe Cory.

Harris opened the door, flicking the light. "Bingo," he said.

"All right," I said, backing away—it always smelled like earth in there, all concrete floors and dusty surfaces and unfinished cinderblock walls. It made me imagine being trapped, in the dark, underground. "I've got to get back to the lobby."

"I know where to find you," he said, already opening the beige box adhered to the wall that abutted the outside.

I headed back upstairs, glad there weren't any guests waiting again. My cell was still sitting on the window ledge of the back office. I finished making the list of date requests that had come through in the email and brought the page out to the lobby computer to check against our reservation system, waiting for Harris's assessment.

The phone abruptly started ringing beside me. I jumped, then relaxed, glad that whatever issue Harris had found in the basement hadn't been difficult to resolve. "The Passage Inn," I answered.

"All set," Harris said, his voice deeper and closer through the line. "Be right up."

I heard the door down the hall, and then the slow amble of Harris's steps coming closer. "What's the damage?" I called when he finally came into sight. "Nothing too bad, I assume?"

His mouth remained a flat line, his fingers running through the base of his beard. "Yeah, nothing major. Just a line disconnected."

I nodded. "Must've been coming loose for a while, I could definitely sense it cutting in and out before it went entirely."

He slid the toolbox on top of the registration desk, pulling out his pack of work orders before sliding them back inside the box. "Let's call this one even," he said. "I was on my way, and it was just reconnecting it."

"No new wire?" I imagined a fraying cable. Exposed wires. Thirty years of age.

He ran his tongue along his top row of teeth, seemed to be thinking through what to say. "The wire's fine." His glassy eyes slid over mine before he leaned one arm on the surface between us. "I don't think it just managed to fall out on its own, Abby. There's nothing wrong with it."

"Could it happen by accident?" I said quietly. Asking, silently, *please*.

Harris did me the favor of not saying no. "Anything's possible, I wouldn't say anything for sure. Just, be careful who you let in down there."

He said it pointedly, and I knew he was picturing Cory coming out of that other storage room. I couldn't help seeing the same, everything shifting through his eyes. Goose bumps rose across the back of my neck as I imagined Cory in these rooms. Cory, hands running over the wires. Cory, who had always had a way in.

But there were others, too. The cleaning company. Various

maintenance workers. People Georgia or I let inside without a second thought, to reach the supplies.

Harris patted the desk once, his silver wedding ring tapping against the surface. "Call me if you need me."

"Thanks, Harris. Hi to the family."

AFTER HE LEFT, I kept running through the possibilities. It could've been an accident. Someone who hit the phone box while storing a piece of furniture, dislodging a wire that had been only loosely attached. Like Harris said, anything was possible.

But the rest of my shift, I couldn't shake the suspicion. Thinking over the last few days, the people who had been in and out. The happy hours we had each night. The people we welcomed into the inn.

I was still shaken and not fully engaged when the group of six finally returned from their hike, asking for a first aid kit. The man with the ruddy cheeks—Mr. Lorenzo—had an arm around his wife, supporting her as she hobbled over with an openly bleeding wound from her knee.

"Oh no," I said, reaching for the supply of bandages kept in a bin under the desk.

"Looks worse than it is," she said with a laugh. I thought, from the look of it and the glint of her eyes, that it would feel a lot worse once the numb of the alcohol wore off.

"Someone should take a look at that," I said. I thought it would probably need stitches, so I handed them the urgent care number at the same time as the bandage kit, along with their reservation for tomorrow.

Even as they were heading for the steps to the second floor, their loud voices carrying behind them, I was imagining a very different sequence of events: a cut knee, and no one to help her, sitting on the edge of a rock and waiting for help that wouldn't come—

The front door of the inn opened again, and Georgia breezed in, several plastic bags slung over both arms, the plastic digging into her skin. "Hey there," she said.

"Hey," I said, making space for her as she deposited the bags on top of the registration desk.

"Refills for the mini-fridge," she said, pulling out two cases of sparkling water in the flavors we liked best. She brought them to the back office, and I considered not asking her, not ruining the change in her demeanor—but I had to know the other possibilities.

"Georgia," I said when she returned with one of the raspberry beverages, "have you let anyone new into the basement recently?"

She turned slowly, bottle already halfway to her mouth.

"I don't mean . . ." I waved my arm between us, uselessly. Her private life was not my business. I started again. "I think we need to start keeping a list of the maintenance workers coming and going."

She took a step closer. "Why?" Her eyes had gone wide, the worry already taking root.

"The phone lines are fixed," I said, "but I think the box was damaged. Would just be good to know who's been down there, in case something bigger happens."

She took a small sip, eyes still fixed on mine, and I wasn't sure if she believed me. She started gathering the other grocery bags, busying herself, not saying, for once, whatever she was thinking. Then she paused, watching me closely. "You know, my dad was always the one person I could trust," she said. "I didn't live with him. But he was the one person who really saw me. Who would tell it to me straight. Even if I didn't want to hear it." I had a habit of closing off when Georgia brought up her father, as if losing a parent bound us together. Meanwhile, her mother was still alive, though apparently they didn't get along. But now I thought she was saying something about me, about us. About trust.

Georgia seemed highly attuned to the potential for danger, but I believed she only saw it in the obvious places: an empty room; a dropped call; a search in the woods.

All these things we saw coming. The real danger came in the places we didn't see it, without warning. *Trey's arrival; the cut phone lines; the hidden flash drive—*

"Georgia," I said, "it's going to be okay."

I was not naive to Georgia's presence here; you don't turn up at an inn and stay on a whim. Not when you have money and resources. Not without cause.

"Okay," she said, almost at a whisper. We stood that way, eyes locked, until the teenager from the Last Stop startled us, stepping inside with the first batch of supplies for happy hour.

HAPPY HOUR WAS JUST about over when the sheriff arrived, still in uniform. I looked for Trey behind him, but he was nowhere to be seen. Sheriff Stamer caught my eye and slowly walked across the room, greeting the few lingering guests as he did. *Hope you're enjoying the stay. Did you make it down to the falls yet?* Keeping things pleasant and surface-level fine.

"Just wanted to check in, since I knew you'd be wondering," he said when he was close enough for the conversation to remain private.

"Everything go okay with Trey?"

He tipped his head side to side. "Just dropped him off. Ended up taking him out to lunch while we went over everything that happened over the spring." He drummed his fingers on the surface. "He seemed surprised by how much was done. How much we all searched."

He waited for the kid to take the trays out to the van before leaning closer. "He showed me the photos. Said you saw them, too?"

I nodded. "What do you make of them?"

"They're just photos. And honestly, they confirm what we assumed. I checked, they were taken the same day and with the same camera specifications we have on file for Farrah Jordan's missing property."

I didn't even think to do that, to look at what other information was available in the photos.

"So someone had the camera?" I asked.

"Seems that way," he said. He cleared his throat. "Could've been someone found it out there, with no idea what it was." That was possible, I agreed. But someone figured it out. Someone put it together. Someone had passed these photos along to Landon West, as a tip.

"What's going to happen next?" I asked.

"Nothing, Abby. Anyone could've found it out there. It was over three years ago. We don't know how it got to Landon West. We'll likely never know." He put a hand over mine briefly, which was maybe the first time he'd ever done so. "Just wanted to let you know, this is an old case. It might feel like a new clue, but it really doesn't tell us much that we didn't already know. As much as his brother might want to hope otherwise, it's not really a break in the case."

As if the last person in possession of these photos hadn't disappeared four months earlier. As if he hadn't been staying in the place I oversaw, and I had missed it. As if history hadn't shown it was possible to happen again.

"You really believe that?" I asked. He looked over his shoulder quickly, then turned back. I lowered my voice. "That it's *nothing*?" *Wishful thinking doesn't help anyone*, Marina had told me. "Did Trey also tell you where he found it? *Hidden*, in that room."

His expression tightened, his mouth a flat line. "I know it's not *nothing*, Abby. It's just not gonna get us anywhere."

And with that, he ran his hand down his tie, turned to face the room, and strode toward the exit. That was all I was going to get from him. That was all he was going to do.

I watched him go, seeing him as an outsider might, as Trey might, for the first time in a long time. The man who couldn't solve the mystery of what had happened to Landon or Farrah or Alice Kelly. Who had let the investigations come to a quiet, unsatisfying conclusion. Who didn't want to invite outside scrutiny and needed to keep me on the same page. I wasn't sure whether he believed what he was saying.

The night came to a close as it always did—and soon I was cleaning up in the silence of evening, doors latching shut, lobby lights dimming.

I stepped out into the night, listening to the sounds of the forest come alive: crickets and a distant barking and the sound of things moving in the branches overhead—a wild cacophony. I crept to the edge of the lot, where the path snaked toward the cabins, hoping to catch sight of Trey. His car was still in that same spot, but there was no sign of him otherwise, and I couldn't bring myself to knock on the door to Cabin Four—*Did you get what you came for? What did the sheriff say? Did you believe him?*

He was a black hole, and I was falling in. Remembering things I'd long since put out of my mind, declared irrelevant. Farrah's pictures had kicked everything back to the surface, and now I was circling the memories from three years earlier, thinking about the pictures—there was something that had seemed unsettling about them. Something wrong.

The truth is—

The truth is, Farrah still haunted me.

The truth is, she'd come into the inn that day before continuing on to the trailhead. We'd been closed for renovations, but the doors were unlocked, and visitors had kept coming in, despite the sign out front.

I'd been painting the baseboards of the open stairwell, leading to the second floor, and I was already on edge. A simple patch had turned into a ruptured pipe, and suddenly there was drywall work, wood work, electrical work. Contractors had been coming in and out, but not in the right order, and the emergency-work calls cost a premium we hadn't budgeted for.

So I was already poised to snap when the door opened again, but it wasn't one of the workers we'd hired. I'd felt her standing in the lobby, just behind me. I'd had paint on my knuckles, a brush in my hand, and I was irritated. I'd told her we were closed, but she'd still stood there, not moving.

I didn't ask how I could help her. I recognized her type from the way she stood with the camera bag over her shoulder, the way she looked around the place like she owned it. I knew before she opened her mouth that she was here for our notoriety. She was here to look around, to pry back the layers, to *find* something.

Were you here, she began, *when Alice Kelly disappeared?*

I didn't answer at first, but I figured the truth wouldn't hurt. *No*, I said, dragging the paintbrush across another section of the board. *I wasn't here for that.*

I met her once. A long time ago.

As if that entitled her to anything more than all the rest. As if crossing paths with someone seven years earlier gave her any special insight.

Like I said, I wasn't here.

But she didn't stop, instead taking a step closer, one foot on the bottom stair. I stood, three steps above her, peering down.

Do you know who saw her? she asked. *Who were the witnesses at that tavern?*

As if we were all in on the information. As if I would just hand it over to her, this stranger. Instead, I said what Cory would've said, understanding, then, exactly why he did—thinking of all the people he was protecting. These strangers, nothing but trauma tourists who saw entertainment in our existence. Seven years in Cutter's Pass, by that time, had dulled me to the intrigue. We were just a group of people, wrapped up in the outskirts of a mystery against our will. As if the town were a puzzle to solve, and we were the pieces. And so I said, in an echo of Cory's own words: *You won't find any secrets here.*

And *those* were presumably the last words ever spoken to Farrah Jordan.

Three days later, when her car was found, when her picture was passed around, and Celeste said she saw her at the trailhead, I admitted to her that I'd seen Farrah, too. That she had stopped by the inn, asking about Alice. *It's not relevant*, she'd told me, with a sort of finality that made me believe her. *We don't need the inn at the center of this, do we?* And then, with a shake of her head: *Poor girl, what was she doing out there, in the snow, all alone?*

She'd told me it wasn't my fault that she was missing, that I didn't owe her anything, that I'd done nothing wrong, and I believed her—because I wanted it to be true.

But I knew that the story told about Farrah Jordan's disappearance was wrong at the core. Farrah Jordan knew exactly who we were, what this place was. She had not stumbled upon the town of Cutter's Pass by accident, drawn in by the beauty. No, she was lured in by something else. The fleeting memory of Alice Kelly.

She knew exactly where she was.

In the three years since, I'd gone to great lengths not to send anyone away who set foot in the inn. Not hikers, coming down from the mountain. Not sightseers, interested in warming up around the fire. And not Trey West.

* * *

THE LOBBY OF THE inn was vacant when I returned from a walk of the perimeter, but there was a blue plate on the registration desk. Dinner, from Georgia. She always left me a plate if she was cooking, saying it was just easier to make enough for two. Breaded chicken and asparagus with a creamy sauce that smelled decadent, on one of the blue ceramic dishes from her kitchen. Her apartment always smelled like fresh cooking, or flowers. Like a home.

I walked around to the other side of the desk, saw a wineglass with a heavy pour of red. I wouldn't normally drink while on the clock, but after the last few days, I let myself relax the rules I'd set for myself.

I took a sip, and it was definitely not the inn-purchased wine to which I was accustomed. I imagined Georgia at a kitchen stool, setting a place for herself, an open bottle beside her. I imagined the dinners she had enjoyed in her past, the person she used to be, before her father died.

And then I pictured Farrah, the ghost of her, standing at the base of the stairs, watching me. Like she was waiting for me to pay attention, to be honest. To find her.

I WAITED UNTIL I was sure the guests were all back in their rooms, and the inn was more or less closed up for the night, before opening the password-protected folder on the lobby computer. Before looking at those photos again, carefully this time, by myself.

I pictured Sheriff Stamer viewing these images, checking the settings, and wondered what it was he saw in them. The story he told himself about this place. The images themselves were flat, definitive—pointing to a specific place and time.

And finally I put my finger on why they'd felt so unsettling.

It was for what they weren't: They didn't feel like Farrah's work. The photos were markers, but they weren't *art*.

Farrah had a public Instagram account, which she had updated every so often with a new landscape photo. It had been untouched since a month before her disappearance.

I went to the back office with my phone, slowly waiting for the inn's account to load. Then I searched for Farrah's account, which I'd done with less frequency in the last year. But in the months after her disappearance, I'd come often, hoping to find a deeper understanding.

Though there was a lot of variety to her photos—mountains and beaches and desert, and even one of a suburban backyard—the one consistent feature seemed to be how she drew in color, so different from the snow-blanched images on the flash drive. On her Instagram page, I had always felt a focus to her images. A purpose.

That's what was missing. The intention behind these images. Of course, these were just a series of shots, lots of images from which she might have chosen only one to work on. But the photos of Cutter's Pass seemed to have a different purpose.

I flipped from her images to the grid of photos she was tagged in, the one place I could find candid shots of her smiling. Something I'd never seen in person.

Perhaps the most unsettling thing was how the number of tagged images kept growing, in the years after her disappearance. Her friends and her students sharing old photos, making her appear so alive. Like she had continued to exist, in a second, secret life.

The most recent new photos she was tagged in were related to the Landon West case. There were several from newspaper articles that shared all of their photos side by side, Landon and Farrah and Alice Kelly and the Fraternity Four. It was the third such post that gave me pause, because of the username.

AliceKellyWasHere

I clicked over to her profile. The description read:

In memory of my beautiful sister, Ali

Love always, from Quinn

The description jarred me. *My beautiful sister, Ali*. A side of Alice Kelly none of us had ever known. What a baby sister might've called her. The user photo showed a younger version of Alice Kelly, face turned down toward a much younger girl—Quinn, I assumed. Both with dark auburn curls piled into high ponytails.

The most recent post was added only three days earlier, and it was a series of photos beginning with a shot of Alice Kelly getting ready for a hike, framed by the woods behind her. She seemed younger than the year she went missing, more carefree somehow. The caption read: *Can't believe it's almost the 10 year anniversary. Miss you every day.*

I took her in. Her beaming smile, her hands on the straps of her pack, a flash of bright orange running down the center. A sudden chill started at the base of my spine.

I scrolled to the next image and was confronted with the haunting image of Alice Kelly walking into the woods. She had turned to peer over her shoulder, looking back at the camera.

The phone slipped from my hand, ricocheted on the table, a clattering that broke the silence, broke everything.

That image was still visible on the screen. I couldn't breathe. Couldn't understand.

I grabbed the phone and started running. Down the hall, employee badge in my grip, hand shaking as I held it to the door. Stumbling down the steps, into the basement, past Georgia's room with the music blaring.

It took three tries for me to get the key in the lock of my apartment, and then I was throwing open the door, throwing on the lights, sliding to my knees before the bag I'd left propped up against the wall, hours earlier.

It was that backpack. Beige, with orange threading down the straps. I felt myself breaking into a cold sweat. There had to be more than one of these. Obviously, there was more than one—it was a mass-produced bag. But it was the smaller details: the label that had been torn off, revealing a darker patch beneath it. I zoomed into the photo on my phone until I could see it clearly: the missing zipper clasp of the smaller pocket, where I'd looped a zip tie. My vision began to swim, even as the image gained clarity.

No. No. Not my bag. Not this place. Not her, too.

This was the bag I'd dug out of the lost and found bin almost ten years earlier, just months after she'd gone missing. Alice's bag. Here, at the inn.

I leaned against the wall, wanted anything else to be true. But there was no avoiding it: For the past ten years, I'd been wearing the pack that had once, a decade earlier, belonged to Alice Kelly. Alice Kelly, who had walked out of these woods, *into the town* of Cutter's Pass, and disappeared. Never to be seen again.

PART 3

Alice Kelly

Date missing: September 2, 2012

Last seen: Cutter's Pass, North Carolina

The Last Stop Tavern

CHAPTER 11

I KNEW THE STORY OF Alice Kelly well. I had arrived in its aftermath—after the search, after the investigation, after the cloud of suspicion over the town had dissipated. The case may have been behind them when I'd arrived that winter, but I could feel it in every aspect of Cutter's Pass.

It was the first disappearance since the Fraternity Four, fifteen years earlier. And that made it all the more notable: *Young Woman Disappears in Same Town as Unsolved Case of the Fraternity Four*. Their story was excavated and rehashed, becoming something bigger, a part of the present. Comparisons were drawn. People who had lived in town for both were given a closer look. It didn't matter that the cases differed in every aspect except for the location. When I drove in, Cutter's Pass was a town on edge; borders pulled tighter, residents grew quieter, everything turned inward.

The story had spread up and down the Appalachian, eventually spilling over to the other side. I'd been living on the outskirts of Nashville at the time, in a third-level two-bedroom apartment with no elevator, because I understood the severity of my mother's illness—that she needed my help, and also that there was a clock, and it was running out. Time bent differently for us, every day moving in a slow monotony while also slipping away too fast.

I'd first seen Alice Kelly's smiling face, high cheekbones and a spatter of freckles, on a local news program my mom kept on all day in our dimly lit living room. My mom then followed the case with a vigilance I didn't understand—there were missing people everywhere, tragedies behind us and tragedies awaiting us—but she held my hand as I sat beside her on that brown couch, eyes trained to the television, as if we knew her. And then, as we continued to watch, eventually we felt that we did.

Alice Kelly, just starting her senior year of college, who had been hiking with a large group from the Outdoors Club over the long Labor Day weekend—a trek that was supposed to end the next day. But her group of three had splintered off, fallen behind, and decided to camp near the intersection of the trails. Alice didn't want to. As her hiking partners explained in interviews, tear faced and noticeably shaken, Alice said she had a test the day after next, couldn't risk missing it. She saw the town in the distance—the dome of the inn and the steeple pushing up through the trees—and decided she could make it by sunset. She was the most experienced hiker among them. She had a plan.

I'd watched those interviews sitting beside my mother, listened as she said, *There's something not right about that place.*

I'd imagined Alice often since then, standing on the ridge in the distance and seeing Cutter's Pass—a town, a safe harbor, an *option*—as she packed up her things while telling her friends she'd be *fine*.

And at first, she was. She'd made it out of the woods and followed the road into town, where the streets and restaurants were packed for the Labor Day weekend. She made her way to the Last Stop Tavern, and her cell phone must've been dead when she'd tried to turn it on, finally back in range. Because, according to witnesses, she'd used the phone behind the bar to place a single call before leaving.

And that was the last time she was ever seen.

It took until the next day to realize she'd gone missing, when the other hikers made it back in cell phone range and tried to reach her. That's when they discovered that something was wrong. That Alice had slipped from her known life. She hadn't returned to school. Her family hadn't heard from her. Her friends hadn't heard from her. No one had heard from her.

All of the calls from the tavern that night were local numbers. None of them had lasted very long. But every call made from that line was traced, and none of the recipients remembered hearing from a young woman, for any reason. Two of the calls had gone to a cab company, but neither driver picked up a girl matching her description. Still: Every cab driver was interviewed, every patron of that bar, every person who had cause to be in the downtown of Cutter's Pass that evening. No one could remember seeing her after she left the tavern.

The story had slipped from the news as the months stretched on, but whenever Cutter's Pass was mentioned, I heard my mother's warning: *There's something not right about that place.* Ironic that I'd come here and found some solace here after her death.

This was the context, the history, I had arrived in. This place that was still reeling from Alice Kelly's disappearance. A reckoning that had never quite happened. A brief destabilization. There had been no answers. No tangible connections made between the cases. No sign of her. No sign of any of them.

Not until this backpack, which I had carried for years, unaware. This backpack, which had somehow made it to the basement where I slept, where I lived. So that now I saw her here in my half dream, auburn hair in a ponytail, dirt across her freckled cheek, eyes wide, and hands gripping the straps of that bag as she stood at the end of the hall of this basement—

A ringing phone brought me back to the surface—at least, I thought it was a ringing phone. By the time I was fully awake, the ringing had stopped. It could've been part of the dream about Alice.

I pushed myself up off the floor, a crick in my neck from how I'd fallen asleep, my head resting on the pack, as if I'd conjured her in the dream, breathing in the scent of earth and the forest. My mouth tasted like stale wine and I still wore my uniform from the day before, stiff and uncomfortable.

The sun was streaming through the gap in the blinds of my living room—I couldn't tell what time it was, only that I'd slept later than usual. I felt disoriented, confused, my entire frame of existence splintered beneath my feet.

I walked through the bedroom into the bathroom, where I stripped off yesterday's clothes and stood in water set too hot, letting the steam fill my lungs. There was a tremor in my hands—like when I'd last had a fever, and Celeste kept coming down to check on me, bringing me soup, resting the back of her hand against my forehead. She'd even called in a doctor, who declared it the flu, said all we could do was wait for the fever to break. It was the one time I'd seen Celeste look truly afraid. She'd stayed on the couch so she could keep a close watch. Something I thought I'd never experience again, after losing my mother.

For a long time, I wasn't afraid of what had happened to Alice Kelly. Because in my mind, I imagined her as someone like me, with nothing holding her in one place any longer. Because, as people soon discovered: She did not have a test the next day, as she'd told her friends; she did not have cause to rush back to school—these were lies.

I believed, strongly, what I had told Trey during our hike. That some people didn't want to be found. And I'd believed Alice had run. Why else concoct the story she had told the other hikers on the ridge that day. I believed that she had taken stock of her life and decided to change course. I believed if there was a secret kept in Cutter's Pass, it was this. I had wondered, back then, if maybe they had all left.

But that story wasn't true. Her bag had been in the basement of this inn, all along.

And suddenly, everything circled back to this place. I could see the ghosts of all of them: Landon, Farrah, and now—Alice.

The woods were not the tie, as much as Trey wanted to believe it. Both Landon West and Farrah Jordan had passed through this inn for a reason. Looking for something. Looking for someone. And now I had evidence that Alice Kelly might've passed through here, too.

I felt like I had when I was standing at the base of the falls yesterday, like I was at the center of a funneling.

The Passage Inn—this was the center.

Alice Kelly's bag had been in the lost and found bin, in the basement of the inn, just waiting for me to find it. And there were only so many people who could tell me how it had gotten here.

THE PHONE WAS RINGING again as I exited the bathroom.

"Hey," Georgia said when I answered. "Sorry to wake you. I just wanted to check. Make sure you were okay—"

"I'm fine," I said, clearing my throat, clearing the fog from my head. I checked the time, already nine, long enough that I'd typically be up, but not late enough for Georgia to be concerned. "What's going on?"

A pause. "It's just, the back office was open this morning, and the dishes were out, and . . . I'm sorry, my mind jumped to the worst possibility." She laughed to herself, high-pitched and fake.

"Oh god, I'm so sorry. I came down for something last night and meant to go back upstairs to lock up, and I fell asleep. I think the wine got the best of me. I'll come clean up, it was delicious by the way, thank you—"

"Oh, no, it's fine, I've got it." I could still hear her breathing, too close to the phone. "I'm having some trouble finding the binder, though. Do you remember where you left it?"

I stared at my reflection in the bedroom mirror as we spoke. The hollows under my eyes and the sharp jut of my collarbone, the birds taking flight.

This place felt, for the first time, like quicksand.

"I'll be right up," I told her, throwing on a crew neck T-shirt and jean shorts, no time to dry my hair. Besides, I wasn't planning to spend the morning at the inn.

UPSTAIRS, BREAKFAST WAS IN full swing, and I barreled out of the employee doorway into the hall without looking where I was going, colliding with a man carrying a plate.

His dish ricocheted to the floor, napkin and an empty butter packet scattering with the pieces of porcelain. "I'm so sorry," I said, just as he spoke, "I didn't see—"

I looked up first—Trey West, in need of a shave, in need of sleep.

"Hi," I said. He paused, looking up. Eyes skimming the long hair, the casual clothes. "Abby," he said slowly. "Hi, sorry. I didn't notice it was you." And then, with a twitch at the corner of his mouth. "You're kind of a chameleon, you know."

I stood, unnerved by seeing Trey here, in this hallway. The same place I'd first seen his brother.

Georgia rounded the corner then, drawn by the noise. She stood at the end of the hall, stopping abruptly. "I've got it," I said as Trey looked her way.

She brushed her hair off her forehead, smiled tightly. "Thanks," she said.

"Who's that?" Trey asked, eyes still taking her in. It was hard not to; she was twenty-four, stunning, one stretch of long legs to a long, exposed neck.

"Georgia," I said. Hoping the sheriff hadn't told him every detail—about who had found his brother's empty room. Hoping he didn't approach her with the same intensity he'd approached everything else.

"She looks familiar," he said, still looking at the empty place she'd once stood.

"She works mornings. I'm sure you've seen her around here." I made sure I'd picked up the last of the broken pieces of the dish before standing.

Trey stood just as I did, but now he was frowning at the faint tremor in my hands.

"I shook you up," he said. I started to protest, but he continued. "Not just now. I mean, yesterday. I'm sorry I didn't come by after my meeting with the sheriff. It was a lot to process."

I waved him off. "No, it's okay. It's your family, you're entitled to some privacy. It went okay, though?"

His eyes drifted to the side. "Yeah," he began slowly. "Everyone's so friendly. Actually between him and Rochelle, I worried they were going to talk me to death."

I smiled. "Well, they're the two people who would know the most in a place like this."

"So I gathered. Hey"—he lowered his voice suddenly—"can I ask you a couple questions later? When you're not clearly in a rush?" A small smile.

I nodded, tucked my wet hair behind my ear. "I've got some errands to run this morning, but I'll be working this afternoon. You know where to find me."

Georgia's call was worrying me—the binder should've been right there. A lost key yesterday, and now a lost binder—too many reminders that things had a way of disappearing here.

Trey backed away, down the hall, out to the back porch he'd just entered from. And I was struck again by the similarities between him and his brother: their builds, their mannerisms. I understood suddenly why I'd felt a pull to him, from the start. Like I could stop him this time, before he slipped away. Alter a conversation, change an interaction, extend an invitation. As if it were possible to pull him back—pull them all back.

I'D FOUND LANDON WEST out in this hall, in a moment eerily similar to the one that had just happened, just outside the employee door. But the lobby of the inn had been mostly deserted then. I'd done a double take when I exited from the stairwell, seeing a man lingering so close, so quietly, to the employee quarters. Something made me pause, pulling the door shut behind me, waiting to feel the security of the latch.

Good morning, I'd said, and he'd looked at the polo I wore, the label on the upper corner, before pointing at the images on the wall. *Is it true, that the owners built this place all on their own?*

I smiled. *Designed and planned from the ground up. Blood and sweat and a little luck.* The same thing Celeste had once said to me. But then I looked over my shoulder, leaned closer, in mock conspiracy. *I assure you there were more hands involved than just theirs. After all, I painted this hallway myself last year.*

He stepped back as if to appraise my work. *Very professional. You hung these, too?*

I did.

I watched as his eyes shifted from frame to frame. *It's like seeing two versions of the same thing.* The image of the structure, framed in wood. The blueprints hanging in the last photo. He pointed to the door I'd just come from. *Do you give tours down there?*

My smile faltered. *No, it's private residences.*

Just like the carriage house out there?

I didn't know why he was asking about Celeste's home. Or mine. But it put me on alert. Made me remember where we were, made me think of Farrah, and the people who had come looking for her, asking in their roundabout ways.

Are you a guest here, sir?

Landon West, he said, hand extended, wide smile with a dimple. *I'm staying in Cabin Four.*

Oh, I haven't seen you around. Though I recognized his name from the log. Figured he'd been using the cabin as a base for hiking. He hadn't been in for happy hour, that I knew of.

I'm working on a book, he'd said, eyes drifting back to the framed series. *What's your name again?*

I hadn't yet told him. *Abby*.

Abby, he repeated. *You've worked here awhile?*

Ten years, I said.

Ten years, he repeated. There was something off about him, the way he circled around a question, repeated my responses. But I had to relieve Georgia from her shift, and I couldn't think of a reason to ask him to go.

Later that night, after I had closed up the lobby for the evening and had just come downstairs, I heard someone trying the back door. Our private entrance. The one hidden under the deck. I wasn't afraid. Instead, I unlocked the door myself and peered into the night, but whoever it was must've heard me coming and fled. I couldn't say for sure it was him—guests sometimes tried other doors, exploring the grounds. Though I believed, in that moment, that it was.

* * *

IN THE LOBBY, GEORGIA was moving around, running her fingers over each surface, checking under tables, around the stacks of logs beside the fireplace. Her purse was on the surface of the registration desk, like she'd just come in, though she'd probably been out here for hours.

"Hey," I called. "No luck?"

"I've checked everywhere up here. Even the restroom, just in case."

The binder usually held copies of the credit cards we made with the slide under the desk. It held check-in and checkout data, license plate numbers, daily orders to the Last Stop for happy hour, our tally of walking sticks. We usually kept it locked up in the back office, but now I couldn't remember where I'd left it last night when I'd rushed out—trying to match the Instagram photo from the *AliceKellyWasHere* account to my bag.

I shuddered, remembering the image of Alice Kelly looking over her shoulder, like she was peering right back at me. *Do you see me?*

"I can't remember if I put it away," I said, running my hands through my damp hair. I saw her gaze trailing my fingers, her eyes flitting around the room, like the binder might still magically appear.

I couldn't remember the last time I'd used it—when the group of six returned from their hike, maybe? Dropping their sticks, exchanging them for a first aid kit and the number for urgent care?

I started searching the areas I might've left it—under the desk, in the drawers of the back office. "I already checked," Georgia said, following behind and clearly irritated, instead of the creeping dread I was starting to feel.

"Shit," I said, standing back, hands on hips. "I don't think it's in the apartment, but I'll look." The final moments of last night had been a blur. "I'll try to recover what we can during my shift. For now, just start a blank one for check-in and checkout."

She shifted her jaw back and forth. "Do you think someone took it?"

The only thing of value inside were the credit card copies; someone would've had to know what they were looking for. I blinked at her slowly. "Is anything else missing?"

Her eyes widened, and my stomach plummeted. I knew we had the same worry: the keys; the safe. I opened the cabinets and my shoulders relaxed—the safe was locked and secure.

"Looks like everything's still here," I said. Luckily, Georgia and I each had a copy of the key to the safe, and it seemed I'd left that one secure, at least.

"I probably just misplaced it," I said. Though I couldn't imagine where it could be.

"Or someone thought it was an extra guidebook," Georgia offered, biting the side of her thumbnail.

I nodded, wanting it to be true.

But I couldn't shake the feeling of someone watching me in the night. Who had noticed when I'd left the lobby unsecured. Who had rifled through things while I'd been falling apart downstairs.

I thought, once more, of Trey West. Maybe he was more similar to his brother than even he knew. Digging and digging, in need of answers, by any means necessary.

"Sorry to wake you this morning," Georgia said.

"I was up. Just have some personal errands to run today."

I left it at that, heading back for the apartment, where I did a cursory search of the surfaces, even though I knew the binder wouldn't be there. I'd barely made it past the front closet last night.

Then I hooked Alice's bag onto my back, grabbed my keys, and headed for my car.

I slipped the bag into the back seat of the sedan, the inside stale and stifling. I felt too hot, like I was hungover, even though I'd only had the one glass of wine.

I turned the key in the ignition, but all that happened was a faint, low-pitched buzzing. I leaned my head back against the headrest, squeezed my eyes shut. I tried the ignition again but got the same result. The engine, as long predicted, was dead.

"Son of a bitch," I said, slamming the front door behind me, pacing back and forth beside the car.

Georgia's midsize SUV was parked beside mine. I'd never driven it before, but I didn't think she'd mind. I strode up the incline to the front entrance, where Georgia was currently helping a guest check out.

I slipped in beside her at the registration desk, caught her eye, reached my hand into her purse, and pulled out her keys. *I need to borrow your car*, I mouthed.

Her face remained frozen, like she couldn't process what was happening. "Oh," she said, one hand in my direction.

"Be right back," I said, and she smiled, running her fingers through her short hair, turning back to the guests.

Her key had an automated lock, and the car beeped in the drive. I moved Alice's bag from the back of my car to Georgia's.

I had to see Cory, and on a Saturday morning at this hour, I'd place money on him still being asleep. He ran his tours late, stayed at the tavern until closing. Avoided downtown during the weekly farmers' market. I didn't call first. It was best if I caught him unprepared.

CHAPTER 12

THE DOWNTOWN OF CUTTER'S Pass on a summer weekend morning looked like a page out of a storybook. Streets carved out of a dip in the landscape, mountains rising up in the distance, trees filling in from all sides. There was an amber glow to the storefronts, still closed at this hour. And the town green was transformed for the weekly farmers' market, tables and booths set up in a mazelike grid, foot traffic spilling over into the surrounding streets, children playing tag on the sidewalks.

I navigated through the downtown with my foot over the brake, until crossing the bridge at the far end of the grid, just past the welcome center, on the way out of town. Some of that water, I knew, came from Shallow Falls. All of it came from the mountain.

Beyond the campgrounds and the stables, the roads were wooded and residential, rising up in parallel tracks along the hillside, mostly with second homes, small but expensive rental properties that could be booked by the week, and a few locally owned plots that had been held on to from earlier generations. Some of the owners continued to hold on to them by renting out the upper or lower floors to visitors.

But most of the permanent residents lived just beyond this area, where the road meandered into the woods, set back in their own enclave of trees.

Cory lived about a mile outside of the downtown, on one such plot of land, with a driveway that crossed over a narrow stream, wood beams spanning the gap. I was never quite sure they were built to hold a vehicle, but everything about Cory was a leap of faith.

His place was an old ranch that he'd purchased from the Langshore family after Nora Langshore had passed, and the younger generations had all left Cutter's Pass, not that anyone was surprised by that. There were people you knew would stay, and people you knew would leave. And there were others who left and returned, like Celeste—as if she had found no match for this place and brought back the things she loved from the outside with her.

Cory was always going to stay, I had no doubt. He lived with his two dogs, Billie and Tuck, both part retriever, and I could hear the dogs already barking as I turned off the engine of Georgia's car. Billie had just been a puppy when we'd met, but Cory often brought them both into town. Whenever he was on shift, those dogs had a permanent spot at the back corner of the outdoor patio, water bowls left out, eager for a head rub from a customer.

I heard the wind coming, rustling the trees first, and then the wind chimes at the edge of his porch. When he'd taken over the Langshore property, he'd kept the hummingbird feeders and patio chairs and the wind chime that sounded just like the rain on the skylights of the inn.

Cory was at the door before I had a chance to ring the bell, clearly expecting someone other than me, judging by his expression. I tried not to take it as a slight.

"Hey," he said slowly. There was a question in the greeting. I didn't just turn up at his place. Hadn't in more years than I could remember. But now I was struck by all the ways it was exactly how I had last seen it.

There was the place I'd sat with my feet propped up in his lap, watching the fireflies; there was the door I'd slammed on my way out of here for the very last time, because I couldn't take the way he brushed aside any question that felt like something real. I'd sat in my car then, cooling off, waiting for him to come after me, but he hadn't.

"I need to talk to you," I said now, waiting to be let in. Hoping I wasn't interrupting an overnight visit with someone new . . . or some tourist he'd met downtown.

Billie raced out from behind Cory, nudging my hand, and I scratched her head until Cory finally said, "Sure, come on in."

"I thought maybe you'd be sleeping," I said, standing in the middle of the living room, same stone fireplace and oversize sectional, but the walls had been recently painted, the stones whitewashed for a more modern look, the carpet pulled up and floors refinished. "This looks . . . wow."

The entire inside had been partially gutted, the wall once separating the kitchen removed to open up the space. It was bright and airy, and I remembered that Cory had told me, once, how he wanted to flip old homes in the area. But he said it in the same way he said he wanted to see the Serengeti and visit the Seven Wonders of the World. I never imagined he would actually do it.

"I've been working on the house on the weekends. Figured it was finally time to make it my own." He ran a hand through his dark hair. "Is everything okay? I heard about Trey's visit with the sheriff."

"What did you hear?" I asked. I wondered if Cory knew about the pictures from the camera, about the evidence of Farrah's case that the sheriff declared unimportant.

He shrugged. "Just that. Rochelle said they were back in the office for hours." Which was different from what the sheriff told me—*Took him to lunch*, he'd said. Maybe both were possible.

Still, if Rochelle had heard about the pictures, she would've known about my involvement, too. The fact that this hadn't reached Cory meant the sheriff was keeping this from both of them. I wasn't sure why. But I made note.

"I'm not here about Trey West, Cory," I said.

"Well, please do share, Abby. What brings you to my door on this beautiful Saturday morning?" He leaned against the back of his sofa, all nonchalant, without a care in the world.

"I want to ask you something. And I need you to answer me this time."

"You need me to answer," he repeated, slowly, like he could already sense it. I could see his demeanor changing, in the tensing of his shoulders, the shuttering of his features.

"I need you to tell me about Alice Kelly," I said.

He stayed still, hand tightening on the furniture, staring at me. "Jesus, Abby, not this again." I'd asked too much, that's what he'd told me back when we were together. He'd said he was going to start charging me, if all I wanted was the same thing as the trauma tourists.

Now he continued to say nothing, a tangible distance growing. Didn't even try to make light of it, how he might've long ago: *You won't find any secrets here.*

No, this time, the question was too direct, too dangerous. I wondered if he knew what I was really asking: *How long ago had Cory lived in my apartment, in the room next door to where I'd discovered Alice Kelly's bag?*

Now I imagined Cory at the bar with her, after she called for a cab, saying, *I work at the inn*, convincing her to come back. I imagined him pushing her, pushing me—

"Tell me what happened back then," I said—I was practically

begging him; had hoped our past had counted for something. But now I was wondering if he was afraid to answer. "I wasn't here for it, and the story doesn't *make sense*." Not anymore. Her bag, at the inn.

"I don't know what you want from me. Or why you're so obsessed with her story. I don't know anything about Alice Kelly that you don't already know."

I closed my eyes, took a deep breath, caught the scent of hazelnut coffee, was transported back to lazy mornings a decade earlier. But then I thought of Cory in the basement. Cory, always with a way in. The phone lines, tampered with. I knew he held his secrets close, but hadn't considered that he could've been involved. I didn't know what he was protecting and couldn't stop my mind from chasing it down, imagining the possibilities—a danger here that I hadn't been aware of.

"Tell me something real, Cory. Please. I think you owe me at least that."

He flinched, and I knew I'd made a mistake. That Cory didn't believe he owed me anything. That, in his mind, I was the one who had changed. "Tell *me* something real, Abby."

I felt the anger surging, alongside the fear—at Cory, at this entire town, at all the ways people talked around and over the fact that there was something very wrong at the core.

"Fine, you want something real, Cory? Come see."

I stormed out the front door and felt him following behind, the same way I believed he would follow after me the day I left him. Though in his mind, maybe I hadn't. It was not the last time I ever ended up back with him in the basement of the inn; it would get so quiet down there, time passing, and sometimes I had to do something just to remind myself I was still here. A different sort of proof of life. But from that day, I understood what Cory Shiles cared about most of all.

I threw open the back door of Georgia's car and pulled out that hiking pack, my throat threatening to close. All the emotion, too close to the surface.

"You want something real?" I said, hearing the crack in my voice, forcing it back. "Here. I've been using her bag for the last decade."

Cory held the bag tentatively in his hands, face contorted in confusion, before raising his gaze back to me. "I don't know what you're saying. This is *your* bag."

I took out my cell, pulled up that Instagram page again: *Alice-KellyWasHere*, and found the photo of Alice Kelly, walking into the woods.

"Look," I said, thrusting my phone in his face. *"Look."*

"Okay," he said, frowning. "So it's the same type of bag."

"No, Cory, for the love of God, *look* at it." I took the bag back from him, put the phone in his hand. Watched as his thick fingers zoomed in on the picture, his brow furrowing. "The label. The zipper. Do you see."

I watched as his eyes switched from the phone to the bag in my hands. Back and forth, back and forth. And then I watched as his throat moved. His face settled into something impassive, closing off. His hand dropped to the side. He had seen it. I was sure.

"I found the pack at the inn, Cory. How did it get to the inn?"

He handed the phone back to me. "I don't know," he said.

"I've been carrying it around, with no idea, all these years . . ."

He placed his hands on my shoulders, and it was only then I could feel that one of us was shaking.

"Cory," I said, just barely over a whisper. "Tell me. Please."

He took a step back, looked down at me. "You think I hurt her?"

I took too long to answer. "No," I said. "Obviously not, or I wouldn't be here asking you about it now, would I?"

He took a long, slow breath, gaze to the side, into the trees, where I could hear the wind coming before I felt it. Just when I thought he was going to tell me something, the secret of Cutter's Pass, he shook his head. "She . . . I have no idea how this fucking bag got to the inn, but you should get rid of it, Abby."

He reached for it, and I pulled it back, our eyes locking over top. He was stronger, we both knew it. We also both knew what it would mean if he took it.

"Abby, seriously. This is bad. This is dangerous."

"I've been using it for *ten years*," I said, my voice cracking, as if I were laying claim to it, not just afraid of losing it. Something that I thought would disappear if I let it out of my sight now.

Just then, there was a rumble of tires over gravel at the entrance to his driveway, and he let go of the bag. I put it in the back seat of Georgia's car and watched as a truck came into view. The navy pickup I'd often see in the back lot of the Last Stop.

"My parents were planning to stop by," he said under his breath.

They were hard to make out clearly as they crossed the makeshift wooden bridge, pulling into the spot beside mine. Marina exited the vehicle first, face tight, looking between us before she pasted on a smile. "Hi there, Abby. We weren't expecting you this morning."

"I was just stopping by," I said so they would know I hadn't spent the night here. Marina and Ray had both warmed up to me after Cory and I had cooled, when I was just someone working at the inn, Celeste's niece, coordinating an order with the Last Stop. I was an outsider to Cutter's Pass. There were some things still off-limits to me, and it seemed they thought their son was one of them.

"She was just dropping off some extra paint they had at the inn," Cory said as Ray closed the driver's side door. Both Marina and Ray wore jeans and sneakers and T-shirts with the Last Stop name.

"Well, that was very kind of you, dear. You look like . . ." She trailed off, but I knew what I looked like. I looked too close to the person I was when I arrived a decade earlier. Unfinished, ungrounded. A little reckless and rough around the edges.

Ray opened the tailgate of the pickup and pulled out a box.

"Let me help you, Dad," Cory said, taking the box from him. Something shifted inside, and it sounded breakable. "Tiles," Cory explained. "For the bathroom."

"Have you seen inside?" Ray asked, obvious pride on his face.

"I did. It looks great."

He slid another box to the edge of the truck. "Got these at cost from a site that had extra."

"Is that Georgia's car, hon?" Marina asked, eyes narrowed at the silver SUV.

"Yes," I said. "Mine wouldn't start this morning."

Cory hadn't even asked. And I realized he rarely asked a question of me, because to do so would be opening himself up to the same.

"Did Cory offer to take a look at it for you?" Ray asked.

Cory's dark-eyed gaze settled on mine. "Yeah, let me know when it's a good time to come by."

Ray sensed something off, his movements slowing. "If he can't help, we've got a good mechanic, Abby, he'll do right by you."

"Thanks, Ray. It probably just needs a jump. I was just in a rush this morning. Don't worry about it."

But Marina was looking into the back window of Georgia's car, at the backpack lying across the bench seat. Orange thread visible, missing label, makeshift zipper. The bag they'd probably seen me with many times before.

"Well, don't let us keep you, Abby." She gave me her familiar gap-toothed smile, but something felt forced in it. "I'll be up again for happy hour this evening. The other night was a nice change of pace for me."

I walked around Georgia's car, opened the driver's side door. "See you soon, then," I said.

Cory nodded at me as I slid into the seat. I watched as they entered Cory's house, his dad with a hand on his shoulder, a feeling in my chest I had to fight down.

I STARTED THE CAR, letting the working AC blast from every vent before shifting into reverse and carefully maneuvering backward over the wooden bridge, Cory's house slowly disappearing behind the trees.

I pulled out onto the road, angled back toward town, then idled on the shoulder.

Alice's bag was visible in my rearview mirror, and I imagined her sitting back there now, eyes reflecting in the mirror. *What next?*

This town was a vault, and I'd been here too long to see it from the outside in any longer. But I still felt a distance, in the way Marina looked at me, in the things Cory wouldn't say. Everyone closing ranks, keeping their mouths shut, faces placid and impenetrable.

If I asked Celeste when Cory had last worked at the inn, I'd already know her response: *Why do we need to know that?* And as eagerly as Rochelle took in information, she doled it out deliberately, like it was a power she wielded. Jack had been here back then, too, but he was a part of their circle—a group I could never quite crack. Sheriff Stamer was as good as family, would never say anything that had the potential to harm someone he cared about.

There was only one person who knew Cory back then who I thought might tell me honestly. Harris had gone to school with them all—with Cory and Jack and Rochelle—their grades overlapping, their pasts seen through a shared filter. And unlike them, he'd left this place for a time.

Cory had stayed in town, working for his parents. Jack had put his skills and passion into a way he could sustain himself, doing the things he loved. Rochelle took courses in the summers but continued to work in the sheriff's office, her job advancing along with her. But Harris—he kept himself apart from them. He'd always lived outside the town boundary, and he had left. I knew this, because I was here when he'd returned.

I sat at the intersection at the end of Cory's lane, no car in sight, and called Harris's cell. Though we didn't have the type of relationship that generally seemed like I could just come out and ask, what choice did I have? Maybe I could ask him to the inn, bring it up casually. But the call went to voice mail immediately: *You've reached Harris Donald. Leave a message and I'll get back to you.*

I remembered his face when he saw Cory down in the basement. His implication, when he'd noticed the line had been disconnected. His pointed warning: *Careful who you let in down there.*

I turned the car around and headed in the other direction—out of Cutter's Pass.

CHAPTER 13

I'D DRIVEN BY THE Donald family property before. It was about five miles beyond the town perimeter, but ten miles before the next, where a rising series of switchbacks through the terrain brought you into Springwood.

But between Cutter's Pass and that rising road was a stretch of cleared farmland, individual homes on larger, flat acreage. When I'd first arrived in Cutter's Pass, Harris was off at college near Asheville, and his grandparents had still owned the property. But they'd let the farming go, so the growth from the surrounding woods had steadily encroached, the fence falling to disrepair.

After they'd passed—one a year after the other—the Donald land fell to Harris, but it wasn't until five years ago that he officially came back as a full-time resident, bringing his new wife and setting up his own business, building his clientele from the people and places he'd once known so well.

It wasn't quite a complete homecoming, though. There existed some gap that couldn't fully be breached—either by him or the rest of the town. Like he, too, could only see this place from the outside in. I wondered what it looked like to him now, after being on the other side.

I pulled into their winding gravel drive, the road splitting into a circle in front of the two-story home. There were two cars parked beside the separate garage—a small white sedan and a pickup truck. A good sign that Harris was home.

I hesitated on the wide front porch, hoping I wasn't waking anyone. But as I got closer, I heard the catchy melody of the end of some Saturday-morning cartoon. Their daughter, at least, must already be up. Still, I knocked tentatively.

The pitter-patter of feet that followed was light and rapid, and I could hear her struggling with the lock, twisting it back and forth several times before eventually managing to unlatch the door.

The hinges creaked, and a small girl in a matching purple pajama set stood barefoot in the foyer, wide brown eyes and thumb going to her mouth when she saw me standing on the other side.

"Elsie, hi," I said, bending down, hands on my thighs. I was never sure exactly how to speak to children, at what age they became capable of carrying on a conversation. "I'm Abby. Is your dad home?"

She ran back through the foyer just as a voice called her name from around the corner. "Elsie? Was that Dad?"

A woman leaned around the wood-paneled wall, taking in the scene in the front foyer. Her face shifted quickly from confusion to a warm and welcoming smile.

"Hi?" she said tentatively, stepping into the room. "Abby, right?"

I tucked my hair behind my ear. "Yes, hi, so sorry to stop by like this. I was just in the area, and I was hoping to catch Harris. I know it's the weekend." I winced, for impact. I struggled to remember his wife's name—she was young, from some other state, Florida, I thought, and not often talked about because the only thing there was to discuss was how infrequently we saw her. She had shoulder-length strawberry blond hair and brown eyes like her daughter and a softness to both her features and her voice that made me see her through Celeste's eyes, thinking she didn't look like she could do the hard things—*Samantha*. "It's nice to see you, Samantha. Sorry to interrupt your morning."

Her smile stretched even wider, if possible. "No, no, come on in." She had a warmth, an innocence, and I could see why Harris liked her, why she liked Harris. Her hair was pulled back into a loose ponytail, and she wore leggings and an oversize shirt. She was barefoot, like her daughter. The house smelled of syrup and home, and I got a flash of nostalgia for Saturday mornings growing up, when my mom and I used cookie cutters to make pancakes in the shape of hearts.

"I'm sorry, though," Samantha said. "Harris is out on a call. But you're welcome to wait, he should be back anytime now. There's coffee, if you're interested."

"Oh, thanks but I've had my quota of caffeine for the morning," I said. I hadn't, but I didn't want to get caught up here. Not with Alice's bag in the back seat, and Trey back at the inn with questions, and Georgia waiting for me to return her car. "I guess that would explain why his cell went to voice mail. I should've taken the hint. But I was in the area."

"Well, it's nice to get to see you again. How's it going out at the inn?" she asked.

I was trying to remember when we'd actually interacted last. When Elsie was a young toddler and they'd both stopped by the inn to bring Harris lunch, during our closed workweek two years ago? Most life updates were passed along through Harris. My world had pulled tighter over the last decade, the inn at the center.

But I was realizing how set apart Samantha was here, all alone, with her daughter. I could feel the bones of everything this place used to be, the past not even out of sight. The wallpaper that still lined the living room must've been here from when Harris grew up, raised by his grandparents in this very house. She'd done what she could, adding a family picture of the three of them at the heart of the foyer, and along the wall of the living room was a series of photographs—a trail in the woods, a meandering creek, a burst of flowers—which somehow worked with the floral beige wallpaper behind it.

"It's all right. A busy time of year." I shifted on my feet, easing toward the exit again.

"He mentioned you had some issues up there." She looked over her shoulder, into the living room. "You're not worried?"

My eyes met hers, and I wondered what exactly Harris had told her—how worried *he* had been, that he hadn't quite let on.

"The missing journalist," she added when I didn't respond, keeping her voice low, in case Elsie was listening—though she was currently sitting less than a foot from the flat-screen TV.

"No, I mean, yes, it's horrible." I shook my head.

She nodded slowly. "It's always a visitor, right?" The corner of her mouth twitched. "Everyone in that town acts like it's *fine*. It's not fine."

I shook my head. "No," I repeated. "It's not fine."

"What do you make of it?" she asked, biting the side of her thumbnail.

I shook my head rapidly, because I didn't have an answer. Because that's why I was here, with Alice's bag in the back seat of my car. "I don't know," I said. The most honest thing I could say.

She sighed, looking around the place. "Living here was supposed to be temporary," she said. "Then there was always a reason to keep staying . . . But after that journalist . . ." She pressed her thin lips together. "I want to go, and Harris promised we would, but do you think he ever can, really? When all his business was built up around the people there?"

I noticed she called Cutter's Pass *there*. That she saw herself as an outsider as well.

"It's a nice place to live," I said, because what could one say when standing in a family home, at the edge of the place that had slowly become my own over the last decade.

She laughed, then stopped. "Okay," she said, drawing out the word. "How long does it take, to feel like that?" she asked, and then she added, "It's just, I've been here over four years, and everyone's friendly, but . . ."

I grimaced. "Yeah, it takes a little while to get a feel for everyone . . ."

"Harris tells me I should go to Springwood for anything I need. Not that I know many people there either . . ."

The question she was asking: Was there something, really, to fear in Cutter's Pass? No wonder she was lonely out here. It helped in this place to have someone vouch for you. Harris should've been enough. Everyone called him in for business, from the sheriff's office to the elementary school, but otherwise he was kept at arm's length, too. And he kept us the same. But I had a feeling Harris knew more about this place than he let on—something he wanted to protect his wife from, and I was disturbing that.

I was struck suddenly with the realization that I shouldn't have come here.

"I have to go. Will you tell Harris I stopped by?" I asked, trying to make a polite exit.

Just then, I saw Harris's work van pull up the gravel drive. "There he is," Samantha said with a smile.

"Thanks," I said, hand on the doorknob. "I don't want to take any more of your time."

"Listen," she said, "we should go out sometime, when Harris isn't busy. Maybe even drive out to Springwood for an evening?" she added with a nervous laugh.

I nodded. "I'd love that. Harris has my number." I made myself smile as I turned away, striding as quickly as I could down her front porch without raising suspicion.

I wanted to ask Harris some questions that would not put his wife any more at ease. And I didn't think he'd be honest in front of her, knowing what I knew now—how much she already wanted to move on. They were both stuck, with this land, with what he'd built from it. But it came at a price, and she was the one currently paying it.

HARRIS WAS WALKING OUT of the stand-alone garage when I caught up with him. He was eyeing the unfamiliar car in his drive, trying to reconcile it with me.

"Well, this is a surprise," he called. And then his smile faltered. "Everything okay at the inn?"

"Sorry, I tried to call first. And then I was driving by," I said, uselessly waving my arms at nothing.

He slid his phone out of his back pocket. "Must've been in a dead zone." He frowned. "There's nothing from you."

"I didn't leave a message. It was more a personal question I was hoping you could answer," I said, peering over my shoulder at his house. Picturing his wife peering back out. I shifted so my back was to the house.

"All right," he said slowly.

"The phone lines," I said, and his gaze also drifted to his home, to his wife and daughter, and I wondered if he feared for their safety more than he'd told Samantha. Whether he hid his concerns, knowing how his livelihood was also tied to this place.

He squinted against the morning sun, hand over his eyes to shield the glare. "What about them."

"You made a comment—" I shook my head. "I felt like you

thought Cory could've had something to do with it, and I was just wondering . . . why you thought that."

He stared at me, silent, trying to read something behind the question.

I shut my eyes, tried again. "I know you grew up here. That you might know something I don't. I do know he used to work at the inn." Here it came, I had to ask. "Did he live there when Alice Kelly disappeared?"

He rubbed one thick hand through his beard. "That was a long time ago. I wasn't here then." He drew in a long breath through his nose. "I think he was at least staying there part of the time." He took another step in the gravel, to the side, busying himself in the truck. "I couldn't swear to it, though. I was in college, we didn't run in the same circle, couldn't say we kept tabs on each other much."

"You were never friends?" I asked.

"Well, in a place like this, you don't have to be friends to be in someone's life, you know?" He closed the truck bed. "But look," he said, and I couldn't tell if he meant in general, or around this place. "I grew up here, with my grandparents, who rarely had cause to be involved in the town. Went to school, came home, got out when I could. Cory was a year behind me, grew up like practical royalty in Cutter's Pass. So no, we weren't friends. He did what he wanted, got away with what he wanted, never outgrew that mind-set now, did he." He looked at me pointedly, and I was sure he'd heard about some level of my relationship with Cory. "Why are you asking me about Alice Kelly after all this time?" he asked.

"Because," I said, "I've been here ten years, and you're the first person willing to answer."

He looked to the house again before taking a slow breath in and out. "My advice?"

I nodded. That's what I'd come for, after all.

"This town isn't gonna let anything happen to him. I'd be careful who you ask that question."

I took a step back, smiling, trying to undo the last ten minutes. I didn't feel any better, any sense of clarity. I felt, instead, like I was pulling farther and farther away from the heart of things. "Your wife is lovely," I said. "Thanks, Harris. Sorry to bother you on your day off."

"You can call me, Abby. Any issues up there, don't hesitate, okay?"

"Thanks," I said, my hands shaking slightly as I slid into the driver's seat of Georgia's car. I watched as Harris approached the front porch, the door opening before he'd set foot on the first step, the little girl running out from behind her mother.

The keys slipped from my hand, and I had to fish them from the space between the chair and the console.

My fingers stretched for them until they brushed against the metal. I clasped the key between two of my fingers, and pulled—the set of keys dangling behind. But in my grasp was a small, half-size key, which I hadn't noticed earlier.

I pieced through everything on the chain, that I'd taken abruptly from Georgia's purse, without permission. I recognized the apartment key, beside the large key to the car. And there was the key that granted access to the downstairs entrance of the inn itself. The only other key was this: small and silver, with a crooked letter *E* engraved on it.

There was something vaguely familiar about it, but I was sure it didn't belong to any room at the inn. It wasn't the key for the safe in the back office, or the back office itself, both of which were kept on a lanyard with our employee badge, granting us access to every guest room. No, this was something else.

I could see Harris and Samantha still standing in the foyer

behind the open doorway watching me, so I started the car, raised a hand in thanks, and drove too quickly on the way out, dirt kicking up in my wake.

I COASTED THROUGH TOWN, seeing every store, every person, through a different lens. The farmers' market crowd was giving way to the weekend lunch crowd, a crawl of cars as visitors looked for parallel parking or slowed to take in the mountain view. I could pick out the residents easily, and realized it was a way of moving that set them apart. A sort of casualness or aloofness, like they were walking through a sea of people who didn't really exist. Like the rest of the players were only set pieces. And in their world, wasn't that true?

There was a young deputy, out of uniform, jogging diagonally across the street through a gap in the traffic. There was Marina, trailing behind Cory's two dogs, unleashed, weaving through the visitors on the path toward the Last Stop.

There was Rochelle, striding down the street in the opposite direction, tapping her knuckles against the large glass window of the Edge, smiling at someone inside. And then there was Jack, backing out the entrance with the cardboard display, coy smile and words I couldn't make out.

I imagined the Fraternity Four walking down the center of this road in that famous picture that now hung behind the bar at the Last Stop. Alice Kelly, walking out of that swinging door. Farrah Jordan, in the very spot Jack was now standing, asking for directions.

A flash of red of a visitor's T-shirt, and my heart leaped into my throat, picturing her instead.

Jack was placing their chalkboard easel sign on the sidewalk, advertising their services. I'd watched him do this several times a day—changing out the offerings based on the time, the season, the crowd. Now there were three lines of writing, in different colors of chalk: *Coffee*, in purple, with a picture of a mug, steam rising; *Gear*, in green, a rudimentary tent drawn beside it, a triangle of sticks; *Lockers*, in white, with an accompanying sketch of a key.

I was still staring at that sign when the car behind me tapped its horn, nudging me on now that the traffic had moved half a block forward.

I raised my hand as I eased my foot off the brake. But my mind kept circling back to that chalkboard display.

A locker. A key.

Instead of continuing on to Mountain Pass, where the road inclined toward the inn, I turned left at the Last Stop Tavern. I circled in a loop around downtown, to my hidden parking spot.

But when I pulled in toward the dead end, I discovered I wasn't the only one here. Now there was a black Audi in my spot, Maryland plates. Trey West's, pulled all the way forward until the bumper brushed up against the foliage.

I couldn't shake the feeling that he was watching me, somehow, even though he'd been here first. That he was checking up on the things I said. That I was not the one in control right now, and maybe never had been.

I angled in just behind him, off the road. Maybe he was visiting the sheriff again, with follow-up questions. Maybe he was seeing what information he could pull from the rest of the locals. Maybe my imagination was getting the best of me, and he was just visiting the Last Stop, or CJ's Hideaway, or one of the other restaurant establishments, venturing into town for a lunch of his own.

But the not knowing made me nervous. Made me wonder what he was up to, and what he hadn't told me.

I turned off the car, and held the key chain in my hands again, staring at the small key.

I'd seen Jack and other employees hand these to hikers passing through, who were looking to store their nonessentials. I'd seen hikers handing these keys back to whoever was working on the other side of the desk, restocking supplies they'd shipped in advance, for their long-distance Appalachian treks.

This was a key to a locker inside the Edge.

I almost backed out of the alley and kept on driving to the inn. I almost let it go. Georgia's private life was her own. But then I thought: She had an apartment with a key, where she could presumably store whatever she needed.

I had not seen Cory for all he was, and it had me reassessing everyone. Everything I had imagined, about what brought people to this place.

It would just take a moment. She never had to know.

CHAPTER 14

THE FRONT ENTRANCE TO the Edge didn't have a bell or chime, but it was still impossible to enter without being noticed. There was an assortment of gear and snacks hanging on the closest wall, and anytime the door opened, it set things in motion—a crinkling of wrappers, a creaking of hooks and hinges.

There were several tourists inside, spinning racks, piecing through the water bottles with hiking mottos and hats with brand logos, moving with a distinct lack of purpose. Jack was at the counter, and the coffee was brewing behind him. He raised his head before the door had even finished swinging shut behind me.

"Morning," he called, which is what he generally used as greeting until deep into the afternoon here, when he could justify a transition to *Evening*. Jack smiled at me with the one he reserved for visitors, friendly but lacking in connection. But his expression shifted as I approached, as he put me in context—without the uniform, without the hairstyle—and he said with a deeper smile, deeper voice, "Well, hey there, Abby from the inn."

Jack had called me this ever since we'd first met, at the happy hour when Celeste had introduced me to them all—the people of Cutter's Pass who were about my age, and would continue to live here alongside me. He continued to call me that a decade later. We never got any closer, even when I'd been with Cory.

He greeted everyone who wasn't from Cutter's Pass with an honorific, something for him to remember—or maybe to remind us instead that we came with qualifications. The owner of the vacation rental storefront around the corner was still *Brad from New York*, even though his parents had moved here when he was in high school, and he'd graduated alongside Jack and Cory.

"Morning, Jack," I said. I couldn't bring myself to return the banter. Especially because I couldn't pin him down: *Jack from the Edge? Jack with the van? Jack of the woods?* "You still in town for a while?"

"Yeah, here till September. Then I'm on for a bunch of school programs," he said. The coffee machine behind him buzzed, and he turned around to remove a pot.

Jack was a permanent fixture here, just like Cory.

His younger sister Jamie, on the other hand, had gotten out as soon as she could. I'd met her once at the tavern, back when I'd first arrived, and she'd leaned in a little too close, whispered too loud, smelled too strongly of vodka for a seventeen-year-old still trying to find herself in a place where everyone knew exactly who she was. *Don't stay too long, whatever you do. The longer you're here, the harder it is to get out.*

The Oliviers were a prime example of people raised in the same environment headed in opposing directions. But lest anyone think otherwise, Jack was great at his job—any job, actually, this particular one included. He could upsell any of these products, though he rarely used them himself, just by his air of authenticity.

He was probably the one person who could decipher the large, detailed maps of the mountain hanging on the back wall, edges overlapping, creases visible. Elevation and terrain and a web of trails—a complex geography.

I drummed my fingers on the counter as he worked. "What do you know about a man who lives in the woods?" I asked.

His hands paused for a second before he looked over his shoulder with a questioning smile. "Listening to Cory's tours again?" he asked.

I shook my head. "I just figured if anyone knew if it was true, it'd be you." He knew who was heading in and who was heading out. Knew the paths that the rest of us didn't know existed. Knew all the things that one could encounter out there.

He walked back to the counter between us, hands pressing into the surface, leaning forward, the imagine of nonchalance. "Well, I've never seen anything that makes me think it's true. But it's a big world out there." He flashed a toothy grin, and I could imagine him giving that line to any shopper, any tourist. "Now, is there anything else I can help you with this fine day?" he asked, changing the subject.

My eyes drifted to the back wall—behind the racks of clothes that filled the common area. Small lockers lined the left side of the wall, in square cubes made for wallets and maybe shoes, like you might rent at an amusement park for a few hours. Larger lockers like those I'd used in high school took up the rest of the space and were apparently deep enough for tents and duffel bags.

I wasn't sure which type of locker this key was for. Or how to get over there without him noticing. I decided to just say it. Less likely it would stick in his mind. And besides, he didn't have cause to interact with Georgia much at all. He probably wasn't even the one to give her this key.

"Just running an errand for Georgia." I held out the small key. "I didn't get the locker number, though."

The front door opened again, and a family of four entered, all with pale legs and long khaki shorts, hiking boots laced up over too-white socks: a mother and father who looked very excited to be here and two tweens, a boy and girl, who seemed decidedly less so.

"Morning," Jack called to them. "Anything I can help you with today?"

"Yes," the father said, definitive, authoritative. "We're about to have our first camping trip."

"Well," Jack said, "you've come to the right place. Just a sec."

He pulled a large brown book out from under the counter, and I got a whiff of old paper as it made contact with the surface. "You got this?" he asked me.

"Yes, thanks," I said as he snaked out from behind the counter, joining the family in the middle of the racks. "Oh, this set is awesome, if you're looking for a full cook setup . . ." He trailed off.

Inside the book he'd left for me, there was an old-fashioned placeholder ribbon, and I couldn't help but imagine an old spell book. But it appeared more like a ledger inside, with individual customers signing in and out. Each page worked as a library card of sorts, with a list of names, start dates, and the scheduled expiration date of the rental. It was somewhat organized by locker numbers, but that didn't seem to be the primary system. Instead, there were sections for daily, weekly, or monthly rentals.

There were yellow tabs sticking out of the pages that still had availability, with all the prior names crossed out in thick black Sharpie, so at least that narrowed it down a bit. The system seemed so rudimentary, this log in mere paper and ink, that a line of marker could erase the existence of any record that had come before. It seemed, suddenly, like something only a place like this could get away with. Like you're not sure whether it comes from the lack of technological progress or a place that craves its privacy.

Either way, in the end, the process involved going page by page, looking for Georgia's name.

Some of the open listings had dates that had already passed, and I could only assume that eventually those lockers would be cleaned out by Jack or another worker if no one came to claim the contents. Sort of like the gear left behind in the guest rooms at the inn, ultimately making its way to the lost and found.

Jack and the family of four had immersed themselves in the cooking section, and the mother was admiring an ultra-light French press. I couldn't imagine them making it very far out there.

I flipped through the pages of the ledger faster, hoping to be done with this before Jack returned so he couldn't ask any follow-up questions. Georgia's name wasn't assigned to any of the small lockers; none of the weekly lockers, either. By the time I had made it to the large locker section, of which there were far fewer, I was starting to get frustrated, wondering if this key wasn't for a locker here after all, that I'd let my imagination run away with me, just like my mother had always said.

And then I stopped. The page for locker 203 was a row of crossed-out names in black, and then a single visible line filled out in looping, cursive blue ink. A chill ran through my entire body. The line read: *Abby Lovett*

I stared at it as if it would somehow trigger a memory. This was not my handwriting. This was not my doing.

I looked over my shoulder, watched as the family followed Jack to the tent section. Then I read the page again. The names above mine had been crossed out in black Sharpie, and according to the ledger, my name had been added to the locker 203 register in *April*. The rental was originally listed as three months, which would mean it had already expired. If anyone had gone through this ledger recently, the locker might've already been emptied.

I didn't know what this meant, why my name was in here. But I did the safest thing I could think of. I took the Sharpie from the pen holder on top of the counter and drew a thick line through my name, so that any trace of me was gone. Then I shut the book and went to check on locker 203.

The racks around the store were high enough that I could move within them, like a maze, and feel somewhat protected. But I could see Jack's head over top, and a scattering of the others shifting across the store.

Each locker had a number plate etched onto a maroon rectangle, adhered to the gray metal. A small keyhole positioned just under the latch.

I stood in front of locker 203 along the back wall and breathed slowly, my vision funneling to this one spot. This one moment.

Sometimes, I could see it coming, a shift to my existence. I heard it in the ringing of the phone before my mother picked up the apartment line with the news that would change both of us forever. I knew from that first shrill ring—something was coming. I felt it again as Celeste opened the door to that basement apartment, gesturing me inside—that there was something here for me.

And I could feel it now, some precursor, in the tiny metal key in my shaking hand.

The rest of Georgia's keys dangled from the chain below, and I gripped them now in my closed fist, to still them.

I slid the small key into the lock, felt the mechanism turn within. I peered behind me once more, making sure I was alone in the back of the store before lifting the latch. The locker was not empty. Not at all. Something black swung from the hook at the side, meant for jackets or backpacks, and it took me a second to process what I was looking at.

A camera.

There were more items inside, a small pile on the shelf just above my line of vision, but I shut the door quickly, breathing heavily. My hands shaking, stomach churning. *What—why—how—*

Laughter, from over by the counter, where Jack now appeared to be leading the visitors toward the register.

What the hell was I supposed to do with this? Lock it all up, pretend it didn't exist? When this locker had been taken out in my name, and Georgia had the key? How long until Jack or someone else opened up the ledger and remembered I had been in here, looking through it?

I twisted the key, checked that the lock was engaged, and wove through the racks of clothing and supplies as quickly as I could. When I opened the front door, Jack looked up, called my name, "Hey, Abby from the inn, did you find it?"

I raised one finger, indicated I'd be right back. I didn't trust myself to speak.

I moved on autopilot across the street, hand haphazardly out to my side, to warn the traffic to *stop*. Rochelle was just stepping out of the sheriff's office as I walked by, and she paused, one foot on the sidewalk, one still on the steps. "Abby?" she called, like she wasn't sure.

I mumbled in her direction—*Running some errands,* or *Picking up some supplies*, or maybe just, *Hi, Rochelle*—but whatever it was, she turned away, and the next thing I knew I was stepping through the foliage and emerging onto that dead-end street where I'd left Georgia's car. Trey's car was still there as well, and I moved quickly, unlocking the door and pulling my bag—Alice's bag—out of the back seat. Then I slipped it onto my shoulders and headed back to the Edge.

There was nothing to be done about the bag. At least it could be explained away.

The only safe thing to do was to get everything out of that locker, and make sure that no one caught a glimpse of anything inside. *Just Abby from the inn, with the pack she always used. Just getting some supplies for a hike*. I couldn't dare leave those things in the locker, now that I knew they existed.

I could feel the sweat on my back as I entered the store again, and all five people turned to look my way. The two tweens had meandered back to the clothing section while their parents were finishing the checkout procedure, Jack filling them in on the best path, the best course, the best campsites.

The girl was scanning the room with her phone poised, like for some social media post. She'd probably caption it: *Ready to rough it* or something equally untrue, considering what her parents were currently purchasing.

Then she was trying on a floppy hat, and I took the moment to open the locker again, dropping my pack at my feet. I unzipped the top and quickly stuffed the camera into the bottom, then peered over my shoulder again. The girl was still busy, but the boy was approaching. I imagined I was probably drawing attention to myself by acting suspicious, and I tried to calm my nerves.

I closed my eyes and took a slow breath, trying to steady my hands, but all I could picture was Farrah, the camera around her neck. And Alice, this pack securely on her back.

One last thing. I stood on my toes so I could see what was on the upper shelf. A small, black leather-bound book, well-worn, edges of the pages warped from humidity or water or time.

I sank to my heels, pressed the back of my hand to my mouth.

The book Trey had been looking for. Landon West's missing journal—

"Anna, you ready?" All heads whipped around, and the girl—Anna, I guessed—dropped the hat to the rack as the group moved for the front door.

It had to be now.

I reached my hand into the locker, pulled out the stack, a cell phone sliding down off the surface. I caught it against my body before it hit the floor, every part of me wanting nothing to do with any of this. Wanting it gone. Wanting to tell the sheriff. To get this all away from me.

I dropped everything into the bottom of the bag, zipped it tight, and hitched it onto my shoulders, closing the locker, turning the lock, head down, toward the exit.

"Have a good day, Abby from the inn," Jack called.

I raised a hand in acknowledgment. The only thing I could do. I had to get out of there. I had to get all of this out of here, as far away as possible.

But I forced myself to walk slowly back to my car, aware of Rochelle just inside the window of the sheriff's office, or somewhere on this street. And Cory down at the end of the block—if his dogs were here, then so was he. And Marina and Ray, and maybe Sheriff Stamer, circling the downtown grid, out in the open summer air.

How many times had the sheriff walked by this very spot? This was his circuit every morning. Coffee at the Edge, the newspaper stand at Trace of the Mountain Souvenirs, his seat at the Last Stop. How many times had he been within reach of Farrah Jordan's camera and Landon West's journal? Within inches? Mere feet? How many times had he seen me with Alice Kelly's bag, with no idea what he was truly seeing?

We were all so unaware.

Finally back inside Georgia's car, the pack beside me on the passenger seat, I locked the doors before starting the car. As if someone was following me.

As much as I wanted to look *right now*, I had to get away from here.

The short drive back to the inn felt endless. Every inch of traffic, a mile. All I could feel was the bag beside me, and how this would look if anyone found me with all of this evidence in my possession. The same if anyone had opened the locker with my name and seen everything hidden within.

I pulled into the employee parking area and drove to the end, parking Georgia's car exactly where she'd left it, beside my own. And then I sat there, staring at the bag, wondering what to do with it. I gave real consideration to grabbing the rest of my things and going. Just going, and going, to a new place, a next place.

It had been so long since my arrival in Cutter's Pass—I'd barely been an adult, barely had a plan. Celeste had given me an opportunity, a purpose, a *home*, and I'd fallen into a daily rhythm, a comfortable existence. But it had been so long since I considered what I was doing here, why I was staying. Whether I should—

I heard steps in gravel, saw long legs in the rearview mirror, and barely had time to prepare before Georgia was knocking at the driver's side window, bent down, peering inside. I turned off the car engine, tried not to focus on the bag beside me—everything inside, that Georgia had presumably hidden inside a locker. All the things Georgia knew.

"Hey," she said as soon as I had one foot on the gravel drive. "I saw you pull up. I've been waiting for you to get back."

"Okay, hold on, let me just put my stuff away—"

"Celeste is in the lobby with a guest."

I let out a relieved breath. This wasn't about the locker or the camera or the journal belonging to Landon West. Still, I felt Georgia hovering as I pulled the bag out of the passenger seat, and she frowned.

"I'll be right in," I said, turning away from her, afraid of my face giving anything away.

"Abby," she said, taking a step closer. When I looked over, she was holding out her hand, and I realized she was waiting for her car keys. "What were you doing?"

I waited until I was sure my hand was still, my breathing

leveled, as I dropped the car keys into her open palm. "Running errands," I said. "Like I told you." Thinking, *I dare you to ask more. I dare you to ask again.*

I started heading for the employee entrance, and she called after me. "Aren't you coming?" She stuck out one hip, hand resting on it. Looked over her shoulder. "Celeste was asking for you."

"I'll be up in a minute. Just let me get changed."

Back in my apartment, I locked the door behind me, felt the adrenaline catching up with me in a steep wave—a shudder rolling through me. I hadn't eaten all day, but my stomach churned, felt ready to turn over. I needed to stash this bag until later. And this was the only place I felt safe enough to do it. There weren't many places to hide things here—built-in shelves in the closets and built-in cabinets and a built-in dresser and armoire.

I reached for the coat closet, because it was the closest door, and because I understood the best place to hide something was in plain sight, where you wouldn't know there was anything worth looking at, or for. Then I changed as quickly as I could, pulling my hair into a bun now that it was dry, slipping on my work shoes.

Just a part of the landscape of Cutter's Pass. Just Abby from the inn, currently needed in the lobby.

CELESTE NEEDED ME, IT seemed, to move the Lorenzos to a different floor—the cut on Mrs. Lorenzo's knee from the hike had indeed needed stitches, and now the steps were proving too much—and apparently I was the only one able to do it.

"Georgia said you lost the binder?" Celeste said, joining me behind the registration desk, speaking low and only to me. It was no longer *we* but *me* who had lost things, who was not careful.

"Yes," I said, "but it's nothing we can't replicate."

She raised her eyebrows at the question neither of us would

voice: *Did someone take it?* I could think of only one person, and I didn't like what that would mean. Whether he was checking up on the things I had told him. Whether he thought there were things we weren't saying.

"Georgia said we needed to check with you, that you were taking reservations by hand. We didn't want to cause any issues, you see," Celeste explained. I wondered what else Georgia had said, but she was currently stacking a pile of fresh towels on the nearby bench, avoiding my gaze.

I checked the computer for current room occupancy—we had one couple due to check in, but an upper room would be seen as an upgrade from the ground-floor room that we referred to as the Outcrop, as if it were a secret home built into the side of a mountain, and not a corner room with slanting ceilings and low natural light.

I gritted my teeth, entered the new information. "Georgia," I said without making eye contact, "let's get Forest View One turned over before check-in time." Then, to Celeste, "The Outcrop is ready for the Lorenzos."

And then they both left, my shift officially beginning in the absence of anyone else.

ROCHELLE HAD SAID THE ravine was full of bones, and sometimes it felt like the whole town was. That I would live here and die here and disappear with all the rest, indistinguishable.

Recently, I had started to feel trapped. That this place was a prison, instead of a sanctuary. A car that was not in my name, and a home that came with the job—everything tangled together, holding me here.

But in other ways, I felt the immortality of the place. The way the names were remembered. The mystery of it, bigger than any one person. The way Jack called me *Abby from the inn*, and I'd become a part of this town, had a role in it that would endure, like the photos that lined our walls. I could picture myself there, alongside Celeste, alongside Vincent. Could picture the people who would come after, taking a closer look, wondering at the mystery of who I used to be. True proof of life.

I disappeared into the back office, where the service was best, and sent the picture I'd taken earlier in the week to Sloane—with the fog lifting off the mountain, eerie and haunting. A reminder that I was here, should someone come looking.

I felt so close to the bones of this place. Something horrible was happening here. Something baser, more disturbing, inescapable.

What had truly happened here was not the same as the mysteries or rumors told at the tavern, or the picture on the wall over the bar, or the last image planted in our collective mind by sheer force of rumor: Farrah Jordan, at the trailhead, staring off into the woods; Alice Kelly, walking out the front door of the tavern, disappearing into the busy evening rush; the Fraternity Four, walking down the middle of the street, the mountain looming in the distance, with the setting sun.

Those images weren't real. Reality was Farrah standing over me in the inn, asking about Alice Kelly. Reality was the photos posted by Alice's sister, trying to keep her memory alive, reminding us who she really was. I wanted—needed—more.

I pulled up Farrah's profile, scanning the images she was tagged in. Then went to the *AliceKellyWasHere* Instagram account one more time, looking not only at her bag, but at *her*. The account was public, and so was the one I was viewing from—a well-followed and long-running account in the inn's name. On impulse, I sent a private message.

Hi, I stumbled upon your beautiful tribute to your sister. We are helping the town collect some photos as the ten-year anniversary approaches, and wondered if you might be willing to share some more recent photos?

The front door of the inn opened, and I went out front to greet our guest, to try and lose myself in the rhythm of the inn, the daily routines that I had come to love. I helped this place run, knew if I left, my absence would be felt strongly. In the same way Vincent's was when I first arrived.

I tried not to think of the others: Farrah, who no one noticed until her car was found abandoned; Landon, and his empty room.

Check-in after checkout, question after request, I counted the hours until I could retreat into my room, into the closet, into that bag. Marina came for happy hour, and I tried to act like the version of myself she knew best, helping her set out the food, nodding in all the right places.

But I couldn't meet her eye, not when I was imagining all the things Cory might be capable of.

Then I helped Marina clean up, escorting the rest of the guests out, checking the clock again. Almost time. Almost done. The sun had set, and I was finally alone, had just placed the sign at the phone to tell anyone how to reach me for any issues.

The front door opened again, and I took a deep breath, dropped my shoulders, preparing for one last guest.

But the only person in the lobby, waiting for me, was Trey West.

CHAPTER 15

"IS NOW A GOOD time?" Trey asked, looking around the empty lobby. I wondered what he was doing in town earlier—who he was talking to. I must've nodded, because he continued. "I was hoping we could talk somewhere in private."

"Sure," I said as his eyes drifted to the back office. But I didn't like the idea of feeling trapped with this man I had misjudged. I had lost the upper hand; didn't know whether he'd been snooping around—following me, noticing when I was gone, taking that binder. Maybe when I thought I was watching him, he was really the one watching me. Should I really have been surprised? He'd played a false hand at his arrival; when I'd caught him in it, he just needed to shift his act.

"We can sit out back," I said, leading him down the hall, flipping the floodlights on before stepping out onto the wooden deck. A place where I could be seen. Where I could get out. His brother's journal was in the basement of this inn, and I needed to keep him far away from it.

Trey sat in a metal chair across from mine, a circular wrought iron table between us. Gnats swarmed in the glare of the light beside the door, a moth gently tapping against the bulb. He wore faded jeans and a partially fitted black T-shirt, and his ankles were visible over the top of his sneakers, and he did not fit in here at all.

He rested his forehead in his hand, then straightened, pushing his hair back, like Georgia might do.

"My brother stopped at my parents' place on the way down here," he said. The hollows under his eyes appeared darker in the shadows, his scar brighter, in contrast. "Spent a night in the same room he grew up in." A twitch at the corner of his mouth. Not quite a smile. "Landon was always the good son. The one who kept up with them. I was the wanderer."

"That must be tough," I said, because I didn't know what was needed from me in the moment. I didn't know why he was telling me this.

He lifted one shoulder slightly, like that was beside the point. "They wanted me to go through the room. Pack it away." He swallowed, like he was steeling himself for something. "They waited for me to come home, and asked me to help them with it. I figured it was the one thing I could do for them."

"I know what that's like," I said. I'd had to do the same, after my mom passed. Packing away her things, the entire apartment, because there was no one else to do it for me. Mostly I'd sold what I could, donated the clothes, took only what fit comfortably in the back of the car.

Trey took a deep breath. "So I'm there in his room with a bottle of beer, looking through my brother's high school yearbooks and concert stubs from fifteen years ago. Just throwing out as much as I could, boxing up the rest, and I find this in the top drawer of his desk." He slammed a lined sheet of paper on the table between us, like it was a trump card. The edges fluttered in the night breeze.

I didn't know when it had gotten into his hand. Whether he'd had this all along. Everything about Trey felt like a magic trick.

I sat up straighter. The paper had been folded up, and I could picture it in the pocket of his pants, all this time. There were several numbers written on the page, but only one sequence stood out.

"Something familiar?"

"Yes," I said. It was a phone number. The area code was local. My throat felt parched. "It's the inn."

"It's the inn," he repeated.

Then he placed his pointer finger on the numbers above it. But I could only focus on his fingernail, down to the quick. There was a roughness to his hands that didn't exist earlier in the week.

"What do you think this is?" he asked.

I shook my head. The other number was in hyphen form: 8-1. "I don't know."

He jabbed his finger at the page, and I tried again. "A date?"

He sank back into his chair, like I'd given the right answer. "That's what I thought, too. Imagine, I'm sitting there at my brother's desk, and I see this date. August first? And the inn's number?" His eyes widened. "I came down, almost straightaway, to make it. Like he was leading me somewhere. It felt like a sign."

"This was just lying around in his old room?"

"He must've written it down and called from our parents' place, then stuffed it in his desk and forgot about it."

"He didn't make a reservation," I said. "Showed up one day just like you did. Georgia checked him in."

He grinned. "Yeah, but that's the thing. I don't think it's a date anymore. I just put it together this morning, when you told me about your shift. I think," he said, punctuating the *k*, "this is a time."

I felt my breath leave me in a quick gust. Because he was right, of course. The phone number of the inn. A window of time of when to call.

"So my question is, why was he calling the inn between eight and one?"

I knew the answer, and he could see it on my face.

"To talk to someone on shift during that time."

"That's what I think, too."

"I'll talk to her—"

"I already tried," he said, and I could feel myself grimace. "After breakfast, I went back to the lobby. She kept saying, *I don't know, I have no idea, I didn't get any call from him that I recall.*" He widened his eyes in an uncanny approximation of Georgia's expression when she was caught on her heels. He shook his head. "But I've seen her before, Abby. I *have*."

Georgia, always nervous about interacting with Trey, worried he would come to the lobby and ask her something—always waiting for me to return so she could keep away.

I thought about the things she'd hidden under her demeanor—a fear, not of the danger to her, but something *more*. Now I pictured her at night, using a master key to the cabin beside Trey's, or sliding into the cabin window if she was afraid of being seen. Trying to get him to *leave*.

She'd opened up a locker with my name on it. Left Farrah's camera and Landon's journal and phone inside. Then made me dinner and talked about her past, and I had bought it all. Hadn't Celeste tried to warn me? I had no idea who she was, this woman who had shown up out of the blue with signs of the mountain on her. A set determination. Someone who, I thought, could also do the hard things. I'd crafted a story for her—a reinvention—and I'd believed it.

"Now I have a question for you," he said while I was still reeling from this new information.

"I didn't know," I said.

He smiled slightly. "That wasn't my question." He sat back, large hands on his knees, so that I was very aware of his size, and mine. "Yesterday, the sheriff walked me through the investigation. He was much more forthcoming than I expected. Told me Georgia had been the one to find the empty room, that she and Celeste had been interviewed. Told me everyone had been cleared, that the general feeling was he'd gone into those woods, gotten lost. And I get that all, it makes sense. I guess I'm just wondering, now, why he never mentioned you."

The night felt alive around us. The sounds of the woods, growing louder. Trey, closer than I'd intended. Like he could push me with one finger and the threads would all come loose.

He leaned close, his voice close, so I could see the overlap of his front teeth, the scar on his chin, a white line made of ridges and not as straight as I'd thought. "Did you not see him, Abby?"

"I saw him," I said, keeping my voice equally low, like it could dissipate into the night, like fog over the mountain. "Just not the day he disappeared."

He raised his eyebrow.

"I only saw him twice. Once, I bumped into him in the hallway. The other"—I pointed to the door, leading back inside—"in the lobby."

Trey grew so quiet, so still, I wasn't sure if he'd heard me. Only his breathing, ragged, unsteady, gave him away.

The last time I'd seen Landon West, it was ten p.m., and I had just shut down for the evening. I'd gone downstairs, but forgotten my cell in the back office, where I'd been letting photos upload to social media.

And there he was, in the lobby, shaking out his arms from the crisp night. He was hovering around the reception desk, like he was waiting for someone, but stood straight when I approached.

Can I help you? I'd asked, suddenly afraid of making my way to the back office, trapping myself. It wasn't often I felt uncomfortable around a guest. It usually involved too much wine at happy hour, or a group of guys egging each other on. It was rarely a man alone in the night. But then, you remembered everything that had come before. The warnings from Celeste, to take care of myself first of all.

How you had no cell service, that the sheriff's office was closed, that between calling 911 and going through your own contacts, the fastest way to get help was to go through Rochelle.

I hope so, he said. *Sorry to startle you. The phone in my room wasn't connecting. I was hoping I could use this one.*

Sure, I said. *That's what it's there for.*

But then, he had placed something inside his coat, and I didn't think he'd come in for the phone at all. Or maybe it was me, appearing there, that had altered his plans.

Should I send someone to check out your phone in the morning? I asked.

Why don't I just try to reset it first. Sorry to trouble you.

No trouble, I said.

Good night, then, Abby, he'd said, and it unsettled me, that he remembered my name.

Good night, Mr. West, I'd said.

By the next afternoon, he would be gone.

"But you weren't interviewed," Trey said.

I brushed him off, pushed back from the table, too close and falling under his spell. "I talked to the investigators, of course," I said. "I just hadn't had much contact with him. I wasn't on shift when he checked in, and I wasn't the one to discover he was missing."

"What did you do, exactly, when you found out?"

I breathed in the night air, looking out to the woods. Anyone could be out there, watching back. I chose my words very carefully. I remembered the feeling, standing in front of that empty cabin. That eerie, haunting feeling, something bubbling up to the surface— "The three of us searched everywhere on the property. His car was still here. We called around, first. And then we called the sheriff."

"Who did you call around to, first. Where did you think he might be?"

"The Last Stop Tavern," I said. "It's the closest place to walk. Our guests often head down there for food."

"Did they know who he was, when you called?"

"Excuse me?"

"You said, you called the tavern to ask about my brother. Did they know who he was."

Cory and Marina and Ray, he meant. That day, it was Marina who had picked up. I remembered it well, the way her voice changed, had dropped and become guarded. The way she'd chosen her own words so carefully, too.

"I don't know. I said we were looking for a guest, a man named Landon West. They took a few minutes to check, and say, *No, there's no one here by that name.*"

"You guys keep track of the guests coming in and out," he said with the vague tinge of an accusation. And it was then I knew it was him who had been in the back office when I'd forgotten to lock it. Who'd taken our binder. Who was watching all of us closely. He was digging, and he wasn't going to stop.

"You snuck in and stole that binder from me?" I stood up, ready to move.

He didn't even flinch, as if we were beyond pretending. "You're not answering any questions, and I have to get them somehow."

"We started doing that," I countered, "after your brother disappeared."

"I think you know something," he said, fingers pressed into the table, "and I'm asking you. *Please.*"

He shook his head, stood up as well. I remembered that the switch could flip so suddenly, and I was glad for the exit: the field, the woods—an escape. "Please, Abby," he repeated. God, he wanted it so desperately. I could feel it coming off him. His entire body practically coiled with it—the need for answers.

"If I knew something, I promise, I would say it. I would've said it long ago."

But now I was thinking of the journal belonging to his brother in the closet of my apartment, the secrets I was also keeping.

"You're heading back tomorrow, right?" I asked. A plea, a reminder. Family members—Celeste had warned me about them.

"Monday," he said. "Unless all the cabins are suddenly going to be occupied tomorrow?"

I shook my head, not trusting my own voice.

"Well, good night, then," he said, but I knew whatever allegiance we'd begun with had firmly cracked. That any trust I'd garnered, with my call to the sheriff, with my answers to his questions, had long worn out. That we stood on opposite sides of a divide now.

AS SOON AS HE was gone, I closed up the lobby and went down to the basement. I couldn't decide where to head first: to see Georgia or to examine the bag in the closet of my apartment.

But the decision was made for me, the door to my apartment slightly ajar, like someone had just forced their way inside, looking for something, too.

I thought of Trey, able to decipher the secrets on my face. Georgia, knowing what I had found.

I stayed in the hall, pushed the door open gently, the creak of the hinge startling us both.

But the only person inside, not even bothering to sneak around, standing there in full view of the entrance, was Cory.

"What the fuck?" I said, storming in and slamming the door behind me. More angry than afraid, with no time to think things through.

But I hadn't seen what he had in his hands then. Alice's bag was behind him, and now he swung his arm around, Landon's leather-bound journal in his grip. "Why do you have this?" he asked.

As if I was the one who had done something wrong. As if he suspected *me* after everything.

"What are you doing in here, Cory?" I said, instead, rage coursing through my veins. Stepping so close, up in his face, pushing him, as I could imagine him suddenly pushing Alice in the basement, pushing Farrah down the icy steps of Shallow Falls—

"What do you think?" he asked, arms held up in proclaimed innocence, except the journal was now out of my reach. "You come by my house with this bag, accusing me—"

"I *wasn't.*"

"Oh, please." His expression was of hurt more than anger.

But I'd been wrong about Cory before, who was maybe not so harmless, who saw this bag as something that could implicate him. "So, what, you decided to break in and take it? Destroy the evidence? Pretend it never existed, just like everything else?"

His eyes darkened, and he didn't deny it. That was the thing about Cory, he didn't lie. Just never spoke the full truth. Circumventing my questions, keeping everything good-natured and on the surface, but keeping his secrets. "I'm going to ask you again. Why do you have this journal?" he asked.

Tell me something real, he'd said. And maybe that's all it took with him. Maybe that's what it took in a place like this, to belong. "I found it, in a locker at the Edge. There was a key on Georgia's key ring," I told him, honesty on display, waiting for his in return.

But his eyes only narrowed, as if this were a story that required too much faith. "This was in Georgia's locker? And you didn't call the sheriff?" He said it incredulously, like all I was doing was casting more suspicion on myself. But we hadn't all grown up in the sheriff's good graces, knowing he would be on our side.

"I didn't tell him," I explained, "because the locker was in my name." His eyes widened and I quickly continued. "I *swear* I didn't set it up myself. But what do you think that looks like?" I asked.

He didn't answer. He didn't have to. Nothing good.

He slowly lowered his arm, the journal within my reach again. "What does it say?" I asked. "I didn't have the chance . . ." Thinking: *Please*. I was imagining a story, an article, the end of the sentence I'd so desperately wanted to read: *The truth is—*

Cory sighed. "I don't know, it just looks like he was going through the investigation. Making lists." A pause. "A list of witnesses. Or suspects? I don't know."

"For Farrah Jordan?"

He nodded. Swallowed. "And Alice Kelly."

He placed the journal on the counter beside us. A peace offering. And I took it.

Landon West had indeed begun with Farrah, his way into the investigation. Her name was at the top, the date she went missing, a note that she'd last been seen at the Shallow Falls Trailhead, and a list of all the people who had been interviewed. He had used their first names only, as if he were intimately acquainted with each. As if he had done his research and felt he knew them. Celeste, Jack, Barbara and Stu—the owners of the Edge, who had to vouch for Jack, who promised they'd come in at lunchtime and he was there, as always, dependable.

There was a phone number listed beside each name, all local numbers.

There was no one whose name I didn't recognize. Landon West was looking here. He was *only* looking here.

The list on the following page was longer. Alice Kelly, date missing, last seen at the Last Stop Tavern. Here, the names stretched down the page: Cory, Ray and Marina, *Patrick*.

A shudder ran through me, realizing he'd been looking at the sheriff himself. That he might've called the number written beside his name. I imagined Rochelle picking up, phone resting on her shoulder, taking his information down. *I'll be sure to tell the sheriff you called—*

But there were other names here, too, a longer list written below, that I didn't recognize. Lacy, James, Caroline. All I could think was that these had been the people who had been hiking with her. On the outskirts of any investigation. Not all of these names had numbers beside them, as if he were still working to find them.

It was then I noticed the tiny blue check marks beside all of the names with phone numbers. As if he'd been making his way through.

"Cory . . ." I began.

"Yeah," he said, "this is about as far as I got before you came in."

My eyes met his over the list of names on the page. Cory's was the first name listed, under Alice's name, with a blue check mark beside it. "Cory, did he call you?"

"Yeah," he said, hand running through his hair. My god, how many people had lied about their contact with him? How had this been missed?

"He called from the inn. Abby, the number turned up as an outgoing call from you, from the inn. So of course I picked it up."

"Cory, my god. What did you say?"

"I didn't say anything. He wanted to talk about Alice Kelly. I've gotten enough calls in my life about that. I told him I'd said all I had to say and hung up. That's it." He looked into my eyes, big and dark and pleading. "I didn't know who he was. I swear."

"He didn't try again?"

"No, he didn't try again." But his eyes drifted to the side; I'd caught him snooping, and it still felt like he was trying to maneuver his way out of something. Giving me just enough, like everyone else.

"He called all of these numbers. All of these people." Jack, and Cory's parents, and Celeste, and the sheriff. All of these people we walked beside each day.

Landon West had been making calls from the inn, so they'd pick up. That time I saw him out in the lobby, the item he'd tucked away in his jacket—had he been looking through this notebook, making the local calls? Had he called the wrong person?

Cory turned the page, and a new list of names stretched in rows and columns. It was like seeing a census of the town of Cutter's Pass—except it looked like it had been limited to everyone over the age of forty.

A list of people who had been here for each and every disappearance, since the Fraternity Four.

"Jesus," Cory said, letting out a sharp breath.

The list of suspects—if this was a list of suspects, and it seemed clear that it was—spanned the boundaries of Cutter's Pass, across the valley.

The truth is . . . *The truth is*, none of us would have wanted this journal out there. Not with all these names. Not with this proof, that Landon West was digging into the old investigations.

"He was looking for the connection," I said. Just as every trauma tourist who had come before, asking their questions, thinking they would be the one to solve it. But suddenly it seemed that he had, or that he was well on his way to it, anyway. The camera had led him *here*—

Cory turned the page again, and stilled. The room stilled. Our breathing stilled.

On the last page, there was a single name, written large, with a question mark. *Abby??*

Cory didn't say anything, didn't need to. We were all implicated here. Anything we asked of one another would open ourselves to those same questions.

"We could burn it," he said, and I couldn't tell whether he was joking.

"Georgia has seen it."

"Georgia," he repeated with disgust. "I wish I could say I'm surprised, but that's not true."

"Oh, please, Cory, I've seen you down here. The same way you came down here when I first arrived."

"That's not—" He closed his eyes. "Look, Celeste didn't trust her when she arrived, the way she just showed up, the way you just took her in. She asked me to look into her, and I did."

I flinched; it stung that she didn't tell me. I'd thought that Celeste was honest with me, but Cory had come first. Cory came first for all of them.

"You 'looked into' her?" I repeated, deadpan.

He waved his hand. "It wasn't like that. I would've told you, if you'd asked." But I'd asked Cory a thousand questions over the years, and he'd never answered any of them in a way that counted. He didn't get to play that card now. "Look, I asked Rochelle to run a check on her quietly. Turns out she dropped out of school when her dad died."

"I know, she told me—"

"Wait. She lived with her mom in Pennsylvania, has her last name, but her dad was from Maryland. I looked it up, Abby, after

Landon West disappeared. Her dad lived in the next town over from his family. How much do you want to bet their paths had crossed in the past? She was probably shitting herself after he disappeared, waiting to see if anyone found the connection between the two of them."

My head dropped into my hands. From the note Trey had found in his brother's room, with the time to call, I knew it was true. Georgia's fear when he had disappeared—it wasn't only that he was gone, but that she was the one who had brought him here. She must've gone to great lengths to erase that trail. Going through his computer, his room, panicking. Afraid. And I mistook her unease as innocence. I had been right about one thing: Georgia was someone who could do the hard things after all.

"I told her to watch herself," Cory said.

"You threatened Georgia? You didn't know anything was connected until after Landon West disappeared."

"Yeah, well, I was right, wasn't I? You don't come here for no reason when you have all that money. She's fucking loaded, you know."

"She wanted a fresh start," I said, but there was no conviction behind my words.

Cory rolled his eyes. "She found that camera and took it to a journalist. Not you. Not Celeste. Not the sheriff. Them." *Them.* The people on the outside. And we were on the inside. Finally, I was a part of this place.

Cory took a deep breath, shook his head. "You trust too easily. You want to assume the best. You want to believe that nothing can hurt you here. But it isn't true."

"I know that."

"Do you?" He looked at that book again.

I felt the emotion rising up, and I wasn't sure if it was anger or embarrassment or fear. "Did Celeste ask you to get a feel for me, too?"

"No," he said slowly. "Why would she do that?"

We were too close—the closest we'd been in years. In the way we were standing, in the questions we were brushing up against. The things that we almost said.

Finally, he was the one to break the silence.

"I'll tell you something real, Abby." His voice was so low, I almost didn't hear.

I nodded, an unbreakable truce forming between us. A trust by necessity.

He ran his hand down his face, dragging the skin, so he looked sickly, older. "Alice. I didn't see her."

"You already said that—"

"No." He closed his eyes. "I didn't *see* her at all."

He covered his mouth with the back of his hand, and I could practically feel the breath, like his hand was my own, hot and afraid, something finally rising to the surface of him.

"That night, I was working, we all were. I was nineteen," he said, as if this would absolve him. As if being a teenager absolved all of us of our youth. "There were so many people in and out of the tavern, it was Labor Day weekend. And I was drinking, behind the bar."

He shook his head, like clearing a thought.

"The next day, the sheriff came around, showing her picture. Said she'd been heading this way, had gone missing. And I don't know, I just said, *yeah, she was here*."

He must've seen my expression, because he said, "You don't know what it was like, growing up in a place like this. With that picture over the bar, always. People telling stories, looking at you. Every single person in town who was alive then was questioned.

Every. Single. One. How do you defend yourself, in something like this? So I just said it. It was an impulse. She was here, and I thought she called a cab."

"She wasn't there?"

"I don't *know*, Abby. Because after I said it, others said it, too. My parents, they backed me up, said, yeah, she was there. They said they saw her, too. And suddenly it was like I had manifested it." He ran his hand back through his hair, roughly. Looked away. "We don't talk about it. We never did. You can't ask something like that. Ever." And I thought I understood. Do you really want the answer to that? That your parents didn't see her, but thought you might've had something to do with her disappearance—and covered for you? Was that any better to believe?

"Jesus Christ." I pinched the top of my nose, trying to recalibrate. Maybe Alice Kelly had never made it to the tavern at all. Maybe she had only made it as far as this inn—

I opened my eyes to the sound of him tearing a page from the book. But it was only the page with my name. The question marks. "We're getting older, Abby," he said. "Do you ever think about what comes next?"

I couldn't. I was stuck. In a way, so was he—his name tied and tangled with this place.

"We need to burn this."

We did, we needed to burn it. And he was symbolically starting with mine, as a way for me to agree.

I watched as he turned on the stove. The *click click click* of the gas, the flame catching. A promise, a bond. He held the corner of the page to the flame, and the ink was illuminated through the other side of the white page.

"Stop," I said, lunging for the paper, extinguishing it with the base of my hand. There was a momentary delay before the pain set in—

"What the hell?" he asked.

I turned the page over, for him to see. One corner charred, and eaten away. But the rest, clearly visible. The words that Landon had written, circled in black ink. Something I'd never seen before, never heard—and I'd been listening for it. Not in a drunken slip, or a far-fetched rumor, or a careful whisper.

It said, with clarity: THE FRATERNITY FIVE

PART 4

The Fraternity Four

Date missing: June 6, 1997

Last seen: Cutter's Pass, North Carolina

Corner of Main Street and Mountain Pass

CHAPTER 16

THE FRATERNITY FOUR. HOW often had I heard that phrase? Always four. Neil and Jerome and Toby and Brian. Never any indication that it had been anything other. Year after year, these four had traveled together. In every picture shown from their prior adventures, it had always just been them.

They were childhood friends who had met at a summer camp in their youth and spent three weeks every summer from twelve to sixteen in the same cabin. When they'd aged out of camp, they continued the tradition—this time, taking their adventures across the country. They were very different young men, from different backgrounds, with different paths they had taken, and would've continued to take. You could see yourself in any of them, if you wanted. Imagine their lives, playing out, as I had often done.

Neil, skinny and wiry, the smallest of the group, but not small by other comparisons, the son of a single mother from Ohio; Jerome, heavyset in earlier photos, but he'd replaced that bulk with muscle in the later years, who'd grown up in DC with a large extended family; Toby, who attended boarding school with his two sisters while his parents moved for business from Boston to Paris and back again; Brian, the jock of the group, who had gone to college on a baseball scholarship. The trips were usually his idea; he was the group's planner. It was his hat, emblazoned with the Greek letters from his old fraternity, that had given them the moniker.

They'd been river rafting in the Grand Canyon, gone skydiving outside Las Vegas, ridden horses across a stretch of Tennessee, fished and hunted in Montana. The news had shown photos from all of these yearly trips. Brian had worn a broken-in ball cap with that faded fraternity symbol on each, and the last image taken of them before they set off had that same symbol, and so they were dubbed: the Fraternity Four.

There was never any indication there had been a fifth.

I watched Cory carefully as he stared at the words on the page of Landon's journal, his brow furrowed, his throat moving, trying to see if those words meant anything to him. Cory, who had grown up in this place, with parents who were questioned, teachers who were interviewed, and friends who had been through the same. Who'd witnessed the investigation receding farther and farther into the past over the years, with no leads. Who watched as the whole town leaned in to the trauma, an identity built around the notoriety. Who stared at that picture of those four young men over the bar, every day of his life. A piece of his history. Of his foundation.

Finally, his gaze rose to meet mine, eyes wide and questioning. I believed I knew him well enough to know this was a surprise for him, too. Of all the stories he'd told and heard, this was not one of them.

"It could just be a guess? A theory," he said, and I nodded, because they had vanished twenty-five years ago, and it was all any of us could do—guess—looking that far back now.

With all of them gone, no one could even say much with certainty about what they'd been up to. No one even knew whose plan it had been to come to Cutter's Pass. Brian's girlfriend said it wasn't his; Toby's sisters hadn't even known he was going; Jerome had booked his flight relatively last minute; Neil had put in for time off work but told his boss it was a family emergency. The shaky foundations of the legend were already in place in the days before their arrival.

One challenge of their disparate lives was that their families didn't really know one another, other than in name. There was no united search. There were rewards given periodically, for any information. But there were certain families with more, who demanded more, who pushed the search in different ways.

Those in town who had been through it, who'd searched for them, who'd answered questions and withstood the suspicions, had come out with a stronger bond forged from it. The entirety of Cutter's Pass had emerged from that time as something different.

"We should burn it all," Cory said, voice low, as if someone else were listening in. "You don't know what it was like, when Alice went missing. It brought all of this back to the surface. All these questions about what had happened, fifteen years earlier. They interviewed practically every person in town. You don't know what it will be like if you turn this over."

"I was here for Farrah," I reminded him.

"There wasn't some great mystery about that, Abby."

"Are you serious?" I stomped over to the closet, where he'd found the journal. Had he not dug any deeper? Everyone here, grabbing the first thing they could see, never digging any further, never wanting to know how it connected with all the rest. "Did you not see this?"

I held, in my hand, a broken camera. Shattered lens, fraying strap. Something had happened to it, just as something had happened to Farrah.

All these things were coming back: Alice's backpack, Farrah's camera, Landon's journal. Rising up from the ground, the earth turning over, like weeds pushing through in spring. Like they were begging for someone to find them, to see them. As if, all along, they'd been waiting for me to put the pieces together.

"Where did this come from?" Cory asked.

I shrugged. "I have no idea. It was in the locker, with that journal."

A noise outside the living room window jolted Cory's attention. He strode across the room and threw open the curtains, staring out into the dark. Then he moved into my bedroom without asking, like this place were his own. He stood close to the windows, light off, peering up, eyes focused on the dark.

"No one can get up there," I said from the bedroom doorway.

He turned my way, and from the look on his face, I knew that I was wrong.

His eyes drifted to the windows again, a sort of nervous energy thrumming in his body. I wasn't sure what he was worried about—whether it was something real he could sense coming, whether it was the things he was afraid to ask, the things he didn't want to know about the people and place he loved so much. Or whether there was something else—something more he was keeping—that he didn't want me to know.

"Don't you want to know what happened to them? It may have been twenty-five years ago, but it happened right here," I said.

He threw up his hands, so unlike the Cory leading tours, or the Cory in the tavern, happy to indulge someone's theories. "They got *lost*, Abby. They got lost, and they died, and animals took care of the rest." I opened my mouth, and he put out a hand. "Or, they didn't. Or, they made it to the next town, or the one after that, and something happened to them there. Or, they were involved in some sort of criminal activity, and they needed to disappear, and they did it."

Those were rumors that we'd all heard over the years. And what was so wrong with believing them?

"Knowing," he said, "isn't going to change anything now."

"Except Alice. And Farrah. And Landon."

"I think," he started, "that you should be careful who you show this to."

I already knew that. All of our names were in there. We were all implicated.

"Whatever you're hoping to find in there, you won't find it," he said.

"How do you know?"

"What would be a good answer, Abby? Really now. Tell me what you hope it will be."

I shook my head, not understanding.

"If the answer's in this town, it's not going to be a stranger."

"I know that," I said.

These men—these Fraternity Four—they had walked by people who were still here. There were people who remembered. Their names were in Landon's journal. A sheriff who was once a young deputy. A couple with a small child, who had just taken over the family tavern. The owners of an inn just finding its footing, getting itself on the map.

And all of the people my age—Jack, Rochelle, Harris, and Cory—had peered out from the background while the police came to the front door to talk to their parents or grandparents. Had felt the silent tension after they left, and watched as those who remained looked at one another with a different understanding.

That's what I had missed, not growing up here. It wasn't a deliberate exclusion, it was a lack of full understanding. The event was in their collective consciousness, a foundation in their bones. They knew what could happen if it rattled. They knew how quickly a crack could spread, and crumble.

Insiders and outsiders, it was a line I'd been desperate to cross for so long, and I'd finally done it: Cory saw me as a part of their world.

It only took ten years. Ten years, in which I had grown to love everything about this place, and myself within it. And now I was in possession of something that threatened the very core of its existence.

The truth is, none of us wanted this journal out there. None of us were safe. All of the stories were tangled together. If you were tied to one case, you would be dragged in to all the rest.

This was the implicit contract in Cutter's Pass, whether we were aware or not: You could be protected, as long as you protected in return. You could live here and love here, be loved in return. Just as long as you promised not to look too closely.

"I have to go," he said, and I didn't ask any more questions. "Do me a favor." He tapped the cover of the journal sitting on the kitchen counter. "Tell me before you do anything with that."

"I will," I said, but that was a lie. There hadn't been a clue in ten years, and suddenly, everything was in my possession. Ten years, and now it was mine.

I wanted to call those numbers, listen to who picked up on the other end. Ask what Landon West was looking for.

He must've gotten too close.

The truth is—he'd written, frustratingly unfinished.

The truth is, I wanted to finish that sentence for him now.

The truth is, you can't make too much noise when you come to Cutter's Pass. You can't let it know what you're looking for. What you know.

Cory took my chin in his hand. His dark eyes searched mine, and I was searching his in return, wondering what he knew, what he wanted to protect: himself, yes—and the secret he was keeping about Alice. But maybe not just that. I had to trust him. There was no other option.

He kissed me, hard and fast, as if it were the last time, and it probably was. And I remembered that I had loved him, once. As much as I loved this place, and myself within it.

* * *

HERE WAS SOMETHING THAT no one knew, not even Cory. According to Trey, Landon West used his phone to record his notes. And now, I had it.

As soon as Cory was gone, I plugged his phone into my charger and waited. When it finally came back to life, a password code popped up on the screen, and I stared at it, stuck. Until remembering what Trey had told me when we'd opened the file on the flash drive. The pass code he'd used for everything since he was little. I tried it now—*9-8-7-6*—and, suddenly, I was in.

IN THE VOICE MEMO app, there had been a folder marked *CP*. And in it was a list of five saved recordings. They were labeled automatically by date, and the first was recorded the day after his arrival at the inn.

Okay, I'm ready, Georgia's voice echoed through the apartment as soon I pressed "play" on the memo labeled *Interview 1.* I scrambled to turn down the volume.

No name, right? she added after a brief pause.

I promise I won't use it. Landon's voice caused the goose bumps to rise across my arms, the back of my neck. Like he was right here with me.

Like I could stop him this time.

Let's start at the beginning. Where did you find the camera?

Here. Her answer sent a chill up my spine.

In the inn?

No, some guests brought it back from a hike. It was in one of those weather-resistant cases, but it looked like it had been dragged around by an animal. They said they found it exploring the section beyond the falls and wondered if it belonged to another guest.

Did you know it belonged to Farrah Jordan?

No, I didn't know whose it was. I took it from them and said I'd look into it. There was no identification, so I pulled out the photo card to see if I could figure out who it belonged to so I could get it back to them.

And?

And, there was the date. The date listed in the pictures. That's how I knew. We close the inn for two weeks in January. I knew that she was last seen during that time period a few years before, at the trailhead. That's how I knew it was her camera.

Did you tell anyone?

No, definitely not. A pause. *Look, you've seen the time stamps, right? The first pictures, blurry, in the snow, those were taken hours before the rest.*

I don't follow.

She sighed a long familiar sigh. *I think something happened, during those pictures. It looks like she's struggling. Or falling.* The silence stretched, then there was the sound of something shifting, and I imagined her pushing the hair off her forehead, looking to the side. She lowered her voice, and I could hear the waver in it. *I think someone else took the rest of those pictures.*

Fabric rustling, like Landon was shifting positions. *You didn't tell anyone here*. A statement, but also a question.

No, I didn't know . . . I didn't know what to do with it. And then I thought of you. My dad used to save your articles, ever since you interned for him in college.

It was quite the surprise to get a call from you at my parents' place over the holidays.

A nervous laugh. *Yeah, well, I knew how to reach them. Hoped that's where you'd be.*

And then the recording stopped.

I looked over my shoulder, at my closed apartment door, imagined Georgia just feet away down the hall. I was struck by her words: that she didn't think Farrah had taken those photos. And wasn't that what had nagged at me, too? They didn't look like Farrah's typical shots, because they weren't.

I hadn't checked the time stamps of the earlier photos, but I knew the sheriff must have. Did he see the same thing she did? *A struggle; something happening. A time lapse. Something changed.* Or did it all depend on what you wanted to see?

She was right, about the photos not seeming like Farrah's. And now I believed she was right about all of it. That this camera was showing not where she had been, but what had happened to her.

But that realization paled in comparison with the next: She'd found Farrah's camera and contacted Landon West instead of telling us. Georgia hadn't told me, hadn't asked me about it—as if she didn't fully trust me. Or trust that I didn't have something to do with it.

I moved on to *Interview 2*, wondering who else Landon had convinced to talk—and how. For so long, this town had remained silent and closed off to outsiders. They'd presented a united, impenetrable front.

The first thing I heard on the recording was laughter in the background. A clattering of glasses, the sound of distant chatter. And then: *Can I get you another?* A man's voice, deep and measured.

That'd be great. Landon's voice then, closer to the microphone.

Want to open a tab?

Paying cash. Hey, Ray was it?

Mmm. I heard the sound of a glass being pushed across a surface. I could imagine it perfectly: Landon West, sitting at the bar of the Last Stop Tavern, speaking with Ray across the bar top. But this didn't sound like an interview. It didn't sound like Ray knew he was being recorded at all.

That picture, Landon continued, *that's the famous Fraternity Four everyone talks about?*

That's them.

I smiled slightly, hearing Ray's terse replies. Poor Landon West, didn't realize he'd picked the one person in the bar least likely to give him any information. There would be no gossip spilled, no rumors shared. He'd be lucky if he got more than a two-word response.

Who took that picture?

Pardon?

I mean, how did that picture get in your possession. Someone must've taken it, right?

Disposable camera. One of them brought it with him. Must've asked someone in the tavern to go out and take it for them. They left the camera behind.

And this was the only thing on it?

Yep. Don't see they had much chance to take any others.

I could picture Ray pacing behind the bar, to another guest, another visitor.

Did you work here then? Landon's voice again, and I imagined Ray passing by him. I imagined the tight, stoic expression on his face.

Yeah, this was my parents' place.

Must've been a crazy time. What, were you around their age then, too? What was that like?

I'm afraid I don't have much gossip for you. I had a toddler then. Was pretty busy with him. A pause, a sudden crack, as if a palm had slapped the surface of the bar. *Your receipt, sir.*

The recording ended.

I sat back, taking it all in.

There were questions people asked often: *Were you here for it? What was it like here? What do you think happened?*

And then there were the less common ones, inquiries bordering on demands—the ones that had slipped my notice. That question—*Who took that picture?*—was one of them. For all the times I'd sat at that bar, staring up at their photo, that was one I hadn't asked.

Did Landon West think the picture came from this mysterious fifth member?

Interview 3 appeared less an interview at all, and more of an attempt at an interview.

Hi, I'm hoping to talk to Sheriff Stamer. Landon's voice, slightly muffled, like it was coming through a layer of fabric. I pictured the phone in his pocket. All these people he was taping, without their knowledge.

Do you have an appointment? Rochelle rarely made me smile, but I appreciated the familiarity of her curt response, realizing her impatience wasn't just directed my way.

No, I was hoping to find some information about the old cases here, for a book—

Sir, I can stop you right there. The sheriff isn't going to talk to you for a book.

What about for curiosity, then?

Still no.

What about for an investigation?

Silence. I felt another twinge of familiarity, of déjà vu. It was the same, slithery way I'd remembered Landon West navigating a conversation. How quickly it snuck up on you, this feeling of *wrong*—that he was not the person you first believed him to be.

Well, Rochelle finally answered, slowly and carefully, *as I'm sure you know, any investigation*—I could picture her air quotes, her wry expression—*would need to go through official channels. So I'd suggest you do just that, sir.*

Landon West, he'd answered, as if she had asked. And then the rustling of fabric as he exited the building before the recording stopped.

I got a chill—I'd had no idea he'd stopped by the sheriff's office, that he'd given his name. That they had any indication of who he was when he disappeared. But suddenly I realized: *Everyone* here knew. Rochelle and the sheriff, Ray and presumably the rest of his family. They knew who they were looking for when we called in the news of our missing guest. My memories of that initial search shifted. I tried to remember who had come out, and why. What they had offered, and when.

The date on *Interview 4* was later in the week, in a morning.

Is it true, that the owners built this place all on their own?

My shoulders tightened, and I held my breath. I knew the words that came next, heard my own voice coming through, distant and muffled. *Designed and planned from the ground up . . .*

My god, he had been taping me, too. That morning when I'd exited the stairwell, surprised to find him there, looking at the pictures that lined the wall. He had repeated my responses often throughout the conversation, which I'd found unsettling but attributed to a quirk of his demeanor, an awkward social affect. Now I wondered if he was only repeating it for himself, to make sure the words recorded, for later.

How had he found this exchange worth saving? I listened to myself, to the haunting echo of my own voice. It was a conversation I had revisited and replayed many times after he'd gone missing. But why he'd kept it, I couldn't understand.

But presumably there was something here that made him go to his journal and write my name: *Abby??*

Or had he sought me out, after something he'd learned? A question he had, just for me? Had he been waiting for me after all? As if he could see straight to the inside of all of us, the things we wanted to keep hidden.

There was only one more recording, and it was unlabeled, taken the evening before we'd noticed he'd disappeared. I wondered if it was from when I'd found him in the lobby.

But when I pressed "play," it was only Landon West, talking to himself. He must've been making notes for the article he had been in the process of writing.

There are a group of residents who have been here for each disappearance. It's a small town—over twenty-five years, it's not an unreasonable number. Those aren't bad odds.

A pause as I heard him typing. I could imagine him working on that document we'd found on his flash drive.

And then, a sudden knocking sound. Three raps, in quick succession. Someone at the door.

Just a second, he said loudly. I heard him curse under his breath, a rustling, and the thud of his feet against the floor, like he'd just slipped on his boots. And then the sound of him packing things away on the desk, a pause—heavy footsteps, another pause, as he hid a flash drive maybe.

Coming— And then the recording cut dead.

I stared at the phone, trying to process. That was it, the last thing he'd recorded. The night I'd seen him, in the inn, standing by the lobby phone. He'd presumably gone back to his room, to work on his article. And then someone knocked on his door.

My god, the person standing on the other side of that doorway—was the last person who saw him. Or worse.

I could feel them, this person out in the night, knocking on the door to his cabin.

I listened to the last recording again, from the start, trying to hear something in the background. Anything. A clue. Footsteps, or the way they spoke, or any words they called back. But it was the same, every time. A frustrating hole of silence.

Like I was losing him. Like I had gotten so close, and all of them were slipping through my fingers again.

CHAPTER 17

I'D FALLEN ASLEEP AFTER midnight more from necessity than anything else, curled up on the living room couch, with the curtains pulled securely shut and Landon West's journal open on my chest. But I'd woken often and then early for good, every noise jolting me, making me picture the worst. Not an animal outside, but a person, crouching down, peering in. My imagination chasing down every thread.

So I was ready and watching the clock, waiting until eight, when I knew Georgia would be up. On Sundays, we held breakfast later and skipped happy hour, but I knew she'd be getting ready for work by now.

I would have to confront her. I would have to ask *why*—why she'd gone to Landon, and not me or Celeste or the sheriff. Why she'd panicked and hidden everything in a locker *with my name* back in April. What she thought I was truly capable of.

There was a safety in the daylight, in talking to her in public, outside the confines of this basement. I stepped out into the hall, and there was no music coming from her room. She must've already been upstairs.

But when I pushed out the employee door into the main floor

hall, the lobby was eerily still. There was only the older couple who'd been staying at Eagle's Nest, early, even, for checkout. The man turned at my approach, keys to his room held out in his hand. "Oh, hi. I was just going to leave this on the desk," he said.

"Thank you, that's fine," I said, even as I was taking the key from him. "I hope you had a nice stay," I said, peering around the lobby. It was otherwise empty. The back office door was shut, nothing set out for the day just yet.

"We did," he said as they pulled their two wheeled suitcases behind them, through the front doors.

As soon as they were gone, I used my master key to check the back office—empty, lights off, register and safe still untouched in the closet.

I swallowed my panic at the empty space where Georgia should be. The things she should've done. Maybe I was wrong; maybe Georgia was still in her apartment after all.

I could feel the beating of my own heart, a cold sweat breaking out on the back of my neck. My hand trembled as I held my employee badge to the lock on the stairwell.

Back downstairs, I knocked on the door to her apartment. The silence was unsettling. The sinking feeling in my gut growing stronger.

These are the signs of a disappearance: A gap. Silence. Emptiness. The realization that *something else* should be there. Music playing, footsteps, breathing. A tremor in your hand, your body understanding before you have time to make sense of it.

They were signs, not unlike when Landon went missing, when I could see the wobble of her step, the tension of her shoulders. The moment before realization fully set in.

"Georgia?" I called through the door, imagining all the ways I could be wrong. Georgia, sick in the bathroom, unable to make it upstairs. Georgia, out for an early-morning run, on her way back right this moment; Georgia, who had fallen in the dark, hit her head, and needed my help.

Only Celeste and I had the master keys for this, and I debated using them now, knowing how I would feel if someone had stepped into my apartment, uninvited. I remembered the rage clawing its way out when I saw Cory standing inside my apartment last night—that sharp betrayal, that breach of my privacy.

But then I imagined the ways Georgia might need help now, and I didn't think again. I just did it. Key in the lock, a twist to the side—but that turned out to be unnecessary. Her apartment was unlocked.

"Hello?" I called as I pushed open the door. "Georgia? It's me. It's Abby."

I was accustomed to the scent of toast in the morning, or coffee from her single serve. But there was nothing here—the kitchen was spotless, every surface bare. I didn't like the feeling I got, standing in her space.

The living area had a few throw pillows scattered on the couch, and a teal ceramic bowl on the coffee table. Nothing else. I checked the rest of the rooms: the bedroom (bed made, room otherwise empty); the bathroom (door ajar, no humidity clinging to the mirror). The ceramic toothbrush holder, empty.

Shit. I started moving faster, the feeling gaining force. Pulling open the drawers under the bed—empty. Checking inside the closet—empty, except for the bare wire hangers. I stood in the middle of the living room, hands on hips, trying to process the scene. There was a corner of white visible inside the ceramic bowl on the coffee table, the one thing it seemed she hadn't taken with her. I walked closer: a folded piece of white paper.

On top lay the gold key to her apartment, and her rectangular employee badge. There was only one word when I unfolded the page, written in her familiar print: *Sorry*

I dropped the contents back into the bowl, stormed out the apartment, out the basement exit, trudging over to the employee lot, even though I knew what I would see: Her car was gone. Georgia was *gone*.

Had she realized I'd been to the locker and bailed? Had she been afraid of what I would say, what I would do? Had she been afraid of something *else*?

I walked up the incline of the drive to where I could get the best signal. But my call to her went straight to voice mail, over and over.

I sent her a text, out of desperation: *Please call me. I just want to know what's going on.* And then, I added: *I just want to know you're okay.*

But the message didn't show as delivered. As if she'd turned off her phone as she ran.

"Abby?" Celeste was standing just inside the front door of the carriage house. She was wearing an orange flowy top, and her long hair was in a braid draped over her shoulder. I assumed she was waiting for her ride to church, as she did most Sunday mornings.

She stepped out of the shadows as I walked down the drive. "Is everything okay?" she asked.

"Georgia's *gone*," I said. I saw it on her face, the concern, the flash of panic. *Gone* was a word that could mean many different things here. "She left," I added.

She frowned at the empty spot in her driveway. "Is she coming back?"

I let out a sharp laugh. "Doubtful, considering she left behind her key and employee badge." I pressed my palm against my mouth, trying to choke back the emotion.

"Okay, come in. Come inside," she said, one arm reaching for me, gesturing me toward the door.

My throat was tight with anger, with panic. I shook my head quickly. "There's no one at the inn. I have to—"

"It can wait. Everything can wait. Abigail, come."

I exhaled slowly, then stepped inside the first-floor entrance, a narrow, dimly lit foyer with a door to the side, leading to the garage, with Vincent's truck. A set of steps led up to her second-floor living quarters, behind us. "Did she say anything?" Celeste asked. "Are we *sure* she's okay?"

"She didn't say anything, no. But everything's gone."

"We should tell Patrick, he'll be here in just a moment—"

"She left a note, Celeste. It just said *sorry*. I don't think . . ." How to explain, that Georgia had not been who we thought she was? I started again. "I think you were right about Georgia, all along," I said.

Realization dawned on her face. She nodded once. "She left, then." It was dark in the downstairs entryway, and the morning light out the doorway was almost blinding in contrast. "The last few months have been hard on her," Celeste said. She looked like she was going to say more, but she cut herself off. Then she lowered her voice, added, "She was never cut out for a place like this, Abby."

Her compliment, in the silence that followed: *You are.*

A car pulled down the employee drive, and I thought, for one hopeful moment, that it was Georgia, coming back. But instead I recognized the sheriff's blue Honda. He stepped out, wearing slacks and a short-sleeve button-down. Same boots, though. "You about ready, Celeste?" he called.

"Just a minute, Patrick," she called. Sheriff Stamer picked her up for church most Sundays, brought her back home after, too. He'd been a part of the orbit of this inn since I arrived, bound to its history in his own way.

"You're going?" I asked. Sometimes I couldn't understand how she just continued on, but then, she'd been through more, lost people before—people she'd cared about.

"It'll just be an hour or so. If you can set up breakfast, I'll handle the afternoon, okay? The inn will not fall apart, I promise."

I nodded, still trying to process—Georgia was gone, and it was just me and Celeste again.

She slipped a bag onto her shoulder. "Just put up the sign if you need a break. Let's just do what we can in the meantime. I'll ask around for someone to cover the shifts. We'll hire someone. Don't worry, there's always a new batch of kids looking for work." She squeezed my arm once, a small reassuring smile. "We've done this before, you and me."

In the early days of my arrival—but that was winter, low season—the two of us were able to make it work with the help of the community, who had all rallied around Celeste after Vincent's death. They'd taken shifts, fixed things that needed fixing, didn't wait for her to ask for help. The sheriff had sent Rochelle over to get the computer system organized. I could still feel the ghost of her in the process and spreadsheets that we continued to use, ten years later.

"Come now," she said, stepping out into the morning light, waving to the sheriff, who was leaning back against his blue sedan, one leg crossed behind the other, the vision of casual—as if there was nothing at all to be concerned about here.

He acted like I wasn't even there as he opened the passenger side door for Celeste, patting the metal roof once after he closed the door. Then his gaze drifted to me, and he nodded once—"Have a good day, Abby"—like he had only just seen me there, before sliding into his seat.

TREY WEST DIDN'T COME in for breakfast. There were two more couples checking out, two more couples who wanted me to *make sure to thank Georgia for her advice*, and I nodded, feeling a pang. Not for her, but for the person I thought her to be. Then I wondered about the person she thought I was, too. When she'd arrived, she saw me as a part of this place—the inn and the town. She never saw me as an outsider here.

Maybe, in hindsight, that's what kept her from trusting me, too.

After the guests checked out, there was a lull—and I used the time to take a break in my apartment. I was tempted to bring Landon West's journal upstairs with me, to keep it on me, but I was afraid of seeing Trey, that he would be able to sense it. I decided I had no intention of that journal ever leaving the confines of my apartment again. For a moment, I understood Georgia hiding all of this in the locker. There was this feeling that nothing was safe here. Not in the basement of the inn, not behind locked doors. Hadn't Cory already shown me how easily others could get in? The past always had a thousand ways in.

I took pictures of the pages of the notebook with my phone to piece through while I waited for Celeste to relieve me.

I couldn't stop thinking of the last words he'd written: *The Fraternity Five*

I couldn't stop hearing the knock on his cabin door, during his last recording.

Everything was in my hands now. The power of it all, to hold the information. To decide.

I picked up the phone line at the front desk, staring at the list of names and phone numbers. I scanned it, stopping at the ones I didn't recognize: Lacy, James, Caroline. Only one of them had a number, and it was local, for *James*.

His name was not on the list of residents that had been here for all of the disappearances—it was only listed under Alice—but it was possible he had sent Landon off in a direction that got him somewhere. Somewhere no one else had managed to get before.

I called it now, phone pressed close to my face, heart speeding up as the ringing continued. Finally, a woman picked up, more irritated than friendly.

"Hi, can I speak with James please?" I asked.

"You have the wrong number," she said, and hung up quickly.

Well then, maybe not. There were no numbers listed for Lacy or Caroline. It was possible the college would be able to put me in touch. Or at least, give me their full names.

In the back office, my phone loaded slowly, notifications showing up on the screen from content that had come through during the night. Emails to the inn, social media tags, and a notice of a new message from *AliceKellyWasHere*.

I felt the breath leave me in a rush, as if Alice were reaching out from across time, even though I knew it was just her sister, Quinn: *Yes! Thank you for keeping her memory alive. Anything for a fresh lead. There's been nothing for years. Hope this will help someone remember something new. Here are some of the last photos I have of my beautiful sister. Let me know if I can help with anything else?? -Q*

I willed the images to load faster, but they came through in painful layers, top to bottom, as I waited for Alice to appear. And then, there she was, in my hand.

There she was at a kitchen island, standing beside a woman who must've been her mother, hands deep in a bowl of dough, head tilted and tongue out as she made a face at the photographer, while her mother laughed.

There she was in the driver's seat of a car, the photographer in the passenger seat, so that Alice appeared too close to the screen, as she kept one hand on the wheel, the other giving a peace sign while she grinned.

There she was in front of the woods, with a large group of students, and a sign that said OUTDOORS CLUB. She was front and center, her hands on the sign, the focus of the photo.

She was magnetic, I could tell just from these images. The way her mother looked at her; the way the person behind the camera focused on her. In the group shot, several people were looking her way. A man behind her, a woman to her right, hand on her shoulder, laughing, as if she'd been the cause of the laughter. I wondered if this was one of the names on the list, someone the sister might've known. Lacy or Caroline, maybe.

I responded: *These are perfect. She's stunning. Would you know any of the other names in the group shot? Would love to connect with anyone else who was close with her, who might have more to share. Also, I had the names Lacy, James, and Caroline as friends to contact—do you know their last names?*

Then I searched for photos of the Fraternity Four. They were everywhere—in blog posts and old articles. The four of them, two in hats, one in dark sunglasses, all facing the camera with the mountain behind them. I'd seen this image so many times. But on the screen, they always looked just slightly removed, out of focus. A picture of a picture. I pulled one of the images up, enlarged it on the monitor—

"Abby?" Celeste called. I'd been lost in my thoughts, didn't hear the lobby door, and suddenly Celeste stood beside me, back from church. I closed out the page, turned to face her. The only change to her attire was the long chain around her neck that held a master key. "I put out the word we'd be looking for help. Already got a few leads. Okay?" she asked, and she smiled, like this was the only cause for concern.

My heart was still racing, from the surprise of her.

"You're worried," she said, frowning. "Is it Georgia? Or is this still about Landon West?"

I shrugged. "Both?"

Her eyes went to the hall, to the photos with her husband. "Vincent," she began, and her eyes turned watery, lost. "He wasn't the same after the disappearances. Didn't like to leave the inn."

The Fraternity Four, she meant. She had to.

She took a deep breath, eyes locking on mine. "You have to make your peace with it, Abigail. Even if there aren't any answers."

I nodded, though I didn't know if I could. I wasn't like her. I thought of Celeste going up on that mountain each morning. Refusing to be afraid, against all judgment. She had a fearlessness I envied.

Celeste nudged me out of the way, moving things around on the surface of the desk, until she found the fresh binder Georgia had started. "Now, let's see how quickly this all comes back."

Celeste had always been averse to technology. Said it wasn't reliable, especially given where we were, and she was right.

"Do you want me to get the reservation page up?" I gestured to the computer. When we used to work together, I was always entering the notes she left behind, following up on the day.

But she raised a hand. "Don't worry about that. I never had much use for it, so I'm not about to start now." Her eyes crinkled in an almost smile. "All of you, you miss too much, looking down instead of out. A screen is no match for reality."

Right then, I agreed with her.

I knew where I had to go now. I knew what I needed to see.

CHAPTER 18

THERE WERE THINGS YOU knew if you lived here. The types of things that had always made me feel like an insider, even if others didn't quite see it that way: A weekly poker game was held in CJ's Hideaway after closing on Wednesdays; you could borrow gear from the Edge without paying if you were a local and Jack Olivier was behind the counter, as long as you returned it in the same condition you found it; and the spare key to the Last Stop was kept in a lockbox tucked behind the light over the back door.

Cory had used it when he took me there off-hours, just the two of us, when he'd make me a drink and call it a date. He never told me the code, but he never made an attempt to hide it from me, either, and so I knew it was his parents' anniversary: 0823.

There was only one piece of real evidence about the Fraternity Four, if you could even call it that—and it was in that tavern, nailed into the wall behind the bar. It had hung there, in plain sight, ever since the establishment changed its name to the Last Stop Tavern. The image had been replicated, digital copies sent to newspapers and websites, but there was only one original, and we had claim to it.

I stood on the other side of the block, in front of the abandoned entrance of the real estate office, where aerial views of available plots were taped to the glass from the inside. And then I slipped between storefronts, into the alley with the entrance to CJ's Hideaway. A menu hung from the window, where the inside matched the alley itself—dim, like a cave, walls of wine bottles surrounded by dark brick and heavy wood.

The restaurant was closed at this hour, and the rest of the alley was deserted. Down at the other end was the back entrance to the Last Stop, and I headed that way.

I checked up and down the alley before standing on my toes to reach the box, wedged behind the back light fixture. The lock mechanism was slightly rusty, the numbers worn down, black showing under the silver etching. It looked like it hadn't been used in a long time. But when I shook it, I heard the sound of metal on metal. I slid the code into place, and the lock flipped open, a single gold key the only thing inside.

The back entrance to the tavern was at the end of the dark and narrow hall with the restrooms. Beyond that, the space opened up to the bar and large dining area with the glass windows beyond, facing the street. I locked up behind me, listening for signs of anyone inside: the hum of the machinery in the kitchen on the other side of the wall to my right; the rattle as the air-conditioning pushed through a vent overhead. Nothing else.

I walked to the end of the hall, where the rest of the tavern remained well lit, even without the overhead lights, from the wall of glass windows lining the street. The sidewalk out front appeared deserted for the time being.

Even from across the room, the framed picture stood out. It had been secured behind a plastic covering, inside a wooden frame that had been screwed into the paneled wall just below the upper bar shelves. It wasn't a large shot—maybe a five by seven—and there were four people in the frame, so it didn't show a lot of details. I'd seen it myself, before I'd arrived—on the news programs after Alice Kelly had gone missing. But standing in front of it, the details came to life; the colors appeared more vivid, the people alive. I understood why people stopped to see it in person. Like Celeste said, there was no match for reality.

What this photo provided was a *feeling*. These four young men had been happy and carefree, and this was the last image of them. Brian, on the far right, was caught midlaugh with his eyes closed, no idea of what was coming for them. The two in the center: Toby and Jerome, were looking over at Brian, instead of the photographer, with expressions of bemusement. Only Neil was facing the camera head-on. It seemed like he was reaching out toward the camera—I could imagine an arm just below the frame, stretching forward—and his mouth was frozen partly open, like he was starting to say something.

Here, they could always be twenty-four and twenty-five. Immortalized. Here, they could still be anywhere, and you could imagine their entire lives stretched out before them.

If they had lived, they would be fifty, or turning fifty. They would be celebrating with family, or maybe with one another still. Sitting in front of them, it was so easy to imagine.

There wasn't a lot of clarity in the picture, partly because of the size, and partly because of the smudging of fingerprints across the plastic layer over top, from visitors coming to pay their respects, sneaking behind the bar, offering up a toast.

Now I dragged a stool around to the other side of the bar, legs screeching against the treated concrete flooring, and climbed up. I used the bottom of my shirt to wipe off the prints as best I could—the closest I had ever been to them.

I could feel them, too. It was as if they were just here, had just been planning their trip. As if I would be able to turn around and see them at a table, watch the good-natured pats on each other's backs, hear the gentle ribbing, the order of *one more round* before heading out.

Brian had that hat on, with the symbol of his old fraternity. Toby wore one, too, but it was on backward, his blond hair escaping out the sides, a breeze I could almost feel. Jerome's muscled arm was slung around Toby's shoulder, the green of his shirt blending perfectly into the background. Neil had sunglasses on, contoured to his head, the type used more for skiing, with reflective lenses, tinted slightly blue.

I leaned closer. *A fifth person*, that's what Landon had believed. He'd been asking around about *who took that picture*, and now I couldn't get that question out of my head.

Who was there, on the other side of the disposable camera? Who was Neil reaching for? Who was Brian joking with? There was no one in the background, nothing behind them but the rise of the mountain, where they'd soon disappear.

I tried to imagine someone else, just out of frame. But there was nothing to indicate it. Only the person taking the shot.

I could almost feel them, gesturing for everyone to get closer, counting down, snapping the button a second too soon, before everyone was ready.

There were no storefront windows that offered a reflection. There were only Neil's sunglasses, but everything was too small, and I had no idea where any original film would be. I did the only thing I could, and took a picture of Neil, close-up, with my own phone—hoping I could see things better on the screen, by changing the lighting or enlarging the frame.

I hopped off the stool, pulled up the photo, zoomed in on Neil's face. God, he was so young. Younger than me, right now.

The corner of his glasses reflected the setting sun, and my stomach sank because I knew it was too late. Too late for any of them to be heading out, just as they had been warned. Too late for any of them at all. I knew they were not alive. That theory didn't hold. Despite the rumors of a cult, or of the people who didn't want to be found, they were just four twentysomething young men, who took a quick trip, left their lives behind. They were not planning some grand escape. They'd left too much behind. Too much unresolved. They were dead. I knew this now.

I zoomed in closer, on the other lens, without the glare. There was nothing but a small blur of white at the bottom of the lens. Like webbing. No, not webbing. As I focused, it looked more like a crack, spreading.

I brought the phone closer to my face. So close, I felt I could reach out and touch his face. The blue of the lens, the white of the crack—

A noise escaped my throat, alone, in this empty room. A logo. That's what it was. White on navy blue. And I knew exactly what it was: a tree, bare branches stretching into the sky. Like they were reaching for something.

It was the logo for the Passage Inn.

My home, the place where I'd lived, for ten years. Someone wearing that shirt, or holding an umbrella, or in possession of something with that logo was on the other side of the camera. Someone who might've known what happened to them. Who might've been *the fifth member*—

The sound of a key sliding into a lock jarred me. I stood straight, shoulders tense, phone still in my hand—only to see Rochelle pushing open the main entrance to the tavern, in dark jeans and a green tank top.

She paused just inside the door, rocked back slightly on her gold sandals. "Well, hello there," she said.

"I was just . . ." I said, my voice wavering. But I couldn't come up with a good excuse, not with that image in my mind. I was doing what an outsider would do, sneaking around, trying to figure out something left unsolved for so long, as if I could be the one to uncover the truth.

"Yes," she said, faintly amused, "I can see that. So can everyone else. We just got a call at the sheriff's office about *someone inside the Last Stop, snooping around*." She gestured to the glass windows behind her.

"So you came to check it out?" I asked.

"Sure, no point wasting resources. Everyone's busy."

As if she were a member of the department herself. As if she decided what calls to pass along and what to check out on her own. "You have a key here?" I asked.

She started walking across the room. "We have a spare key to practically everywhere. The store owners all prefer it that way, so we can check on any issues without waiting for them to arrive." Of course they did. They all trusted one another here. But only one another. "Though I see you found a way in, too."

I held up the key from the back lockbox, placed it on the counter like an offering. Hoping she let me go, kept this to herself. Not a big deal, *nothing to see here*.

But she came closer, not letting me off so easily.

Maybe this was an opportunity. Rochelle might be the one person who would know these things. Who handled every call, set up every system. She had access everywhere, heard everything, and in the past, had shared her own theory so readily. *They fell*, she'd said. That's what she truly believed: They had fallen into the ravine, and animals had taken care of the rest.

But there was a note about the Fraternity Five, and I could see the logo for the Passage Inn reflected in Neil's glasses. And I wondered if she was missing something, too.

"Rochelle," I began, because she'd already caught me, so what was the point in hiding it anymore? Why not get what I came for?

"Do you know, when they interviewed everyone during the investigation . . ." I didn't even have to say which one. She could tell, from where I was standing, what I was doing. "Did they ever have a suspect?"

She tilted her head, came even closer. "Oh no, not you, too," she said. "It's long gone, Abby. It's *over.*"

But it wasn't over. It existed beside us, in everything we did. In every visitor's question, in that picture over the bar. It was the thing that mattered most of all. I took a deep breath, pressing on, "Did they interview—"

She put her hand up, bangles sliding down her arm, then raised a single finger. She joined me behind the bar, leaned back to assess the inventory. Then she pulled a half-empty bottle of tequila from the shelf just to the side of the framed picture. She grabbed two shot glasses with her other hand, placed everything between us on the bar top.

It wasn't even noon, but Rochelle filled both glasses. "One shot, one question," she said with a sly grin. "Keeps you honest. Keeps you from getting greedy."

She placed her elbows on the counter, leaning forward, chin in hands, like she was waiting to see what I would do.

I grabbed the closest glass, could smell the alcohol, feel the burn even before I tasted it. I hated tequila, and I got the feeling she knew this, remembered it from years earlier. I started with a sip, then tipped it all the way back, my throat burning, my stomach churning. I coughed into my closed fist, then set the glass back on the counter.

I pictured the reflection in Neil's glasses; the shadow of a fifth man behind the camera. "Was Vincent ever questioned about the Fraternity Four?" I asked, even though he'd been long dead before Farrah disappeared. And then I coughed again. "Were any of the rumors about him?" This person whose absence I had stepped into so firmly. This person I felt I knew so well, just by existing in the place he'd once occupied. But I had only known him through Celeste's old stories. Through the photos that lined the walls of the inn. She'd told me that he'd changed after the disappearances, that he didn't like to leave the inn.

Rochelle laughed. "What do you think happened here twenty-five years ago? Every person between the ages of fifteen and seventy was questioned and accounted for. Their alibis taken apart backward and forward. I've had access to the files since I was seventeen. I could practically recite them for you." She shook her head. "This town was traumatized. Is it any surprise they don't want to talk about it? If you'd grown up here, you'd know that."

I ignored her dig. "And Vincent's alibi was solid?"

She laughed again, gathered her hair over one shoulder. "Vincent's was the best. *Out of town, confirmed with work and hotel.*" She recited it like something she'd read many times. "Apparently, back when the inn had first opened, he still had to split his time between the inn and the firm he used to work for. So, he wasn't even *here*. He didn't come back until the next day. Which you should know."

"I was *three*," I said. A young child, just like she had been, like Cory, like Jack—none of us with any recollection of that time in our lives. Just the stories we were told.

She waved her hand, standing straight. "And anyway, that guy? No matter how much Celeste says he loved the nature here, I rarely saw him outside when I was growing up. He was not a hiker, didn't seem outdoorsy at all. What would he be doing out there? He was an architect. It was amazing Celeste got him to move out here, honestly."

I didn't understand. Vincent wasn't here, but I knew what I saw— "Did anyone else work at the inn then?"

She waited, not answering, and then I understood. I pulled the second shot glass across the bar top, tipped my head back, poured it down. My entire body was on fire, my nerves fraying, as I awaited her answer. Because I felt suddenly so close, too close.

"No," she said. "At least, I don't think so? The inn had opened a couple years earlier, but it was still pretty new, just getting off the ground . . . They didn't have a lot of guests. I don't think they could've afforded to hire anyone else. They did it all themselves, mostly."

Mostly. I could cling to the mostly. I had to. I didn't like how the scene was shifting, the ghost I could suddenly picture on the other side of that camera. Just because Rochelle had access to the files didn't mean everything was in there. She was the same age as I was, relying on other people's stories, on what was written down or recorded. So much here happened quietly, behind the scenes, passed in whispers and rumors.

"Everyone was interviewed?" I pressed. "Even the sheriff?" He'd been a young deputy then; his father had been the sheriff instead.

Her face hardened, eyes darkened. But she didn't pick up the bottle of tequila, didn't make me take another shot, and I understood—this one, she would not answer. I had crossed some line. Or maybe she didn't know. His father had been the sheriff then, after all. What were the chances there was anything on record that would have the capacity to hurt him?

She lowered her voice. "You've got almost everybody fooled here, Abby. Maybe having Celeste vouch for you is enough for the sheriff. Maybe it's enough for Cory." She leaned forward. "But you should be more careful, Abby Lovett. People are going to start noticing what you're really like."

She picked up the bottle, poured one more shot, and picked it up. But instead of holding it my way, she smiled tightly. "My turn," she said. Then she gulped it down in one fast swallow, wiped the back of her hand across her mouth. "What are you doing here?" she asked.

I gestured to the photo over the bar. "I came in to see—"

"No," she said, all drawn out. "Not here." She slapped the surface of the bar, grounding us physically. "I mean, *here*. In Cutter's Pass."

I shook my head, unsure how to answer. Unsure what she wanted to hear.

She sucked air through her teeth, a faint whistle. "The thing is, I checked you out, when you arrived." I must've made a face, because she rolled her eyes. "Don't take it personal, I do it to everyone, there's not too much going on, a lot of days. And you can't be too careful here." I knew she'd done this for Cory, looking into Georgia's past. It had not occurred to me she did this to others, too. "And what can I say, very on the up and up. One unpaid parking ticket, not that I think anyone will come after you, especially since you were seventeen." A head tilt. "I am sorry about your mom."

I felt myself nodding gently, because I was sorry, too.

"But, here's the thing. I couldn't, for the life of me, connect you to Vincent." She spun the shot glass on the counter. "I told the sheriff that, but he said, *Let it go, Rochelle, extended families, blah, blah, blah . . .*" She said this all like it was inconsequential, like the very fabric of my connection to this place wasn't threatened by her words, her rumors. "But that's his weakness. Celeste, I mean. You know they were together for a while, before she met Vincent?" I shook my head, and she made a face, like, *Well, of course you wouldn't*. "He's a couple years younger, but he's had a blind spot his whole life about whatever she says. So maybe he's not the best judge." Maybe that's why he was drawn to the inn, helping out, picking her up for church each week. Some bond that preceded everything. Even Vincent.

But I was stuck on what she'd just revealed. Imagining when I arrived at eighteen, Rochelle telling people, *I don't trust that girl*. The way it had taken me so long to make a real connection with this place. The way I was invited to some events and weddings and graduations—the big things—but not the smaller ones. For ten years, she had been warning people, *She's not one of us*.

"Who else did you tell that to?" I asked, holding my breath after.

"Cory, obviously, seeing as he was all over you." Of course. The way Cory never let me fully in. Never fully trusted me, until he had seen my name in that journal, too.

"So," she said. "Are you going to tell me the truth?" She grinned. "I took the shot and everything. It's only fair."

But I gritted my teeth, no longer feeling small and off kilter in her presence. All I could feel was the anger gathering. "Isn't ten years enough for you?" My voice was rising, but I didn't care. "Have I not proven myself by now?"

She stared at me, lifted one shoulder before responding. "For some people, I guess. But here you are." She raised both hands, taking in the empty tavern, where I was currently trespassing.

"Rochelle," I said, taking the shot glasses to the sink, rinsing them out, because this wasn't a game. *My life* wasn't a game. "This is my home."

Her face was stoic before breaking into a slow, full grin. "Well, Abby," she said, raising the open bottle, "don't forget it."

We were staring at each other, the air charged, my throat still burning and my thoughts spiraling, when the front door of the tavern swung open.

Both of us turned in that direction, but only one of us acted like we'd been caught doing something we shouldn't.

Jack Olivier stood there with a slightly confused smile on his face. "Hey, this is open already?" he asked, looking between the two of us. Rochelle's expression warmed to him, and it occurred to me suddenly that they were together.

It also occurred to me there would be no secrets kept between us. That this—*me, here*—was not something that would be forgotten. That I was running out of time.

"Sure, what'll it be," she asked, pulling down a fresh glass. Neither of them worried about getting caught. About the implications.

"Hey," Jack said as I brushed by him, heading for the exit. "Abby from the inn. Twice in two days."

CHAPTER 19

HADN'T CORY TOLD ME that there would be no good answers? Nothing I wanted to hear, nothing I wanted to know?

For ten years, there had been no developments. Ten years of listening and observing and learning so little. Until Trey managed to find a thread, and pull.

But this place had become my home. These people had become my family.

And yet.

And yet.

I felt as if I was always the one meant to uncover it. The only one who could. Not quite insider, not quite outsider. A trail left just for me. If only I would see it through.

ROCHELLE SWORE THAT VINCENT hadn't been here when the Fraternity Four passed through town. And who did that leave?

I felt sick, couldn't face Celeste. Couldn't look at the woman who had become my sole family. All the wonderful things she had done—for me, for this place, for us. The place she had occupied in my life. Who we had become to each other. But: that logo. The inn, at the center of all the disappearances to follow. There were only so many places left to dig, if you were going to do it.

I had to be sure. Ask the wrong question here, ask the wrong person—everything hung in the balance. Everything was at risk: the life I'd built for myself, the people I had grown to love, the person I had become.

I ENTERED THE INN around back, through the employee entrance in the basement, to avoid her. It was silent inside, except for the buzzing of the overhead light. But I could see something taped to the entrance of my apartment.

A note, from Celeste, on a yellow sticky note adhered to the center of my door: *The phone lines are down.* As if she'd come here to look for me.

I imagined her standing out here in the hall, knocking. Calling my name, as I had called Georgia's earlier in the day. Taking the key from around her neck—the other person with a master key. Of course she had a way in.

As I opened the door to my apartment, I wondered: Did she step inside? Did she look around, open the closet, find Landon's journal, Farrah's camera? I checked for signs that anyone had been here, but everything seemed exactly as I'd left it.

Maybe all of this was my imagination. Every bit of it. And Celeste was just as I had always known her—fierce and loyal and independent—and she'd come downstairs to borrow my cell to call about the lines.

I walked into my bedroom to check the apartment line—it was dead. *Shit.* But I remembered what Harris had done last time to fix it. It seemed all it took was a cable being reconnected, if it had managed to come loose.

I didn't want to think about that too much, about how it had happened, accident or otherwise. I just wanted the phones back, as quickly as possible.

I headed down the hall, to the storage closet that shared a wall with the outside. The one that didn't require a key, with the cleaning supplies and furniture gathering dust, stacked along the wall. The room was dark and shallow, with unfinished gray cinder blocks, and it smelled like chemical cleaner and earth.

I opened the phone box near the entrance that Harris had pointed out last time, trying to find the issue. All the wires appeared connected. Just in case, I pushed them in securely, one by one. I should've asked for more specifics when he was here.

Maybe there was another box in the other storage area. I used my key to access it, since this one was typically kept locked—filled not only with the linens and the lost and found bin, but with records and finances and the history of this place. There were no other electronic boxes along the walls, that I could tell. All I noticed now were the empty spaces that had been left behind when Cory cleared out some of Vincent's boxes, earlier in the week.

The room felt so much larger, open and light. I peered behind the vacant shelving now, checking any visible wall space, but there was nothing.

I left the door open and checked the storage area next door again, thinking I might've missed something, with the lack of light in the unfinished space. There was nothing along these walls either, but I noticed how much smaller this room was than the one next door. How the back wall, behind the piles of furniture and the bucket and mop and chemicals on a corner shelf, was left raw and unfinished, as opposed to the one next door. As if this room was closer to the earth.

And then I was thinking of Landon West poking around. The things Georgia might've told him, showed him. In the upstairs hall, he'd been looking at the blueprints, asking questions. Looking for *me*. Asking if Celeste and Vincent had built this place all on their own.

What could he have seen in here? What was it, in the blueprints, that had him so curious?

What was it that had prompted Celeste to remove them from the wall soon after, claiming they needed a new frame?

Had Landon called her on her home line? Stopped her in the hall? Did he go to her house, or catch up with her on a hike?

I felt every hair raise slowly across my arms, my legs, the back of my neck, thinking through the possibilities. A faint buzzing sound, and I didn't think it was from any overhead light.

There was no record of any interview between the two of them, but there was a check mark next to her name in his journal. He must've called. He must've asked something.

Had he asked if she'd met the Fraternity Four? If she'd taken their picture? Had he pushed harder, asking if there was something hidden within the walls of the inn itself, and not lost out in the woods? *Your imagination is running away with you again.*

Be careful, Abigail.

She was so *small*. In a decade, I'd seen no sign of threat, or force. She tended a garden, and walked a mountain path, and handed off the long hours and hard work to me and, more recently, to Georgia.

I wasn't sure how long I'd stood there, the room buzzing, my imagination running away from me. I stared at that far wall, breathing too shallow, feeling the room contract on me. And then I slowly backed away and closed the door behind me.

I COULDN'T GET ENOUGH fresh air into my lungs. Imagining what could be hidden in the space behind the cinder-block wall. Thinking about who had built it, and when. *Why.*

I stumbled along the perimeter of the inn, hand to the wall, to steady myself. Trying to talk myself down—my overactive imagination getting the best of me yet again. My feet kicked up gravel as I walked up the incline from the employee lot, to where I could get the best cell service.

And for the first time in a long time, I wondered who I could call. Like Georgia must've felt when she figured out who that camera belonged to, I considered reaching out beyond the boundaries of Cutter's Pass. Saying *There's something wrong, something very, very wrong here—*

I caught sight of movement in the windows of the inn that faced my way, from the back office behind the lobby. You couldn't see through them well—too much reflection, too much protection—but I could just make out the outline of a person at the window, staring out. I recognized her posture, her movements, the hand she raised toward me. Celeste, watching me.

Everything within me stilled. I raised my cell toward her, pointed to it, so she would know—*I'm handling the phone lines, just like you asked*.

I could see the outline of her as she nodded in return. Then I turned around, keeping my back to her as I called Harris.

As often happened, my call went to voice mail. But seeing as it was Sunday, I wasn't sure when I'd hear back from him. He must take a day off on the weekends. He must take time for his family. I debated leaving a message at all, except he'd told me, as we'd both stood in front of his home, that I could call him any time. That I should.

"Harris, it's Abby," I said. "We're having some more issues with the phones at the inn. I checked that juncture box, but it all looks okay. I must be missing something. Hate to bother you on a weekend, but it's not just the lobby phone. It's also my apartment. I'm not sure how widespread the issue is. If you get a chance, can you give me a call, walk me through it?"

I wasn't holding out luck for a response anytime soon. He was probably enjoying the day with Samantha and Elsie, probably drove out with them to Springwood, staying far away from this place—he knew better, after all.

I peered over my shoulder again, expecting to see Celeste still watching. I'd felt her eyes, the entire call. Except I must've been imagining it, because there was no one at the glass window.

A car pulled up the road, turning into the inn's parking lot. New guests, checking in, probably. Celeste would be occupied.

There were some things I wouldn't have considered doing, hours earlier. There were some things I wouldn't have *considered*, hours earlier. But I knew I had one single opportunity right now, and I needed to take it.

I checked over my shoulder one last time, making sure I was alone. And then I headed for the carriage house. I needed to see what she'd taken from the storage area, what was so important to have Cory bring to her home—I needed to be *sure*.

As I took the narrow steps up from the garage-level entrance, I tried to picture it: the Fraternity Four and Celeste. This person who knew every inch of the mountain like the back of her hand. I pictured her as she was in the photos in the hallway of the inn, youthful, adventurous, someone who could see a vision through to completion.

Would she have met them at the tavern? Would she have taken their picture, and then taken them into the woods? And then what? Who was this person whom I'd respected and idolized and taken such solace in?

The door at the top of the steps had an old dead bolt, though I couldn't remember a time when Celeste locked her door. She had always made me feel safe here, by her own lack of concern.

I turned the knob now, and it opened easily. As if there was nothing to hide. Nothing to fear. Though I knew that wasn't true.

It had been a while since I'd been to the upper level of Celeste's carriage house. When I'd first arrived, we'd had Sunday dinners together, and I could feel the loss of her husband still heavy in the places he'd once occupied. I'd helped her move some of his things out, storing them in the basement. Leaving space for her to exist without the specter of him everywhere.

It was a small living area, but she said it was all she needed—she had the entire mountain, after all. White angled walls, exposed beams across the ceiling, and a brick fireplace, centered between the couch and the lounge chair, which no one seemed to use and must've belonged to Vincent. The bedroom was through a single doorway to my left.

The kitchen was closest to the entrance. Appliances along the wall, a rectangular wooden table in the middle. That table now was covered with papers, one of the storage boxes open and resting on a spindled wooden chair.

I didn't have to look very far at all.

I held my breath, bracing myself for what I would find. But the documents appeared old. I picked up the closest paper, and it was a deed of trust. A document declaring who this property belonged to—with both names listed as owners: Vincent Farley and Celeste Farley.

Okay. So these were the papers in Vincent's things that she'd been looking for. This didn't look like something secretive. These were just documents about the inn. Legal paperwork; our history.

Below, there was a larger stack of papers bound in a rubber band, and I recognized it—a will. Thinking it was Vincent's, I picked it up. But this belonged to Celeste. It was thick, and seemed to be awaiting signatures, but the thing that caught my eye, as I flipped through the pages with no understanding of what I was looking for, was the same thing that caught my eye in Landon West's journal, and in the Edge's ledger: my name.

I stopped at the page, reading closer. Reading again. It seemed that Celeste was trying to add me as an owner of the inn. That she was going to leave this place to me.

I sucked in a breath, and this time, I pictured everything I had always believed her to be: a parent figure, when I had no parent left. Someone who loved, most of all: this mountain, this place, and me.

I wanted to sit with this, stop digging—but this wasn't what I'd come for.

I dropped the stack, piecing through the other papers, searching for the blueprints. There was nothing here but legal documents and financial statements about the founding of the inn—its accounts, the permits. There were no blueprints or architectural notes here.

I didn't see the other boxes, but I was sure Cory had brought more over. I knew they were here, from their absence in the storage closet. But there was nothing else in the living area. Just this single box.

I crossed the room quickly, heading for her bedroom. Inside, her queen-size bed was neatly made, the surfaces of her furniture clean and bare.

No boxes here, either.

Just a framed photo on the dresser of her and Vincent, hiking sticks in hand, from long ago. There were trees on either side of them, open air and the mountain ridge in the distance—the same overlook I'd showed Trey on our hike. Standing beside Celeste, Vincent looked so at home, so outdoorsy and capable, not at all like the man Rochelle remembered growing up.

The only place left to check was the closet, on the opposite end of the room, and the longer I searched, the more guilty I felt.

But I was so close now.

I opened the closet door, the hinge crying. Her clothes—khakis and flowing tops in blues and greens—hung from the bars that spanned the three walls. Hiking shoes and sneakers and her walking stick leaning in the corner. And there, along the back wall, were the stacks of boxes, all with Vincent's name.

A brown corner was poking out from behind the stack—the edge of a frame. The same style that matched the other pictures that lined the walls of the inn.

This was the frame she'd removed, claiming it was damaged, that it needed to be replaced.

But here it was, and when I turned it over, everything appeared exactly as it always had. There must've been a reason she didn't want these blueprints out there anymore.

This time, I knew exactly what I was looking for. The basement. I ran my finger down the protective glass over the blueprints, followed the path of the hall, the juncture to the two lower-level apartments. And then the closets. They were labeled: Closet A, Closet B. Both with the same dimensions—

"Can I help you with something, Abigail?"

I dropped the frame, the corner smashing into the wood floor, a collision I felt in the reverberation of the floorboards.

God, she moved so quietly. I turned around slowly. Celeste stood at the entrance of the room, piercing green eyes, waiting for an answer.

CHAPTER 20

THERE WERE TIMES, WHEN I first arrived, that I was afraid of Celeste. Not because of what I thought she could do physically, but because of how much of my life was in her hands, how much of my future at her whims. I was intimidated by her expectations of me, and her presence, this person who was so clearly revered by everyone around us. Whose opinion of you could lead the way for others.

I'd come to learn that her praise was unspoken; it was given, instead, in the decisions she left in my hands, the property she left in my care. To be loved by Celeste was a feat. But maybe it had kept me from seeing the truth about this place. About her.

"I was looking for this." I picked up the framed blueprint and held it out to Celeste, because the truth was the safest answer.

She frowned. "Yes, I can see that. You could've asked me, you know."

I couldn't get a deep breath, couldn't slow my heart, but I wasn't afraid. Maybe I should've been, but I still couldn't make it fit. Celeste, who had been my place of safety. I couldn't surrender that, not after all we had been through.

I needed to ask. And it felt like she was finally giving me permission to do so. "Celeste," I began, "what did you do?"

She stared at me, as if trying to read what I was really asking. She pressed her lips together. "Come out here, Abigail," she said. "Come out where we can talk."

I followed her into the main living area of the carriage home. She pulled out a chair at the dining room table, wooden legs scratching against the floor. "Come sit. I need to sit. I'm very tired," she said.

I slowly pulled out the chair across from her, placed the framed blueprint at my feet. It did not escape my notice that the pile of papers sat between us. A physical promise: *Look. Look what I am trying to do for you—*

And yet.

And yet.

"You took that picture, Celeste." There were no good answers, because I could feel my eyes tearing even as I said it. This person who had taken me in, made me a part of this world, become my family—all the good things about this place, because of her. "At the tavern. The logo from this inn, you can see it in the reflection. It had to be you."

And still, I wanted her to deny it. I was waiting for it: *What picture? What logo? No, that's not possible, dear.*

Instead, she let out a long sigh, her head dropping onto her hands, and she looked so old, so frail, suddenly. So incapable of any of this. "I always knew this day was coming. I wondered," she said, "how long it would be. Who it would be."

"Celeste," I said, and I was begging now, begging for it to be a misunderstanding. Wanted her to say that I was wrong, that it was not her in the photo, that there were others who had worked at the inn and Rochelle was *wrong*. That she had not been the fifth member of their trek. But she did no such thing.

And so I repeated the only question that mattered: "What did you *do*?"

"You have to *understand*," she said, and I could feel that she was pleading with me, too. To believe her, or to understand, or just to listen. But she stopped whatever thought she'd begun, shook her head, took a deep breath. "Everything happened so fast. It felt like forever, but it was so fast."

"What?" I asked. "*What* was fast?" My voice was too high, too tight, and I felt my hands balling into fists under the table.

"Okay," she said, as if coming to terms with something for herself. "The beginning was an accident," she said, and my ears started ringing.

"An accident," I repeated, imagining a way to make it okay. A slip into the ravine, like Rochelle had said. Someone tripping, and a hand, reaching out for another—a terrible, horrific accident.

Her hand was shaking as she reached for me, but my arms stayed in my lap, under the table.

She took a deep breath, started again. "That's not the beginning, really. The beginning, well. It started in town, where I met them. There was something off from the start. With their entire dynamic. It was like they didn't really want to be here."

In all the versions and rumors I heard, there was never mention of anyone else. Never any mention of who they'd interacted with before setting out.

"It was just luck, that I was there." And I thought of how much all of our lives came down to luck. "I was heading down to the tavern after work, for a drink." Her eyes drifted to the side, and I wondered if she was meeting up with Sheriff Stamer, a young deputy then, while her husband was out of town. I wondered how much of Rochelle's implication was true.

"And there was this group of boys out front, they were just *boys*, and they asked me to take a picture." Her eyes drifted shut. "Yes,

I took that picture for them. They set their packs on the bench, and I took the shot, and then they were arguing, and somehow the camera must've gotten left there, on that bench, when they picked up their packs again."

"They were arguing?" Had people from the tavern seen them, out the window? Or were they too far down the road, out of sight?

"Yes, about whether they should start. They said they were heading toward the Appalachian, and I told them, *You won't make it, it's too late.* Apparently, *everyone* told them that. But Brian, the one with that hat, he was adamant. He was the athletic one. Said he didn't come all this way to waste a day in some shitty little town. Like I wasn't even there." I had heard that everyone told them not to do it, down at the tavern. The thing I had never heard was Celeste.

"The others were right. It was obvious to anyone who looked at them. Their gear, they were *amateurs*. They'd had a round of drinks, maybe more. They had no business setting out into the dark. They reached some sort of compromise as they were arguing, that they'd go if they could find a guide. They asked me if I knew anyone. And for some reason I just said, *I can do it.*" A pause. "I think about that often."

"Why? Why would you say that?" I brought my arms up on top of the table, leaning forward.

"I was worried. Look, they weren't going to make it all the way. We all knew this. But I thought, I could get them somewhere good, safe, convince them to set up camp. I thought I could keep them from getting hurt. You have to understand, Abigail. I thought I could help."

I could imagine it so clearly, a young Celeste, unable not to help, as she had once done for me.

"It wasn't long after we started that I realized this wasn't just a camping trip."

She put up a hand as she saw my expression, the question she knew was coming. "It *was*," she said, "and also, it wasn't. Something must've happened on their last trip. I didn't know them, so it was hard to put my finger on it then. I could only read between the lines of the conversations. It seemed that Brian hadn't been doing well, over the year. Since college, really. Getting more reckless, with the drugs, with his activities. Jerome, the one from DC, he hiked up with me for part of it, filled me in a little while the others trailed behind. Brian had been a serious athlete, went to college for baseball even, but nothing came of that. There was a hole to fill. An adrenaline void. I think the trip was really a push to get him help. Sort of like an intervention."

"An intervention?" Of all the things she could've said, that was one I hadn't imagined.

"Yeah, came as quite the surprise to Brian, too. I don't know the details, but the others started broaching it slowly as we hiked. But they hadn't planned it, not really. Not *well*. It became my understanding that, whatever had happened the year before, most of them had decided not to go away again that summer. Brian kept bringing it up, like he'd won an argument, saying, *See, I knew you guys couldn't stay away. I knew you'd come around.* I think the hike was Toby's idea, though. He seemed closest to Brian, mentioned getting together with Brian the month before, when he was passing through Chicago. I think Toby had reached out to the others after he saw how bad things truly were, and they threw the trip together impulsively to get him alone, away from anything else. To help him."

It explained how, afterward, no one could be sure who had planned it, only that it wasn't Brian this time. That Jerome had bought his tickets last minute, and Neil had told his boss it was a family emergency. Because it *was*, in a way. They were a found family, even for all their differences. Four people who had stuck together through all of it—from middle school to adulthood. Who saw the changes each summer, Brian growing worse. He was in need, and they all came.

"We only made it to Shallow Falls," she said. "We stopped to rest. It was too dark, I told them, to go any farther. The ravine was a killer, and there was some argument over that. Brian, again, wanted to press on. Whatever was waiting for him that night, it was like he could feel it. And he was trying to outrun it."

I imagined them, at the open expanse at the base of the falls, at the center of a funneling. Celeste convincing them this was far enough, with the ravine ahead. I imagined the accident coming: A slip. A fall. The beginning of the end—

"Things really started escalating then," she said, and her hands ran down her long braid. She wasn't looking at me anymore—it was like she was *there*, twenty-five years earlier. "They kept saying to Brian that he wasn't himself, that he wasn't listening. That he was going to get them hurt, or worse. And then Toby, he was going through Brian's bag, to see what he brought—drugs, I assumed. And Brian was telling him to stop, and then Toby—he pulled out a gun from somewhere inside Brian's bag." My head shot up. "And then he was yelling, *Why do you have a gun? Why the hell did you bring a gun on a camping trip, Brian?*"

Celeste's eyes were closed, but I could see them moving back and forth under her eyelids, as if she were watching the scene unfold.

And then her eyes shot open. "It was dark. It was dark, and it was hard to see what was happening. But there was a struggle—Brian, lunging for the gun, Toby, pulling back. And then it happened." Her throat moved as she swallowed, the words quiet, raspy. "A quick, *crack*, and the shot had gone right through Toby's chest. Right there." She gripped her heart, like she could stop it.

I wasn't breathing. I felt like I was there, so close, standing where Celeste stood, reaching out and trying to stop it.

"You think everything goes silent after a shot. But that's not what happens. The woods came alive, instead. The animals, the birds. Everything was moving. Running. It was hard to know where to go. What to do."

I closed my eyes, willed her to run.

"Everything happened so fast after that. So fast," she repeated, in a whisper. "Brian had his head in his hands, and Jerome took that as his cue to rush him—but he turned, quick. *Bam.*"

I felt the jolt with each word. Saw Jerome fall, eyes wide in shock and confusion.

"And then it was just me and Neil, and both of us, we were the smallest ones. Neil had his hands up, so I did the same. Neither of us made a move, and then Neil started talking, just low and calm. *Brian, it's okay, put the gun down.* And of course Brian couldn't put the gun down, he knew there was no going back. Two dead, and we were witnesses. I was just terrified. I didn't see a way out. But Neil kept going, like maybe it could still work."

The terror was in the room with us now. The truth, not at all what I'd thought. Not at all what I wanted to hear. I wanted to tell her to stop, but I couldn't. Not now.

"I think about that a lot. The hope he still had, when I knew it was too late." She breathed in slowly, and I could hear the shudder of her exhale. "He tried to humanize himself. That's what you're supposed to do, you know. *Please, Brian,* he said. *It's me.* He was smart. It makes it harder to pull a trigger when you're putting a human face to it. When you're not just reacting to someone in a physical struggle, but making a choice. It's a different type of killing, you know. He did his best," she said, reaching for me across the table. And this time, I let her. "He really did his best."

She put her cold hand on my arm, a faint tremble to it. "He said, *Please, Brian, I have a daughter.*" The room hollowed, and my ears were ringing, and I couldn't hear her say it. But she continued.

"Brian didn't believe him. He said, *You do not.*" She was looking at me now, asking me to see it with her. "But Neil kept going. He said, *I do, and I haven't even met her yet. But her mom lives in Tennessee, and I send them money when I can.* He said, *I have a daughter, and she's beautiful, and her name is Abigail Lovett.*"

PART 5

Abby Lovett

Date of arrival in Cutter's Pass: January 7, 2013

First seen: Main Street, outside the Last Stop Tavern

CHAPTER 21

S*HE KNEW.* I COULDN'T get the words out—couldn't ask how, or when, or *why*.

Every memory, every interaction, my understanding of her, of *us*—everything was realigning. Of course Celeste had known. Celeste had known of my connection to the Fraternity Four before even I did.

My mother's fixation on the Alice Kelly case was not about Alice Kelly at all. It wasn't that she saw her as some manifestation of her fear—a girl about to be abandoned, set to navigate the rest of her life alone. It was about the location: *There's something wrong about that place*, she'd said, her hand gripping mine between us on the couch.

It was the place where my mother's entire life had forked, though she'd never stepped foot there. It was the place that both of our lives had forked, though I'd never known it.

She told me once, and only once. *Your father was Neil Smith. He was part of the Fraternity Four.* They were the last words of record of Tasha Lovett. Before I'd lost her to the drugs, and then the cancer, a day later.

The facts she had told me about my father before then had not been lies. Not *really*. She'd said, *It was a short-term thing*. She'd said, *I told him about you after you were born, and he sent us money. He wanted a better life for you.* She'd said, *But then he disappeared.*

I didn't press her on it; a disappearance to me back then was a very different thing. As far as I was concerned, my father had made a choice, to leave us. To leave me behind, in the past. She let me believe that; and I was not interested in a person who had no interest in me.

But after she told me who he was, I could only imagine another life stretched out before me. An *almost* life. Another future I could've had, another person I could've become.

There was a single photo of him in her things, though I might've passed right over it, if I hadn't been looking for it. It was her, and the group of them—the Fraternity Four, on horseback, at the stables where she worked, when they came through Tennessee. Neil beside my mother, her looking over at him, a slight grin.

It was worse than if there had been nothing at all. This one image, four inches by six inches, a bread crumb, a trail, to follow.

We were not so different, Neil and I, both only children of single mothers. I looked her up—this person who would've been my grandmother—but she had long since passed on. There was no one who held his memory, or his past to connect with, to search through.

There was only this place. And with Alice, a new disappearance prompting a fresh look at the Fraternity Four case—it was all anyone was talking about, on the news—there was a possibility that I could discover more. About him, and about myself. In Cutter's Pass.

I did not expect to stay. I did not expect to keep a secret for the last decade, but then, it had always felt like a secret: my mother had kept it, herself, for eighteen years. History had a way of pulling you back, like quicksand. How to explain that I was here because before Alice Kelly, my father had been the last to vanish.

And then I *had* found something here—it just hadn't been the thing I was looking for.

THE DRIVE IN FELT like the type of place where one might disappear, hands gripping the steering wheel, the tunnel of trees and the slick pavement, patches of ice and dangerous curves in the dark. There were a thousand ways I could slip off course, and I imagined all of them as I drove my mother's old car, with no one to look out for me. With no one to look for me at all. But eventually the trees opened up and Cutter's Pass presented itself: a beautiful oasis.

The downtown was a snow-drenched wonderland when I first coasted into the valley, lights in the shape of snowflakes hanging from the awnings, a sidewalk full of puffy hats and gusts of cold air escaping from people's mouths and steam rising from the hot chocolate in their gloved hands, and I thought, *How could anyone go missing from a place like this?*

I'd stopped in front of the tavern, exited my car, stood in the middle of the street, like my father had once done, with the mountain rising behind him, and I could almost feel him there. Hear what he would sound like. Feel the details. Find the context. Like he was just out of frame, in my peripheral vision.

You looking for the inn?

I turned around to see a guy about my age standing behind me. Maybe he'd noticed my car parked out front—the luggage piled in the back seat. Or maybe he could read something else in me. I said, *I* am *looking for the inn.* Because I did need a place to stay, and I saw no other obvious accommodations in town. He extended his arm in a straight shot up the mountain, a sharp whistle as he pointed the way.

Thank you, I said.

Thank me later. You can find me here. And he gestured to the tavern behind him. *The Last Stop*, it was called.

Everything felt like a sign.

When I stepped into the lobby of the inn, I knew I couldn't afford it. Not more than a night or two before I maxed out what was left of my credit card limit. But it didn't matter, because the woman at the registration desk—*Celeste*, though she'd barely looked up at me then—wouldn't give me a room. She said the inn was closing for the two-week stint of winter, which was both bad luck and good luck, depending how you looked at it.

She wouldn't give me a room: bad luck. But when I saw the construction being set up just off the lobby, I said, *I'm also looking for a job*, thinking it would give me some more time here, and she'd said, *No openings at the moment.* Bad luck.

I had nowhere else to go, and it was getting dark, and I was desperate, so that night, after the inn turned dark, I took up residence in the abandoned cabin farthest away, where a window had been left unlatched at the back—in hopes of a warm night before I figured out where to go from here. *My foot on a log, my elbows on the windowsill, and I was through*. Good luck.

She'd found me there in the morning, possibly tipped off by my car, tucked around the curve, leading toward the trailhead. But she used a master key and walked right in, like she knew exactly what she'd find. It wasn't even light yet, and I bolted up in the bed, disoriented.

Listen, kid, you can't just stay without paying.

I wanted to pay, I insisted, sliding out of the warmth of the sheets, taking out my wallet from my bag on the desk, to hand her a credit card.

Listen— She held that credit card, searching for my name, to continue. She squinted, like she couldn't make out the small print. *What's your name?* she asked.

Abby, I said. And then, when she kept looking: *Abby Lovett.* I hoped she didn't call the police. I hoped she didn't kick me out, tell everyone in town about the drifter who had broken in.

Abigail, she said slowly, as if correcting me, and I nodded, because she was right, and because I was in a bed that was not mine, in this room that was hers instead. I would be whoever she wanted me to be right then.

Well, Abigail, what are you doing here?

I told you, I'm looking for a job. A pause. *Also, my mom died*, I said—another truth, though it was irrelevant. But it was the only thing I could think that would appeal to her.

She kept looking.

I have nowhere else to go, I added, the emotion balling in my throat. I almost told her then, about *my father* and *the Fraternity Four*, but she spun around, so I was staring at her back, at the open doorway behind her. Like she was debating something.

Then she turned back. She looked at me closely, her green eyes sharp and focused, like she was reading something in me. *Look, Abby, the truth is, this place is only good for people who can do the hard things. And you don't look it, no offense.*

I can, I said, determined to prove it to her.

Well, then, get up and get moving. There's a lot to do. Get ready.

And I had.

Now I thought back on the secrets I had kept for years. Afraid she'd have me sent away, cut off, if she knew the truth. She *knew*, from the very start.

More than that—she covered for me. Gave me a story, for others to believe.

Celeste, who said to Rochelle and Jack, when they'd started peppering me with their rapid-fire questions, *She's Vincent's niece*—and told me after, offhand, like it was inconsequential: *Trust me, it's just easier this way.*

"You knew who I was," I said, forcing out the words. From the very first day. Had known exactly what mattered most to me. This person I thought had taken me in, grown to value me, love me, even—had she been working me, all along?

"It was the last thing he said," she explained. I saw her again, squinting at my name, asking me to say it. *Abigail.* "It's haunted me for years. You were the appeal he gave for his life."

But it hadn't worked. I hadn't been enough to save him. I had to know. Quietly I asked, "What happened to him?"

"Oh," she said, a long sigh escaping. She sat back on the chair, her entire body shrinking, and she looked so small. "Well, I made a mistake."

I stared at her, eyes burning, until she said it.

"Brian was going to shoot him. I believe he was. And then, I would be next. I had only a moment, you only get one—one single moment to decide." She raised her green eyes, and they were pleading, and sad. "I went for the gun."

Her eyes snapped shut, and I could imagine it before she said it. *Bam*, so fast. I imagined Neil, eyes wide, mouth open, my name the last words ever spoken, still warm on his lips.

I was so stuck in that moment that I almost didn't process when she kept speaking. Because she was still there—*alive*—and she was the only one to tell the story now. "It fell from his hands from the impact, but it was too late."

"Celeste, what did you do." Because she wasn't looking at me anymore, and she had *hidden* this, had let the truth be buried for twenty-five years, no closure, no answers—for anyone.

"It all happened so fast," she repeated, and now I wondered which part she had meant. Whether it was the lead-up; whether it was this. "You think you know what you'll do, Abby. But you don't. You don't always."

She stared out the window, toward the mountain. How was that place not a nightmare for her? How could she stand to be here?

"I scrambled for the gun in the dark, and I found it, and I shot him." *Bam*. "He was so much bigger than me. What was I going to do? Run?"

Yes, I thought. *Run. Get help. Go, fast.* She had the gun. No one knew these woods better than her. She could've made it, slipping through the trees—

She dropped her head into her hands, and I thought she was coming to terms with something. But then I realized she was still there, still watching it play out. "Neil was still alive, and I tried to stop it, but there was just so much blood—" She held her hands in front of her face, like she could still see the blood on them as she pressed her hands to the wound. "I wrapped him up, where he was shot in his stomach, told him to hold on. I told him I was going to get help." She sucked in air. "But you know how long that trail is. You know how much longer it takes in the night." She shook her head. "By the time we got back, it was too late."

"We?" My head shot up. *We?* She had gotten help? Someone else was *there*? "I know Vincent was gone," I said. If not Vincent, who?

Her mouth twitched. "Well, you have done your research." Her eyes drifted shut. "Patrick and I, we go way back. He was here, at the inn, when I came out of the woods. He had been looking for me, and so—there I was, running from the woods, holding a gun and covered in blood, begging him to help me." She swallowed. "He didn't even think, just took the gun from me and started following. He wasn't on duty, we had no cell phones, it was just us, running through the woods. Or him, following me, thinking he could help."

"And?" I asked, feeling my temper rising.

She let the silence stretch before responding. "There was nothing to do."

I slammed my hands on the surface of the table between us. "Oh, but you did *something*. Where are the *bodies*, Celeste?" Thinking: *Please*, let it not be that I have been living in a graveyard. *Please* let it not be that I had been surrounded by their bones. So close, all along.

"Look," she said, and I could tell she was getting irritated, too. Like this was not what she had expected of me, after all this time. But for ten years, I'd been listening, and looking. Ten years, I'd been waiting—the hardest thing. "We ran it through, a hundred different ways. The gun, and me, and the blood. I'd fired it, too. And now I'd dragged Patrick into it. His prints would be on it, too, and he was going to be sheriff someday, and the inn was just getting off the ground, and there is a *difference*, Abigail, between a disappearance and a fucking bloodbath." She was shaking then, and so was I. "None of us would've survived it. Not Patrick, or me, or this place you call your home. Not the town, either."

"So, what? You told *no one*?"

"I told Vincent. Called him at his hotel as soon as I got back here, and he drove home right then, in the night. Went straight out with Patrick, to help."

"To help . . ." I repeated, feeling sick. "Where are they, Celeste," I repeated, through my clenched teeth.

She pushed back from the table, clearly exasperated. "That, I do not know. That, I cannot give you. They sent me back here . . . I was in no shape to . . . There were guests and people had to see that I was here, if it came down to it."

But I thought of the blueprints, hidden away in the carriage house. The thing Landon must've wondered, when he saw them. The back wall of the storage area, pulled closer in. The horror I imagined.

"Celeste," I whispered, and even as I said it, I didn't want to hear it. "Are they here?"

"On the mountain? Yes, I assume. I pay my respects, as often as I can." Up and on that mountain every day before dawn. A cairn, a grave marker, at the sight of their deaths. A flower cut from her garden, left as homage. For my father?

"No, *not* the mountain. Here." I grabbed the framed blueprint from the floor, dropped it onto the tabletop between us. Pointed to the room in the basement, my finger noticeably shaking. "The wall in the outer storage room, it's not as deep as the other one, like it's supposed to be. Like someone changed it." I covered my mouth with my hands, like I couldn't believe I'd said it. Made the possibility solid and real.

She stared into my eyes for a beat too long before waving her hand between us, severing the moment. "Don't be silly. Of course not. These blueprints were a guide, but they're not definitive. More like a draft. You know how the landscape is here, too much uncertainty. That area, in the basement, there was a big rock outcropping, goes down pretty deep. We couldn't dig into it. So we built around it." She shrugged, like it was so obvious.

It was easy to believe if I wanted. It was just as easy to disbelieve, and I was wavering.

"The inn had *guests*, Abigail. It's not possible. Two people, in the night, on that trail, could not bring four . . ." She trailed off, not wanting to say the word. *Bodies.* There were four bodies, and she had covered it up. Her gaze returned to mine. "We wouldn't bring that back here to this place. That would be a very dangerous thing." She blinked rapidly, and every word she said made sense, if only I would accept it. But I thought of how hard she worked to keep the investigation away from the inn, with Farrah. I wondered if she wasn't sure, either. If it haunted her, the not knowing.

"You *never* asked?"

"We never spoke of it again. Not any of us. Vincent had to make it back to his hotel for checkout, so he'd be seen there.

Patrick was on duty the next day. There was no *time*. We all had to keep going. You make a decision, and then you live with it." Her breathing shuddered. "I ruined them that night. The both of them. If he hadn't been here, if he hadn't seen me . . ." It took me a moment to realize she was talking about the sheriff and Vincent, not my father. "They were never the same. Stuck, the both of them. Because of what I did. Vincent lost sight of the beauty of the place, could only see that night in it. Could only picture what had almost happened to me. And Patrick, well. *You* see. His life never moved forward. Like he's always circling back here. Like he still can't escape that night."

I saw him differently then: the sheriff, never moving on. Living a life of atonement, picking Celeste up for service each Sunday. The connection they had. What must they have been thinking each weekend, sitting side by side, heads bowed? As if they were bound by trauma, as opposed to love. Maybe we all were. Could any of us even tell the difference anymore?

I closed my eyes, trying to make a decision of my own. "You just got rid of the evidence and let their *families* . . . you let them wonder, for years?"

"What do you think would have happened to this place? Not just me and Vincent and Patrick, but this place—bankrupt, gone. This inn, this *life*—it was Vincent's dream as much as my own. It would've ruined *all* of it. This *town* would never be the same." And then she shook her head. "Do you believe in this place, Abby, like I do?" Not in a god, then, but in something else. The magic of the place. "Because in the year after Vincent's death, when I was more alone than I'd ever been, and the nightmares returned after so long, you arrived on my doorstep. Like a second chance, to make things right. To pay it back to him."

An obligation; a debt. Guilt. Motivations were slippery like that.

"I always wondered if you knew," she continued. "I assumed there was something that brought you to me. But you never asked. You never said anything, in all this time."

Ten years, and I'd given up hope that there was anything here to find. I'd been right at the center, all along.

"I thought you'd tell me to go. And—" The unspoken truth. She was all I had.

She sucked in a breath. "I did the best I could, Abigail." I didn't know whether she meant that night, or with me—all these things she was leaving for me now, the longest atonement.

"What about Alice? And Farrah? And Landon?"

She frowned, straightening in her chair. "What about them?"

"Landon West thought . . . everyone thinks . . . that all the disappearances are tied together." I'd heard his voice on the recording. He was looking at the residents who had been here for each disappearance. He believed he could find the thread connecting them all.

"It isn't true. It's been twenty-five years. I don't know anything about the others. What would a college girl have to do with something that had happened fifteen years earlier?" She shook her head. "Tragic, every one of them." She leaned forward. "But a different sort of tragedy."

But she wasn't the only one with secrets.

She placed her hands on the table, pushed herself to standing. "Okay, listen, let's get back to the inn. Get some rest, and let's talk again tomorrow, in the light, in the open air. You need some time."

"They're not down there," I repeated, needing it to be true.

"I promise you," she said at just over a whisper. "They're buried somewhere out there." She gestured behind her, to the mountain.

"One day," I said, "someone might find them. Someone will see that they didn't die of exposure or animals or an accident."

She ran her hand down her braid, a faraway look in her eyes. "Yes, Abby. One day, they might."

I RETURNED TO THE inn in a daze. Went through the motions on autopilot.

Every door slamming shut sounded like a shot. *Bam.* Every voice, and I imagined my father, the words he'd pleaded with, for his life. Every peal of a man's laughter, and I imagined Brian in that picture in the tavern, head thrown back, no indication that by the end of the night, he'd have killed the others and be dead himself. This person I could never bring to justice, for all he had taken from me.

That is, if what Celeste had told me was true. But she wasn't the only one who had been out there that night.

There was a sheriff who knew more than he ever said. Who was stuck. Haunted. Who knew that Landon had been asking questions, and what could happen if he found them. Who knew everything that had happened or would happen in town by nine a.m. on any given weekday. Who, I had to assume, knew who I was, too.

CHAPTER 22

IT WAS LATE, AND the inn was quiet, and I was thinking of all the people with something to hide. It wasn't just me, who had been so careful, because, as I had learned, *Families made people nervous.* The way they kept digging, beyond reason, even when there's nothing left. Driven by something deeper.

I was thinking of Cory's parents, lying for him, without even asking whether they needed to. And a young Patrick Stamer following Celeste into the woods, when she was covered in blood. And Celeste never asking her husband or the sheriff what they did next, after they sent her away.

No one here seemed to want the answers. Not then, not now. Not *really.* As if they were scared of what they might uncover about one another, or themselves.

I was locking up the safe for the day, my phone balanced on the ledge of the back window, in case Georgia reached out, when there was a knock at the lobby door. Which was unusual. We didn't lock it.

Just as I stepped out from the back office, the door pushed open, and a head poked in, peering around the lobby—curly brown hair, a beard that matched. Harris smiled when he saw me there. "I was worried it was too late," he said, stepping inside.

"No, perfect timing. I was just about to close up for the night. You're a lifesaver."

He strode across the room, reached over the registration desk, and picked up the phone, listening to the dead air. "Hmm," he said, brow furrowing. "Can I check out the basement again?"

"Of course. I just need to finish shutting things down at the front desk." I led him down the hall slowly, aware that most of our guests were sleeping, the rooms locked and quiet for the night. I stopped just before the employee door. "Can I ask you something, in confidence?"

"Go for it," he said.

"What do you think of the sheriff?"

His eyes drifted to the side, and he ran his tongue behind his teeth. "I think," he began, with the tiniest smirk, "that he hires me sometimes. And that he's the reason I'm hired by others."

"Fair enough," I said, pressing my employee badge to the lock.

He pushed the door open, then held it there, pausing. "What are you really asking me, Abby?"

He knew exactly what I was asking. And I remembered how Cory told me I needed to be careful about that. "I feel like I don't really know what people are capable of," I began, edging my way into it. "I feel like I missed so much, not being here for all the disappearances."

"Well," he said, "neither was I." He took a step downstairs, turned around. As if the privacy of the stairwell kept him safe, allowed him to say it. "What I think about the sheriff is, there are people who are everything to him. And there are people who are nothing to him."

I nodded once, in thanks and in understanding.

I finished securing the lobby, waiting for Harris to finish up so I could go downstairs, to my apartment, process everything Celeste had told me. Decide what I was going to do with it all.

Walking into the back office, I saw an alert on my cell phone. I had hoped it was Georgia, sending some sort of message. An explanation; an apology. Or Sloane, checking in, reminding us both that we were safe.

But the notification on the screen was for a new message that had just arrived from *AliceKellyWasHere*.

I perched against the windowsill, feeling the cold of the night against the glass on my back. I navigated to the message: *I don't know their last names, sorry. But I remember them. They're in that group shot. I know it's hard to see, but here's a closer picture: Lacy on the left. Caroline on the right. They were the ones on the hike.*

She didn't have to say which one. The hike where they left her, let her go off on her own. Where she disappeared, never to be seen again.

The photo started to load below, in painstaking fragments. And there she was again, Alice Kelly, at the center of the frame, a close-up of the front row standing behind the sign. Quinn must've taken a closer snapshot of the picture. Lacy with a hand on Alice's shoulder, turned her way, Caroline smiling at the camera. They were all so young. I pictured them hiking together, packs that seemed to weigh as much as they did, and what Alice would've looked like, ten years later. Where all of their lives would have gone from here. Where the others' had. If they thought of her. If they sometimes thought they caught sight of her in the aisle of a store, or while picking up their kids from school. If they were all still haunted by it.

A new message chimed. Quinn was online *right now*.

James was her ex-boyfriend. He didn't hike as part of that group. I'm surprised he went at all. He really only joined the Outdoors Club for the pictures.

I read it again twice before responding: *He was a photographer?* There was something here. Something between Alice and Farrah.

A note that she was typing. And then: *Yes, that's how they met. A photography class outside of school taught by some nature photographer. Alice joined for the nature part. He was there for the photography.*

Footsteps approached from slowly down the hall, and then Harris was standing in the door frame, watching me type out a response to Quinn: *Was he ever questioned?*

"Who are you talking to this late at night?" he said with a smirk.

"Alice Kelly's sister, actually," I said, raising my eyes to him. "I found her on Instagram."

"Huh. You're really worried about the sheriff?"

I made some noncommittal gesture. I wasn't sure. Didn't want to start rumors I couldn't stop. "Any luck down there?"

He ran a single hand down his face. "Unfortunately, no. It's a bigger issue," he said. "I'm gonna check outside."

"Okay," I said, only half paying attention. Watching the screen of my phone again, waiting for her to respond.

Finally, it came through: *No, not that I know of. Everyone on the hike was cleared. They were looking at people in town.*

Except. *Except*, she'd never made it into town. Cory hadn't seen her. No one had.

Is he in that Outdoors Club picture, too?

I squinted at the original shot, but everyone was too small to see clearly, since she'd taken a picture of a printed-out photo.

More typing:

Yeah, hold on. I'll take a clearer shot. He's the guy standing behind her.

I waited for the photo to load. Fragment by fragment came through, zooming in on one slightly grainy face: brown curly hair first, a sort of widow's peak. I couldn't see his eyes because they were turned down, toward Alice. And his face was smooth, free of a beard. But it was him. My god, this was *Harris*.

"What?" I spoked it out loud. This wasn't James. This was Harris Donald. I went for our safe, where we kept our old invoices, and started piecing through them now, until I found a pink slip with his company's heading: *J. Harris Donald*

I shook my head, turning to the photo again. It was ten years ago. A lot of young men looked like this.

Coincidence. My imagination running away with me.

Wouldn't he have told me, if he'd known her? He'd said he wasn't *here* for the disappearance. Because he was away at college. But surely he would've mentioned *knowing her*? That he had dated her, even?

I'd never seen Harris with a camera, never asked him about his interests, his hobbies. But I remembered the pictures I'd seen in his house. The photos on their living room wall, of the trail, the creek, the flowers—had they been taken by Harris? Had he also known Farrah? Had Farrah known *him*?

My ears were ringing, something sharp and tinny, and I checked my phone for the picture of the numbers Landon West had written in his journal. A local number, beside the name *James*. The woman who answered had said it was the wrong number when I called before. But I pulled up that number now and called again.

It kept ringing, but I didn't hang up. Ring after ring, until eventually someone answered. A woman, sleepy, confused. "Hello?" she answered, and this time, with the context, I could place the voice.

It was Samantha.

"Samantha?" I said, holding the phone close to my face, keeping my voice low, urgent.

A rustling of sheets. "Who is this?" she asked.

"Abby, at the inn."

"Abby, is everything okay?"

No, it was not. "I called before, asking for James. Is that your husband's first name?" I asked, watching the front door of the lobby. He was out there. Right outside—

"Wait. What? Why would you . . . It's the family name. James was his grandfather, and he's been dead a long time. Anyone calling for a James is just a sign for a spam call—"

"But is it his *name*," I repeated, my grip tightening on the phone. *J. Harris.*

"Yes, but he doesn't go by that—"

The door to the inn swung open, and I heard Harris call my name.

I hung up the phone, hands shaking.

"Yes?" I called back. Trying to defuse the moment. Put a stop to this.

"I've gotta show you something," he said, still standing at the entrance.

"Can we do this in the morning?" I asked, thinking, *Please, walk away. Walk away.*

"Can you come out here for just a second?"

Not Harris, who was steps away from me now. Who had access to the inn, who we invited inside, hired for work. Harris, who could've cut the lines or disconnected them, just as well as he could've repaired them, to have a reason to be up here, keeping an eye on things. The danger, a stain upon this place—something I had let happen, with my silence. And it was here; he was still here.

"Abby," he called again, and I was afraid he would come inside. That I would be trapped in this room. That there was no way out.

"Be right there!" I called.

Who to call, how to get help, the fastest way here? I texted Rochelle. *It was Harris. Please get the sheriff. He's here.*

And then I left my phone on the sill, to ensure that the message went through.

Chances were, no one was coming. Not in time.

I stood, my head swimming, strode past reception, with the walking sticks—useless. I passed the fireplace, with the piles of logs in perfect pyramids. And then I grabbed the iron fire poker, from where it was angled just so, and stepped out into the night.

CHAPTER 23

THERE WERE NO LIGHTS on the path that snaked to the side of the inn, toward the cabins. Everything was extinguished. And as I stepped out into the night, the lobby lights behind me also went out.

We were bathed in darkness.

"The lines are cut." Harris's voice came from the side of the inn, and I knew it had been him, since the start. Since he'd heard about Trey's arrival in town, he'd always had a reason to be up here, keeping an eye on things, finding out what he knew. Discovering, instead, what *I* knew.

Shit. All I had was a fire poker and an expanse of time until the sheriff maybe, possibly, showed up.

I imagined Alice, arms gripping the straps of her bag, hearing a step behind her in the woods, recognizing him, her confused smile faltering. Looking around for help, for anyone—

Farrah turning around on the snowy trail—

Landon, opening the door to a knock in the middle of the night—

Run, I wanted to tell them. *Run. Faster.*

"Abby? You there?"

I thought of Celeste, and her warning—that we were alone up here, and I needed to look after myself first of all. My car was dead. The lines were down. How quickly would Harris hear me if I took off now—toward the town? How quickly until he caught me?

Goose bumps rose across my arms, the back of my neck. The night was too expansive, too unknown.

"Just grabbing a flashlight," I called tightly before retreating inside. I turned the dead bolt behind me, backed away from the entrance. Behind the thick wooden doors, and the reinforced glass that could stop a bullet. This place that would keep me safe.

I gripped that fire poker and listened hard, waiting for the sound of his footsteps, the shadow of his body passing in front of the tempered glass—but there was nothing. I started thinking maybe I had been wrong about him, about everything—and then I heard them: footsteps, in the distance, a soft thud near the back of the inn.

I spun around. Stared into the darkness of the hall. He was coming up the wooden steps to the deck, with the back entrance to the inn, which would be unlocked—

I started sprinting, racing him for the door, but he was already there, the handle turning, the hinges creaking, and it was all I could do to pivot to the side and hold my employee badge to the red light of the battery-powered lock, slipping inside the dark stairwell, toward the basement.

His shadow passed the door just as I pulled it shut.

"Abby?" he called.

I held my breath, could hear the rapid beating of my own heart echoing in my head. I clutched the poker in one hand and backed down the steps quietly, surrounded by darkness. The dark stairwell, the dark hall.

I thought of the blueprints that had once hung on the wall, with all the entrances and exits labeled clearly, and I moved on instinct, hand tracing the concrete walls. I knew every inch of this place. This was my home. Five more steps to the bottom.

"Abby!" he repeated, louder this time, just on the other side of the door. I thought of the guests, the inn, all the things in my charge, that I was supposed to keep safe.

"I'm here," I said behind the safety of a locked door and thick walls meant for structure and protection. I needed to keep him in one place, hope Rochelle got my message, got the sheriff—

But then I heard the familiar click of the lock disengaging, the door opening, and I saw the shadow of him for a brief second before the door fell shut again.

We stood, mere feet away, in total darkness.

Of course he'd had a way in here. Of course he could come and go as wanted, for who knew how long.

"I think someone's been out there," Harris said, voice low, as if he hadn't followed me into the basement in the dark.

And I thought: *You*, you've been out there. The first day Trey arrived in town, Harris was working downtown where the news had begun to spread, and it was all my fault. He knew. Someone was looking. Families, digging long after everyone else. Driven by something deeper.

I remembered what Celeste had said, what my father had done when faced with his killer, to try to humanize himself. To humanize all of us. "Does your wife know you're here, Harris? I just talked to her on the phone," I said, taking another step down.

"You did what?" he asked. He didn't move. I'd caught him off guard.

"Your number came up in a list of people who were friends with Alice Kelly," I continued. "I didn't realize you knew her, Harris."

"It was a long time ago, Abby," he said as if this could still be salvaged. As if he could talk his way out of it, even though he'd cut the lines, the lights, and used a key he shouldn't have to come after me. "What did you talk to her sister about?" he asked, like he was covering his bases, finding out how many people knew, how far gone this was.

He started moving again, a slow shuffling down the stairs—less sure of himself in the dark than I was.

"Just some old pictures," I said. "You were in them, you know. And about how you met Alice. In a photography class."

His footsteps continued down the stairs as I slipped around the corner, hand on the wall, thinking of options: my apartment; the back exit. Holding that poker in my grip. Feeling the safety of it, but only in theory.

"It's okay," I said as I kept moving away, slowly. I had learned something, living in Cutter's Pass. You couldn't keep your secrets if you wanted someone else's. You had to trade them all. It was only fair. "I keep secrets, too, Harris. Did you know I saw Farrah? Did you know she told me that she met Alice once? I'm guessing she knew you, too."

"You didn't tell the police?" His voice had shifted—he was closer now. Down in this long hallway, with me.

"No," I said, my hand brushing against my apartment door. Did I have time to get inside and lock it? And then what? Then *where*? I was only trapping myself, hoping he didn't have another way in. "I didn't say I saw her at all."

"Why not?" he asked.

I thought of Celeste, the way I'd let her guide me. "Because someone told me not to."

He laughed, one loud bark, echoing off the walls. "This place," he said. "This fucking place."

"I know," I said.

"I didn't want to come back here," he said.

But I thought I understood. Alice. He had to. "I know you

were on that hike, with Alice." It didn't matter what I knew, now. Only how I connected with him. He was going to harm me if I gave him the chance. I needed to keep him talking. Make my way to the exit, get a head start—

"She disappeared from Cutter's Pass. From the Last Stop," he said.

Except, not really. "No, she didn't. I know she never made it out of the woods. Cory *lied*, which I doubt will come as a surprise to you."

The silence stretched, and I thought he wouldn't respond. But then he did. "It was an accident. I promise, it was an accident." He was whispering, and he was so close, I knew if I reached out a hand, I'd be touching him. That he could reach out and grab me before I had time to get away. My options were running out. What I needed was time. More distance. My hand brushed against the first storage closet now. If I turned to run, he could catch me, and who would even notice? How long until someone came looking? Would I become just one more name in a list of people who had vanished here?

Another step, the second storage unit—so close now.

"I just wanted to talk to her, but she got spooked," he continued. "I just wanted to *talk*, and she started running. She tripped, hit her head." His breath caught. "I panicked. Abby, I panicked. Brought her down the trail, and I swear I didn't know what I was going to do. But I got out of the woods late that night, and there was Vincent's truck, just parked there. His keys in the visor." No one here was afraid of any of the things we should be. "Like it wasn't even my idea."

Like it was this place. Always this place, making people do things. Everything outside our control.

"Where did you bring her?"

"Home." A chill ran through my entire body, imagining the land I'd stood on. His wife and daughter, playing out there. "Then I brought the truck back and kept going. I don't know, I just kept going. And nothing happened. Cory said he saw her at the tavern. So did others. And it was like, it hadn't even happened. Like maybe I'd dreamed the whole thing. A terrible nightmare, an alternate existence. And we could all pretend she was still out there somewhere. It's better that way, Abby. No one even asked me one question."

"Until Farrah." I stepped back again, knowing, for sure, what he had done. Knowing I had to *get away*.

"Yeah." A pause—he was so close, and I was out of space. Did he know where we stood? How he had me cornered, with only one place to go now? One palm on the handle— "She saw me in Springwood. I was with my *family*. They were checking out after a doctor's appointment and I was waiting outside, and she walked right by me. I didn't recognize her. Not until she called my name. Even then, took me a second. Around here, James is my grandfather. Only people from college called me James. Seven years, such a long time." *Run*, I wanted to tell her now.

Go.

It was time. There was no other choice. I pushed my body against the door and turned to run. The cool night air, the crunch of grass under my shoes—and Harris, a step behind, lunging in a flash, hand around my arm, pulling me back against the rough exterior of the inn.

"Where are you going?" he asked. The poker in my other arm; time stretching; everything in a balance. God, he was faster than I thought. *Alice. Farrah.*

I was shaking, the adrenaline with no place left to go. Trapped, again. "I need air," I said, breathing heavy. "I just needed air." And the air *did* help. The stars were overhead, sharp and clear, and the universe felt so close, and alive. I could see the shadow of the mountain ahead. The shadow of the cabins, to my left. And there, beside me, the shadow of a man.

"Farrah remembered you, though?" I was Celeste, in over my head. I was my father, trying to defuse the tension.

I felt his grip relax, his hand drop from my arm, and I held my breath until he continued. "Yeah. Said she thought of me often. And Alice. Especially now, she said—we were so close to where it had happened, and what a coincidence, running into me here, too. And then Samantha came out with the baby, and I had to introduce them. My *wife*," he said, "is too friendly. Said she should come to see my photos at home if she was heading toward Cutter's Pass." He sighed. "I could see everything change in Farrah. She said, *Wait, you live there?* And it was my wife who said, *I know, trust me, I know. But his family has been here for generations. So we can't leave.*"

"Your wife had seen Farrah, too?" I asked. I pictured her telling me about the disappearances, asking, *What do you make of it?* Asking something more. Asking if her imagination had gotten the best of her. I started inching away again. Those woods—people could disappear in there. *I* could disappear in there.

"You should know better than anyone, it's best not to say anything here. Everything is so fucking tangled together." When I didn't respond, he said, "Abby?" and I knew he could see the shadow of me shifting away, just as well as I could see him. A shape, coming closer.

"I do know," I said. "I know that." Look where I was right now. Look what I had brought to the doorstep of my home.

"I told Farrah, I *told* her," he said, like it was her fault, instead of his. "I said I was on that hiking trip. I had an alibi."

But she was digging. Like she owed it to Alice, all this time later. Like she was the only one who realized it.

"You followed her." Just like now, as I tried to maneuver away. But every step I took, he followed.

"Once I saw what she was doing, where she was going . . . I just tried to talk to her before she started talking to the wrong person."

But she *had* talked to me. I'd told Celeste. And we'd done *nothing*. He'd been able to bury all he had done, with our silence.

"She just . . . wouldn't stop." His hand was on my shoulder now, a weight, holding me here. Holding me to him. "I didn't mean for her to get hurt. I just didn't know what to do." Even though he seemed in very sound mind after. Even though I knew he had taken the pictures on her camera. Had left it out there for us to find one day. So we'd think she was lost to the woods, too.

I could feel him, deciding. Weighing the risk. His van, the dark. The people around. The trail I might've left. I couldn't get away. Couldn't get a big enough lead.

I knew what to do. Hit him, catch him off guard, give myself a chance. *Run.* The trail? The street? To Celeste, screaming for someone to hear me? His breath was too close, and suddenly I was Alice, trying to escape, tripping, footsteps coming closer. I was Farrah, in the snow, eyes wide, trapped.

"Okay, it was an accident," I said, a chill rolling through me. "But the camera," I said. "It got to Landon West. I found his journal. He had all our names in it, and a bunch of phone numbers. *Your* name was in it. I know he called you. The last time I saw him, he told me the phone in his cabin wasn't working. And I heard a recording, from that night, his last night, someone was at the door—"

"God, I didn't *want* to, Abby. I didn't want to hurt anyone! But he kept digging. He called my house, and I just had to find out what he knew, I have a daughter now, I have to protect her. I'd do *anything*—"

"Okay," I said, trying to keep him off balance. I could feel the tension in his voice and he was growing more agitated and it had to be *now—*

A flashlight turned on, to our left, a third person. A man's shadow. My heart leaped, thinking it was the sheriff. But instead, Trey West stood there, holding his cell phone in front of him, the only light we had. "No, it's not *okay*. What the fuck did you do to my brother."

Escalating everything.

"What the hell," Harris said, arm up to block the light, his shadow thrown onto the stone wall behind him. The light catching off a glint of metal in his hand—a gun. Something that must've been there all along. Hanging between us, in every word. Always a possibility. *Bam.*

I could see how it had happened. The knock on the cabin door. *Here to take a look at your phone lines, can I come in?* Looking around the room. *Can I get your help with something from the van?* Pulling the gun, getting him inside, and then it was too late, it was always too late.

"Shit," Trey said, the beam of light sliding away, onto me. My eyes wide with panic, the fire poker held out in my grip, for protection.

Exposed.

"Hold on," I said.

I needed more time.

But there was no way out, and no time, and I thought of Celeste, standing in the dark, and my father with his hands up, doing everything he could.

"Harris, the police are coming," I said, my voice pleading, panicking.

Trey had dropped the phone, and the light pointed upward, and all I could see were our shadows, stretching. People, moving.

"No," Harris said, his voice suddenly behind me. "No one is

coming, Abby. No one ever comes. No one ever looks. You know that. You're one of them."

But he didn't know I'd been looking for a decade. I had always been looking.

It all happened so fast.

I heard Celeste's whisper, felt the impact of her word: *Bam*. Just like that, and everyone's life had changed. Hers, theirs, mine.

I thought of Harris's daughter, the large brown eyes, and her life—her future. The things she would one day search for.

You only get one shot. I swung the fire poker fast, across the space I imagined him to be. I felt the resistance of his body, heard the sharp intake of his breath.

The moment was suspended in animation, his arm in shadow, held outward, until Trey collided with him, both of them making contact with the stone wall. I heard the gun skitter to the ground, and we were all desperate for it. Scrambling for it.

But it was Trey who came up with it. Standing over Harris, who was still crouched on his hands and knees, probably bleeding from where I'd cut him. "I wasn't going to *hurt* you, Abby—" He pulled his hand from his shoulder and groaned, falling to his side.

"Go get someone," Trey said, voice flat and emotionless. "Go!" he yelled at me.

But I couldn't. I wanted to run for Celeste, but I couldn't leave him there, alone with the gun and the man who had killed his brother. Couldn't trust what he would do when I was gone. Couldn't let anything else happen; couldn't ruin him, too.

"I already called for help," I said, my grip still unrelenting on that fire poker. I could still feel the vibration in my hand, from when it had made contact.

Harris laughed into the dirt, and Trey was saying, "Go ahead, move again," and I was trying to figure out how to get Trey to give me the gun instead, when headlights crested the hill.

I could've sobbed, and maybe I was, because I was sucking in air, and my voice was wavering as I yelled, "Here, over here," as the wheels skidded in the gravel lot and the door opened and a man stood in the beams of his headlights.

The sheriff stumbled out in gym shorts and a T-shirt, gun haphazardly in his hand, like he'd just rolled out of bed. "Abby?" he called into the night.

"Here!" I called.

"She attacked me," Harris was shouting from the ground, trying, and failing, to push himself up. "She fucking attacked me."

The sheriff had a flashlight on the scene, at Trey standing over Harris, and he was pointing his own gun now, shouting, "Put down the gun, slowly, put it down!"

That was it, one car, one man as Trey stepped away from Harris and lowered his weapon to the earth.

But not thirty seconds later, a second car pulled up, and Rochelle raced from the driver's side, Jack following behind, flashlights dancing as they ran.

And then a third, a fourth.

Cory, Ray, Marina.

Until the road was blocked by them, the people of Cutter's Pass, who had been waiting for a very long time. Who were being absolved as they watched; and their parents and friends and loved ones absolved, in turn.

Celeste rounded the corner, shawl wrapped around her shoulders, pushing through the crowd until she could reach me. A hand on my shoulder, which she squeezed tight, and said, "My god, Abigail. You're okay." Which was both a question and an observation, and required no response.

I dropped the poker to the ground, felt her hands on my face, on my hair, on my shoulders. One rough thumb under my eye, though I wasn't sure if I was actually crying.

"Okay," she said, "let's get you home."

"Celeste," the sheriff called. "We need her at the station."

"Well," she said, her words weighted with everything between them, "it can wait."

She had that kind of power.

THE QUESTIONS STRETCHED DEEP into the night, after we made it down to the station, and there was a recorder positioned between me and the sheriff, dark circles under his eyes. Wanting me to walk him through it again, but I was tired, and so was he. Finally, he pressed "stop," leaned back in his chair.

"Stop holding back, Abby," he said, as if he knew there were pieces missing, people I was protecting. "How did you know?" Things I wouldn't give him.

"I told you, the picture with Alice, from her sister. Harris told me everything. Trey heard us outside. Harris practically admitted that he hurt Landon, that he'd gotten too close."

"But before that." The journal, he meant. The locker with my name. The secrets I would keep.

"Maybe if you hadn't been so afraid of digging, this wouldn't have happened," I said, and he looked at me sternly.

"You know who I am," I said. It wasn't a question.

"It doesn't have to be part of this." He gestured to the recording.

"I know who you are, too."

He continued to stare, hollows under his eyes, a reddish-gray stubble running down his jaw. "I don't know what you mean, Abby."

"Where are they buried," I whispered, leaning forward. "Please."

His throat moved, and I thought he'd pretend not to know what I was asking, and maybe he would've if he'd slept, if he wasn't so tired, if he hadn't just realized there were likely three victims buried nearby. "I don't know," he began, voice scratching.

But his eyes were still locked on mine, deciding. He dropped his voice even lower, even though it was just the two of us now. "The scene. The bullets. The gun." His throat moved. "I did that. But the rest?" He shook his head, closed his eyes, like he never wanted to look again. "Only Vincent knows," he said. "And he's gone."

I opened my mouth, closed it again. I couldn't imagine it, didn't see how it was possible for one person to handle that, all alone. But right then, I could choose to let it go, choose to leave it with him.

A history, wiped clean.

The sheriff opened his eyes again, then raised them to mine, in question. We stared at each other for a long moment.

He pressed "record" again.

LATER THAT NIGHT, AFTER the interviews, Trey was waiting for me. I saw him in the headlights of the car, where he was sitting on a log, in the dark, at the edge of the lot. He ran his hand through his hair as I approached.

"You okay?" I asked. I pictured him again, gun held over Harris. I wondered if he regretted his choice. If he was playing it back through, imagining pulling the trigger instead. Whether I would've backed him up, said he'd had to do it—

He stood, the sound of his steps in the gravel cutting through the night. "The journal," he said, voice low. "I want it."

He'd heard me, the things I'd said to Harris when I tried to escape outside. Trey had been drawn outside by the lack of lights, the feeling of *wrong*; the locked door of the inn, knowing something was happening. He had been waiting and listening in the dark.

But I couldn't give him the phone, the journal. They had to go. The photo over the bar, even.

"It's already gone. There was nothing in there for you," I said.

"Why are you protecting them?"

But how to even begin; it would take ten years to make him understand.

"Good night, Trey." Goodbye, I meant.

I KNEW WHAT I would do, as soon as it was safe to do it. I'd light a fire for the guests in the pit out back, and when they went inside, I would watch as it all turned to ash, bit by bit.

Reshape our history, the whispered path it takes. I had the power to change it. Smooth it flat, something safe to look at. Something we could all be okay with.

I'd watch as the smoke drifted up over the mountain, and I would watch as it disappeared, into nothing.

SEPTEMBER 3, 2022

CHAPTER 24

IT WAS LABOR DAY weekend and the town was overflowing.

We wondered, for a brief time, what this would do to the town. But the killer wasn't from Cutter's Pass, after all, had grown up beyond our boundaries, had never really been seen as one of us.

And the threat was behind bars: Harris didn't fight it, in the end. Not after the bodies were found on his property. A trace of Landon's blood in the back of Harris's van. A gunshot wound, matching the weapon he'd pulled on us that night. The trail of evidence, leading decidedly back to him. His wife took their daughter and left this place, back to her family in Florida, before they'd even started digging on the property—severing all ties. A buried fear that she'd never given voice to, proving true.

It was the talk of the news, for weeks. Each of the stories rehashed, back to the Fraternity Four—though there was still no sign of them.

WE WORRIED MORE, AT the inn. A man taken from one of our cabins. A killer, steps away from the rest of our guests. But the crime didn't seem to put a damper on our reservations. The danger was behind us. If anything, the calls and bookings only grew.

Sometimes, I could see the guests looking at it, the spot where it happened, beside the inn. Where a worker on shift took a fire poker to the perpetrator before he could hurt anyone else, and Landon West's brother held him there until help could arrive.

The story was good for business.

PEOPLE DIDN'T ASK ANYMORE about Alice and Farrah and Landon. Tragedy had a different shape than a mystery. The acreage around the Donald Farm was a graveyard. Three bodies, buried far out, and separately, in the parts of the farmland that had run wild, gone to disrepair. Areas no one would have cause to go, that nature had already started to creep back over.

Most people took the long way around that abandoned land, to avoid it. But sometimes, I drove past: I could imagine it, in the years to come, how quickly it would happen, the trees pushing closer, and the wildlife encroaching, and how fast a place could be swallowed up, so that you didn't even notice it as you drove by. Just a groove in the pavement where a driveway used to be, without even knowing what you were looking at.

BUT THEY ASKED, STILL, about the Fraternity Four. That mystery, almost the same as a memory, keeping them sharply in focus. How they'd heard that the famous photo, the last shot, the one that hung over the wall at the tavern, had disappeared. Stolen by some enterprising tourists who'd managed to sneak in, undetected.

This place was littered with the dead. But it was also a place where they could still be alive, if you wanted to believe it.

We hired new help, like Celeste promised. Ashlyn was twenty, and she grew up here—it was safest that way. She was the daughter of the elementary school principal, and she seemed so young. Three days into her trial period, she looked overwhelmed, but she kept moving. By day four, she wore her hair like me, in a low bun, and she seemed more confident, more at ease.

That morning, I was taking a group of guests out on a hike. I stopped at the front desk, and there was an envelope on the edge, which Ashlyn pushed my way. My name and our address, written in a familiar print. "Someone just left this for you," she said.

I raced out front, envelope tight in my grip, just in time to catch her. Georgia, hand on the open door of her car, turning at the sound of my exit. Her hair hung almost to her eyes, and she pushed it to the side now. But she looked out of sync, and I was overcome with the feeling of passing someone on a street and trying to place them, out of context.

I stopped halfway between the lobby door and Georgia's car.

"I got your letter," she said.

I'd sent it to the address I'd found for her mother. I wanted to know she was okay. I wanted her to know I forgave her, that we were okay. But still: I wanted to know *why*.

She looked over her shoulder, at the road leading out, then turned back with a frown. "I was going to mail this. An explanation." She waved her hand. "An apology. I was just on my way to the post office. And then I kept driving." Her eyes skimmed the inn, the mountain. "I just wanted to see for myself. See if it was all real."

I tried to see what she was seeing: a building of wood and stone, emerging from a clearing, like it was always meant to be here. The fog just lifting off the mountain behind it. I had plans for this place, for what it could still become.

"You can stay," I told her. Meaning: the night; longer. Ashlyn lived at home. The apartment was still open, for now. Believer or disbeliever, Cutter's Pass welcomed you equally.

But she shook her head quickly. "This was an escape. This was only ever an escape. Something to prove to myself. And then, that camera—I thought I could prove something, but all it did was get him . . . I wish I could go back." She shook her head, stepped closer to the car, as if she feared some unnatural pull. A force this place held over her. She gestured to the letter. "I just wanted to apologize. And to say, I'm glad you're okay."

And then I watched as she drove off, knowing it would be the last time I saw her.

THERE WERE FOUR GUESTS on the hike this morning, and we set out in a single line. We'd just passed the first curve, where you turn around, and the trees and rhododendron have already closed around you in a tunnel of shadows, and you can't see your way back out.

The sound of their breathing, the rustle of hiking pants, the thud of the walking sticks making contact with the trail.

"Is it true," the woman directly behind me asked, "that the Fraternity Four were last spotted heading this way, to this very trail?"

"Yes," I said, looking over my shoulder, "it's true."

She shuffled into position beside me, breathing faster, keeping pace. "A man down at the tavern, he said he could take us on a tour, tell us about what happened to them."

"That so?" I said, and thought I saw, through the trees, a flash of a red scarf. A cardinal, probably, if I looked again. But I didn't.

Instead I looked over at the woman, her gaze trailing in that direction, too. After something she saw—or almost saw.

"Ask me anything," I said. "I know everything there is to know about this place."

ACKNOWLEDGMENTS

I'm very grateful to the many people who helped guide this story from the initial spark of an idea to the finished book.

Thank you to my brilliant editor, Marysue Rucci, and wonderful agent, Jennifer Joel, for all of the guidance, insight, and feedback on each and every draft. And to the entire team at Scribner, including Nan Graham, Stu Smith, Brian Belfiglio, Katie Monaghan, Brianna Yamashita, Sasha Kobylinski, Jaya Miceli, Laura Wise, and many others who have had a hand in bringing this book into the world.

Thank you to wonderful friends Elle Cosimano, Ashley Elston, and Megan Shepherd, for the brainstorming, the early reads, and the encouragement along the way.

As always, a huge thank you to my family. To Luis, who joined me on every research trip (and hike) while I was working on this story. And to my parents, who brought me hiking every year when I was growing up and first introduced me to the mountains.

MEGAN MIRANDA is the *New York Times* bestselling author of *All the Missing Girls*; *The Perfect Stranger*; *The Last House Guest*, a Reese Witherspoon Book Club pick; *The Girl from Widow Hills*; and *Such a Quiet Place*. She has also written several books for young adults. She grew up in New Jersey, graduated from MIT, and lives in North Carolina with her husband and two children. Follow @MeganLMiranda on Twitter and Instagram, @AuthorMeganMiranda on Facebook, or visit MeganMiranda.com.